DEAD MAN

BLACK MAGIC OUTLAW
BOOK ONE

Domino Finn

BLOOD & TREASURE

Published by Blood & Treasure, Los Angeles
First Edition

Cover Design by James T. Egan of Bookfly Design LLC.

ISBN: 978-0-692-64407-2

DominoFinn.com

DEAD MAN

BLACK MAGIC OUTLAW

BOOK ONE

Chapter 1

Waking up dead is the worst. Trust me. I know these things.

The last time I woke up this hungover I was naked, soaking wet, and wrapped in a Cuban flag.

This time, at least, I had clothes on. I couldn't see them in the pitch black, but I could feel them. I could feel other things too. Raw pounding in my head. Enough tightness in my chest to make every breath a chore. I was in ten kinds of pain. Apparently that wasn't enough because my leg was asleep too.

There was more. Cold, wet, grimy more. Flies buzzed around my face, circling the stench of death. My arm was slimy. I shifted my weight and something crunched beneath me. My hands and feet pressed against the tight confines of a box.

Smell of death and decay. Check. Some kind of giant coffin. Check. I'm no mathematician but things were starting to add up.

Despite the evidence of my apparent death, I didn't panic. You see, I'm a necromancer (among other things) so I know a little about the subject. I couldn't tell you where I was or what happened the day before to get me here, but I had an inkling I was still alive. Even if just barely.

I tried to sit up. A stabbing pain pulsed through my body until I relaxed again. Request denied.

Okay, deep breath time. I focused inward to calm myself, then reopened my eyes. A thin sliver of light crept through the seam of my crypt overhead, but it was too weak to illuminate the interior.

Good thing I knew a trick or two.

I stared into the darkness, more deeply than before. Not into the box or any physical place, but into a place within me. The pupils of my eyes leaked and my green irises filled with black, and with a blink I could see.

And you thought the necromancer thing was all about wearing black and growing your hair long. I hate to burst your bubble but I'm not a walking death metal stereotype. I don't wear a trench coat and I have a crew cut. I live in Miami, for fuck's sake. It's hot and humid *in the winter*. No sense getting a heatstroke to appeal to northern sensibilities.

Not only that but Cisco Suarez (that's me) isn't just a necromancer. He's a shadow charmer too. That's the magic I just called on. The darkness all around me, it was still there—I could just see through it now.

The thin razorblade of light now stung my eyes. I avoided looking directly at it and checked the rest of the tomb. Crushed cardboard boxes. Stuffed plastic bags. My accommodations weren't as morbid as I'd feared. This wasn't a coffin but a dumpster.

Maybe I wasn't dead after all. Just down for a nap. A bed made of beer bottles. My pillow? A dead sewer rat.

That would've made most men jump, but remember: necromancer. I scrunched my nose and reached for it.

The simple act of limberness was a battle of pain. My muscles were sore. Dry and withered like the old husks of a toppled tree. My bones creaked and my joints were half-dried cement. I stirred up more dust than the Mummy. But I pushed through the agony until I dangled the dead rat by its tail.

It had been decapitated. A tribute. Sacrificial magic, and not mine. That spelled trouble.

I checked for other signs of ritual or binding. Charms. Runes. Burnt sacraments. Scanning the contents of the dumpster, I spied a couple of dark-red cowboy boots on my feet and literally hopped in place. (I almost knocked my head on the dumpster lid.) You see, the rat I could handle. My wearing a bona fide pair of alligator boots was unacceptable.

Don't get me wrong. There was nothing magic or cursed about them. It's just that the modern Cuban doesn't wear cowboy boots. Cisco Suarez doesn't wear cowboy boots.

That's me again, by the way. Shorter and catchier than Francisco, it always reminded me of a comic book name. What kid didn't want to be a superhero? I liked the sound of it so much I picked up referring to myself in the third person. My fatal flaw.

Enough about my name. Let's talk spellcraft. I'm what you call an animist: an everyday human who happens to tap into spirits for magical energy. Wild, huh?

I know what you're thinking: A cleric deals with gods and a wizard with books, right? Well, put the Player's Handbook away and forget everything you think you know. Gods and books have plenty of overlap. (The most famous book in all history is a notable example.)

Fact is, magic is a universal force in the world, pure energies known as the Intrinsics. They're the building blocks of all creation. People like you or me can only manipulate them through spirits. That makes us animists.

Everything else is just a title. Wizard. Cleric. Learned men like to use mage (it's more sophisticated). You see shaman or witch doctor applied to primitive peoples. Or if you wanna vilify animists, call them witches and warlocks. You get the idea. I'm sure some academic somewhere compiled a list of unofficial "official" definitions—but you'd have a hard time running into that terminology on the street. And the street is where the real stuff happens.

Case in point: the dumpster I was lying in.

Some alarm in my head screamed that I was hurt. Maybe fatally. The thing was, besides stiffness, there wasn't anything wrong with me. I wasn't dying, anyway. I kinda felt like a homeless vampire more than anything else. Which would be a lot funnier if I didn't know vampires actually existed. After all, right now I had a hangover from hell—maybe hell was where I came from.

You're probably bored by now, right? Sorry. I think too much. It's a problem I'm trying to address.

With a strained kick of an alligator boot, the lid of the dumpster flew open. Blinding light engulfed me and seared my senses. I literally hissed and uselessly threw my hands up in defense. Maybe I was a vampire after all.

But I didn't burst into flames. After I took another second to get my head on straight, I realized I was still drawing upon my shadow sight. I drained the darkness from my eyes, my lids pushing out black tears, until it was safe to look.

A blue sky. Fluffy clouds. Palm trees.

I was in South Beach.

Not the pretty coastline with white sand they show on TV during football games. That was never far in Miami Beach, of course, but the back alleys were far less picturesque. I was just off Washington Avenue somewhere, outside a dive bar. The alley was empty. I heaved myself over the dumpster wall and landed on the concrete with a thud. I wouldn't win any vaulting medals but it got the job done. Standing and walking involved entirely new kinds of pain, but either it was wearing off or I was getting used to it.

Normally I'd assume this predicament was my doing—it wouldn't be me if I didn't go big—but the dead rat was a bit much. It was also a dead giveaway that someone else was involved.

I padded at my jean pockets. I had a cell phone but no wallet. Was I robbed? It seemed unlikely given the evidence of spellcraft. A beatdown, then?

I frowned. I'd annoyed people, sure. I'd had minor run-ins with gang tough guys and stirred up the local talent, but that was life as a small-time hustler. I was too young for real enemies. No reason anyone should wish me dead.

The preternatural fog in my head wasn't going away. I couldn't think clearly. No amount of head-scratching helped.

With my head on a swivel for danger, I staggered to the pink sidewalk. (Miami Beach, remember?) I was ready for anything. What I didn't expect was to be ignored.

Small groups of shoppers strolled up and down Washington Avenue. Horns honked and cars inched forward and came to a stop at the light. I got a few odd looks but nobody confronted me or threw any blood curses my way. It was just your average whatever-day-it-was in South Beach.

A man strolled by and held his hand out to me. While trying (and failing) to make eye contact, I accepted his offering. A nickel and two pennies. He avoided my puzzled expression and continued on his way.

That was random, but I couldn't be accountable for the South Beach crazies. Cisco Suarez needed to stay on task. Since everything appeared normal outside, I considered pumping the bar employees for information.

The car that was stopped on the road in front of me clicked its doors locked. I looked and the woman in the passenger seat averted her eyes. Bitch. Then I got a glimpse of myself in the window reflection.

I would've locked the doors too.

Besides my healthy tan, nothing of my disheveled appearance was recognizable. My usually close-cropped hair hung over my shoulders in a wild mane. My eyes were permanently frantic, sporting the raised-by-wolves look. The full-on homeless beard didn't help. And my clothes. Besides my jeans and red cowboy boots, of all things I wore a yellowed and bloodied tank top.

Tank tops were never really my look but, to my surprise, I actually filled this one out. My chest strained against the thin fabric and my bare arms looked carved from marble. Still in disbelief, I flexed a bicep at my reflection. Maybe the car windows were made from magic fun-house mirrors.

This warrants an explanation. I may be a little cocky and reckless at times, but one thing I'm not is a gym rat. I was always that scrappy skinny kid who was too stupid to stay down. Yes, that means I lost a lot of fights. I wanted to be a superhero but lacked the dedication. What animist would spend time working out anyway? The power of the world at your fingertips, wasted by repeatedly picking up and putting down heavy things.

No, I was never out of shape, but I was supposed to be thin. Now I suddenly felt like Peter Parker after running into that radioactive spider. I was straight buff, is what I'm saying.

My jaw glued to the floor, I stared like a lunatic. The driver floored the gas at his first opportunity. In their place, a matte-black jeep slammed on its brakes. Which was weird since the light was green and the cars behind it honked. I snapped out of my shock as the group of Haitians in the jeep focused on me, anger in their eyes.

They yelled, "Dead man!" and dismounted, brandishing light automatic weapons.

I threw seven cents at them.

Chapter 2

Let's get something straight before we start. I can't shoot lightning from my fingers. Magic is often more subtle than that, but not always. (Heck, who am I kidding? I don't do subtle.) The point is, magic is most powerful with preparation, thought, and patience. Getting jumped right after waking up dazed in a dumpster? I was a little behind the eight ball here. If I fought, either I died or they did, and I didn't like my chances.

I chose door number three: Run like hell.

I scurried back down the alley and cursed how empty it was. As the Haitian gangbangers lifted their guns, I knew I couldn't make it to cover in time. The dumpster was too far away.

On some mysterious impulse—call it instinct—I lifted my left hand behind me and felt my palm tingle. The firearms erupted into repeated bursts just as a blue glow sprang from my hand and formed a partial sphere (think Captain America's shield.) Bullets deflected into the concrete floor and stucco walls until I slipped safely behind the trash bin.

As the energy rushed away, a symbol on my palm glowed faintly, then faded into a normal tattoo. The ink resembled a snowflake. Another tat ran along the outside of my forearm, a line forming a rough arrow. I didn't remember getting tattoos, but the runes were Germanic and related to Norse gods.

Okay, necromancy, shadow magic, Norse runes... Slow down, right? I wish I could. But I'll break it down for you.

Like I said, spellcraft involves channeling spirit power. That means all magic is shamanistic in nature. But don't make assumptions. It's not dancing around a fire.

Magic, real historical magic, based on the knowledge of every culture since the dawn of time, has always been spirit-based. You don't go to prep school or study tomes. You aren't born with it or without. Magic is spiritual. Not religious. Not enlightened. But *of the spirit*.

Spirits are energy. They live in an alternate world, a dead place, with free access to the Intrinsics. For numerous reasons, countless civilizations have become exposed to spirits throughout time, and you'd better believe people turned it to their benefit. The Egyptians did this with their gods. The Native Americans prayed to the sun and the moon and the hunt. Consider these spirits anything from supreme deity to lowly trickster. They're called patrons, and without them there'd be no spellcraft.

Nobody really knows what the patrons are or where they come from. I don't even know that they're real, sentient beings. My take is that, if enough people believe in something, that's a kind of power in itself. Magic boils down to the mind tapping into spiritual energy, so it makes sense that enough belief can create it.

The tattoo on the palm of my hand, the rune magic, is a shortcut to a symbol of power. I can't even tell you what patron it represents. For some reason, despite never seeing it before, I was well-practiced in the flow of its energy. With little conscious thought, I had adeptly defended myself.

Speaking of which, said defense was still ongoing.

I peeked out from behind the steel dumpster and zeroed in on my opponents. Four Haitians. Three of them held machine pistols in plain sight, their jeep left straddling the sidewalk. For some reason they weren't concerned with making a public spectacle.

The fourth man had white lines drawn on his face. This was Miami Beach, but that wasn't sunblock. It identified them as members of a street gang called the Bone Saints. The ones with the guns were flunkies, unimportant goons who mostly hustled street corners, but the one with the face paint was different. He was a bokor.

Once again, more titles. Magic is as varied as the societies that practice it. Haitian voodoo practitioners are called bokors. I'm a bokor to some because I know a little voodoo on the side. Even though this Bone Saint was only dressed in a track suit and wore very little of the makeup and flair, I could see him for a bokor a mile away.

The gang fired on me again. I threw up my shield and took stock of my enemies. I had no idea why they wanted me dead, but they were adamant about it. Odds were good they'd left me in the dumpster in the first place.

The closer they drew, the less cover I had. Normally I would go on the offensive with a shadow manifestation, but that kind of spellcraft was too difficult in direct sunlight. Even though we were in an alley, it was midday. The sun bore down from almost directly above, and the surroundings were well lit.

Don't ask me why a shadow charmer lives in the Sunshine State. What can I say? Life's boring without challenges.

Another volley of bullets screamed my way and I raised the shield again. Blue sparks exploded under the onslaught but the energy held. I may have been near death, but my magic was still strong.

In the corner of my eye, the bokor jerked an arm. It took an extra second to realize he wasn't casting, and that slowed me down. I saw the flying knife too late. My shield was raised but the heavy knife clanged right through it, not unscathed but not deflected nearly enough. The blade gashed my shoulder. On instinct I knew the shield was meant for small projectiles only. Luckily, the trajectory was altered enough or it would've stuck my neck. I winced in pain as the knife clanged off the alley wall, now spattered with my blood.

With my hand jarred and my shield lowered, a bullet cut into my gut. I buckled backward against the stucco building. The street thugs converged on me, removing my cover from the equation. I feebly pressed closer to the grimy dumpster.

They saw their opening and opened fire.

The only shadow in the entire alley was cast by the dumpster, just a sliver of darkness immediately adjacent. It was no accident I was now huddled within it.

I phased backward into the wall, slipping into the shadow. I became slightly embedded, a part of the wall, visible as a protruding darkness. The bullets whizzed through me and shattered the stucco in a hailstorm of dust.

I wasn't fully ethereal. Not really. Shadows are all about blurring the lines between dark and light, between the known and unknown. I was still there, only I wasn't, and I watched as the Haitians emptied their magazines in frustration.

I couldn't stay like this long. While physical attacks would prove useless, the bokor was coming up at the rear, chanting in response. Against magic, my fortified position was a straw house.

I slipped forward and solidified, smiling as the gang reloaded. It was the perfect chance for a counterattack, but I was still reeling from the gut shot (and whatever had left me half dead in the dumpster). I snatched the bokor's knife and strategically bolted for the other end of the alley.

Before I got there, more gunfire came my way. The shield held strong. Well, except for the one bullet low enough to graze my thigh, but who's keeping score? I tumbled to the cement as the barrage whizzed over my head. Rolling over, I lay low and parallel with the alley, like a surfer paddling on his board. With my shield up, the position provided full cover. The energy at my palm didn't feel as strong as it should have, but it held as another round of mags was spent.

My leg complained about getting tagged, though. That's the weakness of my patchwork Norse protection. No one ever asks how Captain America blocks incoming bullets with his relatively small shield, but trust me, it's difficult.

The Bone Saints began approaching but the bokor called them off. I squinted and watched him step aside. My eyes followed his to his feet.

A snarling pit bull raced from behind him and headed

straight for me. To him I must've looked like a giant ham hock. I scrambled to my feet and burst out to the next street like nobody's business.

This road was much less busy than Washington. I easily avoided the one car in my way while crossing the street. I had a decent head start on the Haitians, but that dog was quickly gaining on me. Who sics dogs on animists anyhow?

I cut into a small produce market. The glass door jangled against the chimes and closed with a satisfying click. I turned and took a breath as the pit bull silently reached the sidewalk and stopped short of crashing into the glass. I plucked a mango from a box for defense but I didn't throw it. The dog didn't come inside. It didn't bark. It just stared at me with cold, dead eyes.

Oh wait. I got it suddenly. A bokor? Siccing a dog on another practitioner? I may be slow but I ain't stupid. This was no normal attack dog.

It was a zombie pit bull.

Chapter 3

On the plus side, the dog wasn't thrashing around and causing a scene. It barely looked dead, really. Bloody, matted fur. Glazed over eyes. Half an ear. It easily passed for a neglected ghetto dog. It stood still, like a pointer, and that's what it was doing. The necromancer controlling the zombie knew exactly where it was, and in turn, me.

That didn't give me a lot of time to think. I'd wanted to keep things low key, but that was pretty much out the window when he cut the zombie dog loose. My best bet was to try a bit of necromancy myself.

I calmed my mind, visualizing the connection between master and thrall. The Baron was the primary Haitian loa, the one I was familiar with. Unfortunately, the bokor channeled a different patron. Besides that, the connection was stronger than I expected from a low-level banger. I couldn't sever it, but I did my best to cloud the energy, to make it difficult for its master to home in on us.

Busy with exploring the dark energy around the dog, I didn't notice the little old lady inching her walker towards the glass door. She admired the hound with a beaming face. "*Ay, que lindo,*" she squealed.

Right before opening the front door and trying to pet

the thing.

With a vicious snarl, the pit bull bowled past the woman. She clutched her walker for support and barely avoided falling and turning into a spokesperson for a medical alert commercial.

The store owner, more prescient of the danger of rabid dogs, hopped over the counter with an aluminum baseball bat in his hand.

"*Coño, perro!*" he exclaimed as he feinted with the slugger.

He wasn't trying to hit the thing. I mean, who really wants to beat another living thing with a bat, especially man's best friend? But the pit bull isolated the threat and caught the aluminum in its mouth. Sharp teeth spilled to the ground like marbles, but the dog had made its point and yanked the weapon from the store owner's hands.

The man bolted towards the door with a "*Carajo!*", shoved the old woman outside with him, and slammed the door. His eyes met mine and he mimed a halfhearted shrug in response. So much for being a hero.

My mango went flying like a cannonball and bounced harmlessly off the pit bull's snout. It lunged for me, going for a leg bite with half its remaining teeth. I picked up the entire cardboard box of mangoes and upturned it over him. The hail of fruit didn't do much, but the box fell over the dog perfectly. I side-stepped and the whole bundle of fur and produce crashed into the plantains display.

The bokor and one of the gunmen were crossing the street. I hadn't seen where the other two men went, but I knew it was time to go.

I ran to the back room and navigated around the

disorganized store inventory. An upside-down mango box with bananas on top gave chase. The blind dog looked like a pinball as it bounced off various obstacles, but its single-mindedness made up for its other failings. Eventually, the box fell away and the dog bounded after me. It wasn't fast enough, however, to beat me to the back exit.

The metal door banged as I hefted my weight against it. It didn't budge. Unable to halt my momentum, my head bounced loudly against the door. It still didn't budge.

Damn. The exit was locked from the inside. If I ever made it out of here alive, I could file a fire code violation. For now I scrambled up the adjacent utility shelf just as the pit bull snapped at my heels.

Straddling the top shelf, huddled against the wall and the low roof, I wasn't overly proud of myself. But I was out of range of the zombie pit bull. It barked and howled and leapt at me, but I was safe for the moment.

Back to necromancy, then.

Death magic is a patient art. Its most powerful applications are heavily threaded in ritual and preparation. Even its flash magic utilizes tokens and tributes. None of which were handy.

Fetishes aren't completely necessary. Like rituals, they're used to amplify magic. The most common scenario is an animist who has no power without them. I'm not that kind of animist. I can do plenty on my own. I can tap innately strong power for my age. (Cisco Suarez is no slouch.)

But you may have noticed I'm not a specialist. I've always preferred the jack-of-all-trades route. Being confined to a single patron's power is boring, but there are schools of thought that believe the only way to truly master a discipline is to specialize. While I'm a good necromancer, this bokor had likely studied nothing but this brand of voodoo his entire life. And here I was, without a fetish to stretch the boundaries of my spellcraft.

That meant I had little chance of deanimating the drooling zombie trying to make me its lunch. But I was right next to it. Far closer than its master. Odds were I could exert *some* control over it.

I got inside the dog's mind again. I didn't bother with clouding its position. I didn't try to break its link with the bokor. Instead, I pushed a suggestion.

"Stop," I commanded.

The barking halted immediately. The pit bull ceased jumping, even though it still paced side to side in anticipation.

"Stay."

The dog stopped cold in its tracks.

"Um... Sit?"

The pit bull retained a mask of fierce hunger but parked its butt on the ground without hesitation.

Like I said, no slouch. I may have been a little rusty, but I still had it in a pinch.

I dropped to the floor cautiously and took in a relieved breath when the pit bull didn't move. "Good dog," I said.

Around its neck was your standard tough-guy dog collar, black leather with spiked studs. I like dog trinkets. One can be a fetish in the proper hands. Fetishes with an emotional connection to the animist work best. I'd say hanging from a metal shelf and nearly pissing my pants was emotional enough. I carefully reached around the zombie's neck and unclasped it. As I did, the pit bull whisked its head around and gave my arm a lick. I drew away but the dog didn't move. It now stared mindlessly ahead. I shrugged and wrapped the collar twice around my right wrist like a bracelet. Cisco Suarez, master of improvisation.

With the zombie neutralized, my next problem was the exit. I studied the door and wrapped my hands around the metal handle.

In line with my jack-of-all-trades persona, I knew an artificer who had introduced me to metallurgy. I'm not very good at it. (In fact, I'm downright awful.) But I can weaken the structural integrity of base metals. It takes too much effort, I'm limited to small objects that are mostly breakable anyway, and my face knots up like I'm taking a dump when I do it. It's embarrassing and I don't like people watching when I work it, but the undead dog wasn't much of an audience.

I grunted and squeezed and rocked back and forth, but I could feel it coming loose. The handle clunked to the ground and I smiled.

Daylight.

Without bothering to wipe or wash my hands, I burst through the door and ran toward Collins Avenue. The street was a slow current of passing Corvettes and convertibles, one of which happened to be the jeep with the bad paint job. That was where the other two flunkies had gone. On my side of the street, a thin shadow ran along the storefronts. I backed into it to hide.

Too late, of course. A hangover from hell, a step behind—I wasn't getting any breaks today. The passenger of the jeep jumped out twirling a machete in his hand.

He was either out of ammo or he preferred to get up

close and personal. Judging by the glee on his face, he had plenty of ammo.

Chapter 4

"You should be dead," growled the Haitian. He approached slowly, with confidence, and flashed a yellow smile. "Maybe we kill you again, yes?"

The bokor was nowhere in sight. As I was on a main thoroughfare, it was only a matter of time before he spotted me. I needed to shelve this brawler quickly and quietly and get on my way. Instead of running, I remained in the shadow of the storefront and waited.

In broad daylight on a packed street, the gangbanger wiped the rusty, two-foot blade on his grimy shirt and stepped onto the pink sidewalk. No attempt at subversion or secrecy. The Bone Saints must have had a real beef with me to risk this. Too bad I didn't remember a damn thing about it.

"Tell me how to fix this," I urged as the man got closer. "Whatever it was you think I—"

I didn't have time to finish the sentence. In a smooth stroke, the Haitian lifted the machete high. I crossed my left hand over my head, and the blade crashed down on my forearm.

Right on top of that second Norse tattoo of protection.

This one resembled an arrow. A straight line ran the

length of my outer left forearm, with fettered sticks at my elbow and a sharp point on my wrist. In the center were three hardening runes, crosshatched lines cutting through the shaft. This was a shield as well, similar to a single branch of the snowflake on my hand but on a grander scale and distilled into its most powerful form. To make my third comic book reference of the day, it's like I had adamantium encasing the far side of my forearm.

This didn't form visible energy like the palm sigil. It didn't extend away from my body. It was crap for bullets and projectiles, but this machete right here was its bread and butter. Once again, I instinctually knew how the tattoo worked, but it was muscle memory more than anything. I couldn't tell you where the ink came from or how I learned the spell. Frankly, I was surprised it worked.

The heavy blade sparked against my arm. The Haitian nearly lost his grip on the knife and took an extra second to secure it. In his unreadiness, I brought my right fist up under his guard and socked him in the belly. As I connected, I called on the shadow I stood within.

For the uninitiated, black magic is a vast umbrella of spellcraft. Anything dealing with death and darkness and the afterlife. If I'm a specialist at anything, it's the darkness.

Now armed with the dog collar as a working fetish, I could channel the full power of my patron, Opiyel the Shadow Dog. He's an old Taíno god of the underworld, relatively unknown in spellcraft circles, and his domain is the shadow.

Here's the thing about shadow magic. As far as spellcraft goes, it's not the most powerful, especially in terms of pure evocative destruction. It's mostly ethereal. An absence. It's how I did the phasing-through-bullets trick back in the alley. But don't assume the shadow can't be manifested into something solid. Something strong. It takes a lot of power and can't be done in direct sunlight, but it packs one hell of a punch.

And boy did it. My fist propelled the Bone Saint through the air and onto the hood of a yellow Lamborghini stuck in slow traffic. The car was dope, but I didn't have time to ogle it. I stepped into the light and picked up the dropped machete, daring the gangbanger to come back at me. He tumbled off the car and hit the asphalt. He wasn't even getting back up.

The tough guy in the Lambo hit the brakes and laid on his horn. He opened the door and screamed at us.

"Watch the car, idiots!"

His attention fixed on the blade in my hand, and he squirmed under my icy stare.

"Chill out," I said. "It's only a Gallardo."

He wanted to take me to task for the comment but wisely kept quiet.

Unfortunately, the police are either less wise or more brave.

"Put the knife down!" yelled a cop down the block.

The uniformed police officer skipped his bicycle from the street to the sidewalk and sped my way.

Bike cops. Faster than slow traffic. Faster than fleeing pedestrians. And most people don't realize they're trained to hop off the bike and flip it forward, tackling you with the back wheel. That didn't sound pleasant.

Great, now I had a Haitian voodoo gang and the Miami Beach police after me. Another beautiful day in paradise.

"We'll see about only a Gallardo," taunted the driver of the Lambo, no longer cowed.

I let the machete clatter to the floor and hopped onto the hood of the Gallardo. The driver tugged at his hair in distress, but I didn't stick around to gloat. I leaped to the hood of an Impala, then into the bed of a pickup truck. It was like playing Frogger, except the street was only three lanes and I cheated. When I landed on the sidewalk on the other side of the street, I spun around and smiled.

Let's watch a bicycle do *that*.

The Haitian driving the jeep was still watching me, but with the officer present, he kept a low profile. Unfortunately, I couldn't exactly ask the cop for help with my gang situation. Appealing to him was a risky proposition. First off, nobody trusts a black magic user. It's not that they believe in magic, necessarily, but there's a vibe they can sense. Or maybe I'm a smartass. Either way, it wasn't worth taking the chance.

In front of me was a premier boutique hotel. Not quite on the sand, but a resort oasis all in itself. I'd never been able to afford a room, but that didn't stop me from taking shelter there now. I barged through the marble lobby with two kinds of trouble right behind me.

A giant chandelier with old-timey light bulbs, hip lounge furniture, a trendy beat—these were all nice things. Part of me wanted to kick back and revel in the decadence. But being chased by gangs, police, and zombies kinda gives you an appreciation for the simpler things. You know, like staying alive.

I ducked into a rear hallway. Nice. The area was covered in thick shadow. I waved my hand over the floor as I passed and the nether thickened. It was invisible, but the shadow was sludge now. It wouldn't stop my pursuers, but it would slow them, just like they were running in a dream. I'd finally bought myself some time.

I rushed out to the back patio and passed a bar with the thinnest flat screen ever. I mean, I was being chased by the cops and I stopped to gawk. I'd never seen anything like it.

Football highlights captivated two men on stools as well as the bartender. A tattered wallet sat on the granite bar top beside an empty plate of food. I winced but I swiped it anyway. Don't call me a thief, call me an opportunist. The thing was begging to be picked up and I was in a tight spot.

I raced to the pool section. Women in bikinis and men with the kinds of muscles I didn't use to have loitered in deck chairs and cabanas. I slowed as I passed a group of Brazilians in thongs because I'm only human. Next was a blonde with breast implants reading a magazine and, uh, let's just say I passed her completely before I realized it wasn't a magazine in her hands.

My feet slid on the wet concrete and I wiped out on the floor. I wasn't embarrassed, just confused. The woman held a weird little TV thing, thinner than the one at the bar. She let it drop to her lap and scowled at me, but all I noticed were the words scrolling on the screen.

Holy crap. What the hell was that thing?

"Stare much?" mocked the woman, rolling her eyes. I noticed her face for the first time. She had the look of a spoiled brat who was used to getting her way with everything except time. She hid the beginnings of wrinkles under a gallon of makeup and even more plastic surgery. A porn star playing with a sci-fi gadget. I couldn't decide which was the bigger teenager's wet dream.

"Paul," she called out, her tone rising in fear. "This guy's creeping me out."

Crap, I forgot about my wolfman eyes. I didn't waste time checking how big Paul was. Whoever it was, I could take him. This wasn't about winning. I needed to catch my breath. I just couldn't do that without running first.

I sprinted away, fully aware that if I kept moving east, I'd eventually run into an ocean.

Chapter 5

South Beach in Miami consists of three main roadways: Washington Avenue, which houses most of the bars and clubs; Collins Avenue, which has all the hotels; and Ocean Drive, which, besides being on the sand and having a beautiful view of the Atlantic, is crammed with restaurants and hotels and whatever hotspots you can imagine.

There are two alleys between the three avenues. I was now in the second of them. Only Ocean Drive remained, and while there were a lot of people to mix in with, I stood out like a sore thumb. I needed to find a place to lie low, and fast.

This alleyway was more claustrophobic than the previous one. A large cement wall blocked my path like the battlements of a castle. This particular building was built like one as well. The wall was part of the blocky structure, with a Spanish-styled roof and window grates. This obstacle spanned a good portion of the block on either side of me, and I debated which direction to run.

The thing is, I was tired of running. And tired of fighting too. I just wanted to stop. I lamented my bad luck until I realized what the giant building was.

The Versace Mansion was a decadent residence of the

infamous Italian fashion designer. An honest-to-goodness house on Ocean Drive overlooking the palms and the sands and the water. When the designer was shot dead on his front steps years ago, the property languished in auction. Who had the money to afford a place like this?

That neglect was gonna pay off for me.

I shoved a double-wide dumpster underneath one window and hopped on top. The metal security grating was locked and I didn't think I could break it. Remember, my metallurgy's only good for weak metal. This steel was designed to keep people out. But that wasn't a problem. I scaled the bars and pulled myself up to the window above it, then higher to a tiny balcony wall constructed of the same grating. I hopped over the edge and snuck a quick breath before I turned to the double doors.

Once again, the security bars were sturdy. Fortunately, one of the doors was open. User error: locks only work when they're locked. I slipped inside and shut it behind me, leaving no trace of my entry.

I immediately felt like royalty. Everything—from the lavish curtains to the stained glass to the bedsheets to the cushions inset into wall benches—was patterned maroon. The furniture and floor were impeccable, turn-of-the-century hardwood. The cream-colored wall faded into a baby blue at the top and was detailed with painted vines and flowers. The single chandelier was modest but still probably cost a fortune, and I was thankful its bulbs were dimmed.

The room was surprisingly organized. Every single throw pillow (and there were a lot of them) was carefully placed. The bedroom was fully stocked and spotless.

A joint like this, the furniture sells with the building.

Many of the accents had been designed by Versace himself and would likely increase resale value. It stood to reason there'd be staff maintaining the place.

You know, so random vagrants don't break in to take a load off.

That meant I needed to keep an eye out. This wasn't the perfect long-term hideout, but it would do in a pinch. I sat still, waited, and listened. I wanted to make sure I *could* relax before I actually gave in to the impulse.

Nobody interrupted the silence. Not the Miami Beach police. Not the Bone Saints. Not even Paul from the pool. I sighed and melted to the floor.

Some people might consider me fortunate given my escape but, as far as I was concerned, I had a bullet in my belly and a graze on my thigh. Worse, the Haitian banger had said I was dead. That they had killed me.

Is that what I'd been doing in that dumpster? Busy being dead?

It was ludicrous to imagine. Between my headache, the fog in my brain, and the fact that I felt like absolute crap, the evidence was pointing more to life than death.

I felt for a pulse. It was racing.

Whatever I had been, I was alive now. If the Bone Saint was telling the truth, that meant I'd been resurrected somehow.

That kind of magic was supposed to be impossible.

Don't misunderstand me. There are no real rules to spellcraft. Rules are just theories written down by those who want control. Rules range from mostly true to flat out wrong, and there are always exceptions.

But not for death, right? That's the one true law of the

universe. You live, you die. Period.

The end of your life, but not the end of your story. You still exist. Your spirit still exists. What it does at that point is open for debate, but every necromancer knows about the truck stop of life called the Murk. That's where spirits live, tapping the Intrinsics, the lifeblood of the universe. Magic is the blood of life, and life is the blood of magic. Every animist knows that.

Now that I had some peace and quiet, I gazed inward and searched for answers. If I *had* been part of some resurrection ritual, I wouldn't very likely remember it. But I did feel a kind of dirtiness about me. Not just the physical grime. I had that in spades, but there was something else. A lingering aftertaste of dark magic. With my necromantic leanings, it should've been more familiar, but I couldn't recognize it. I'm far from an expert. No one truly is.

Here's the thing: There's no singular authority on magic. There's not even a single *kind* of magic. It's ethereal. Natural, but exotic. Knowledge, but unknown.

This works to our advantage. The reason people don't believe in magic is because there's no one thing that *is* magic. People pray for miracles but discount the supernatural. Others see ghosts but don't believe in monsters. Psychics discount telekinetics, and so on.

There's a natural order to only believing what you see. It's smart, most of the time. But since nobody can be everything, we're all guilty of pushing away new ideas.

Like an astronomer arguing with an astrologist, people will fight to the death over their perspective. Think of the scattered opinions on religion, race, sex, and identity—just in the United States alone. Then add all the other countries and cultures in the world. Consider then that the present is a single point and place in time, and you'll concede there are many more outlooks than your own.

That, my friends, is magic in a nutshell. A complex interweaving of subjects and understanding. Something entirely different depending on who you ask.

Is that *my* view? Sure. Like I said. It depends on who you ask, and you asked me. So even though I'm falling victim to the same frailty I just explained, I *still* say resurrection magic is impossible.

Yet here I was. Living proof.

Enough reflection. When I think too much, I contradict myself. If I kept at it, I'd find myself in a full-fledged argument.

The phone in my pocket rang.

The relaxation I'd worked so hard to find bolted. I pulled a solid Nokia candy-bar phone from my pocket and answered. "Go." I saw someone say that in a seventies cop show once and thought it was cool.

No one said anything. I waited a moment before asking who it was. No one spoke, but I swore I heard someone breathing.

Chapter 6

I ended the call and checked the screen for the number. Blocked. I frowned and wondered who would call a dead man.

That wasn't my phone. Like the tattoos, I didn't remember getting it. Maybe I really had died. It would explain not recalling anything in the hours and days before the dumpster. I couldn't tell you a thing about that time. It was gone. I had no memory of that stuff whatsoever, and maybe I never would.

The long-term stuff—who I was, my friends and family, my talents—I could remember all that. I even benefited from residual muscle memory in some cases, as with the Norse shields. That gave me hope the information I needed was somewhere inside my head.

I checked the rest of my pockets. Besides the bokor's knife in my waistband, all I came up with was the stolen wallet. Cisco Suarez, a regular pickpocket. I apologized to Richard Greene of 3032 Temecula Street as I thumbed through his ID and the other contents. I took the bundle of cash. Ninety-two bucks. The bills looked different, like the Fed had just minted a new, high-tech design. As long as it spent, it was good with me. I kept the cash in a front pocket and stuffed the wallet in the back.

I stood on shaky feet that weren't ready to support my weight yet. I sighed, trudged to the bathroom, and closed the door. It was safe in here to flip on the bright light without being visible from the windows. I ignored the Italian marble countertop and the brass fixtures and all the other mind-numbing amenities. A couple of days ago, I would've felt like a king. Today I realized it was all bullshit. Living mattered, not possessions, not stuff.

I rubbed my eyes and focused on the wall-spanning mirror. The car window had been kind to me. I was a mess.

Besides the sexy new muscles, there was nothing else to cheer about. My hair was tangled and knotted, almost to the point of dreads. My chin and neck were covered in a coarse beard. Besides the expected dirt on my skin and clothes, my tank top was flaking dried blood. Probably mine, if what that Haitian had said was true.

I pulled the shirt off and considered my new pecs. The resurrection magic had been good to me, but I'd still been to hell and back. Literally. A large purple bruise covered my heart, which explained the stiffness. Luckily, it was just a bruise.

I checked my lower belly. I could still feel where the bullet had tagged me, but there was no wound. My stomach ached from the hit and a red mark was spreading, but nothing had penetrated. The same with the graze on my thigh. The jeans sported a horizontal tear and there was a burn on my skin, but no blood.

In a way, that scared me more than the alternative.

I smiled at my dark-red alligator boots, wondering if they were a joke from the devil. Then I pulled the knife from the waist of my jeans.

It was a bronzed little thing with runes etched along the blade. A slight curve to the edge and an opposite curve in the decorated handle. Nothing I recognized, and nothing powerful from what I could tell. It was probably a keepsake more than anything. Something used by a necromancer in ceremonies. Something that someone might want back.

I shrugged and leaned over the sink, grabbing a handful of hair and raking the knife as close to my scalp as possible. The bokor had kept a good edge on the blade. It cut through my mane so well that I had a familiar crew cut in no time.

I drew a hot bath. No showers here. I'd been dead—I deserved the hot spa treatment. I steamed up that room real good. While I waited, the sharp knife served as a straight razor and left my chin and neck real smooth. I soaped and soaked. I even nodded off for a few minutes there.

Somewhere in that luxury, I got to thinking about my situation. A lot needed figuring out. The Bone Saints had killed me. I didn't know why. Someone had resurrected me, and I *really* didn't know why (much less who or how). And then there were the tattoos and the fact that bullets had bounced off my skin. I didn't know how I'd managed that, but it sure was new to me.

There are various pursuits of spellcraft. Offense is a common example, but there are many more. Some animists care more about seeking knowledge. Others, utility. But protection is something every animist covets. It's a biological imperative. It's what makes us durable.

Imagine having all this power but no defensive magic. The secrets of the universe are helpless against a large fellow with a baseball bat. So aside from some purist specialists, every animist learns some secondary protection. How far you wanna go with that is up to you. Do you want to stop knives? Bullets? Bombs?

That's the part that depends on practice.

Shadow isn't the most potent force out there, but it's hella good at defense. But hardiness against bullets without conscious effort? New to me.

I wondered if it had to do with the dark energies in my aura. The thought sickened my stomach. I drained the black water from the tub, dried off, and wrapped myself in a towel. When I wiped the condensation from the mirror, I introduced myself to the new, clean-shaven Cisco Suarez.

It was me. But it wasn't.

I looked different. It wasn't just the extra mass on my frame. My face was weathered. Older, if that was possible. I definitely didn't look twenty-four anymore. It might be an oxymoron, but death had really aged me.

I dressed myself in the only stinking clothes I had, wondering exactly how long I'd been dead. That's when the real-life considerations hit me. The social ramifications.

What did my family know? What did they think when I never came home one day?

(So what? I still lived with my mom and dad and little sister. Sue me.)

But darker questions came to mind. For instance: if someone wanted to kill me, was my family in danger as well?

I needed to warn them. I needed to protect them.

Rest time over, I marched from the bathroom with a mission. And that's when I saw the drunk couple having sex on the floor by the door.

Jeez, they hadn't even made it to the bed.

The girl screamed when she noticed me and rolled off her partner. The guy stood up and, to his credit, put himself between me and the girl before vanity took over.

"Who are you?" he demanded, grabbing a teddy bear from a shelf and holding it over his privates.

"What are you doing here?" I returned, stumbling to form an excuse.

"Me? What are *you* doing here? This is my room!" He turned around. "Brenda, go get security."

She was hunched into a corner, clutching her shorn clothes over her body. "I'm kinda naked right now."

"Oh, right."

I threw my hands up and looked away in my best gentleman impersonation. "Chill out, guys. Maybe this is my mistake."

"Maybe?" yelled the man.

"Okay. Definitely. But what do you mean this is your room? This is Versace's room." I inched closer to the far wall, circling away from the couple and the bedroom door.

"Dude," he said, readjusting his teddy bear. "What are you, a stalker? That was years ago. This is a hotel now."

The look on my face must have been priceless. "No, it's... Since when?"

"A year ago, you idiot." The man stormed over to the phone beside the bed and pushed a button. "Security?"

I ran to the balcony door. "Speaking of security," I said, slipping outside. "Little tip: make sure to lock these up at night."

And then I bolted.

Chapter 7

Miami Beach is an island. A series of islands, really. A lot of people don't know that. Downtown Miami is on the coast, then you've got Biscayne Bay between it and the beach. Everyone's familiar with the downtown skyline view from the MacArthur Causeway, the highway bridge that connects the two.

That's what I watched from the Metrobus as I crossed over. Yes, I was using public transportation. You might think it's been an especially unglamorous day for me, but I was used to the bus. My family was dirt poor.

Seeing the skyscrapers in full sunlight brought a smile to my face. I didn't know why. I'd seen them countless times before but I recognized that, this time, I was fortunate.

I'd been dead. For a year apparently. That was a lot of time to lose. A lot of time for things to change.

The urgency of finding my family grew muddled. I realized they wouldn't be in danger anymore. The time for that was long past. Now I just wondered if they knew what had happened to me. If they'd be happy to see me again.

Of course they would, right? But it's a little complicated. (Family always is.) As the firstborn, my parents were a bit disappointed in me. First in the family to reach higher education, I wasted the opportunity by dropping out after two years of community college.

I was a lousy student. I couldn't concern myself with the banalities of academics. So I read a lot. Novels, comic books—anything that required imagination. I used that background to imagine something more. To be open to the impossible. And when I found it, the magic, it felt like it had always been a part of me.

Luckily, my sister had gone down a different path. Seleste knew about my skills, but she hit the books with more dedication than I ever had. She was on track to go to law school. I was proud. Our parents were too, of course, but I always felt I'd let them down.

Honestly, I didn't always honor them as I should have. The whole black magic thing ran me in secret circles. I kinda closed off to them. Didn't pay enough attention. Things had never been crazy at home but constant disappointment has a way of souring things. I wondered what disappearing for a year could do.

The bus cruised past the city proper and headed down Flagler Street. Miami's laid out on a grid system, streets running east to west and avenues north to south. Flagler Street is the heart of Miami. Street zero. North 1st Street is above it and South 1st Street is below. It doesn't mean it's the best part of Miami, but it's Miami all right.

We passed all the run-down strip malls and *mercaditos*. This was Little Havana, and it was my stop. I rang the bell and exited the Metrobus with an uneasy sigh.

I strolled down the sidewalk. (It wasn't pink here.) When I passed a mailbox, I dropped Robert Greene's wallet inside. It wasn't certified, but I hoped the postal carrier would be in the mood for a good deed.

On the corner was a small cafe. No interior, just a windowed bar running along the sidewalk. Old men and hustlers leaned confidently on the counter, laughing and debating local politics. Who was corrupt, whose parents were real Cubans, even a mention of Castro. There was always talk of Fidel, but now they were referring to his brother Raul as *el presidente*. I supposed the old dictator had finally kicked it sometime while I was dead myself. I wondered if we toasted beers in hell. I paused with a frown, the manifestation of change sinking in.

As I stood, the scent of marinated beef and toasted bread caught my nose. It was instantly recognizable. My stomach growled. For some reason, I was ravenous. I kept my head down, pulled out a small wad of cash, and stepped up to the sidewalk counter.

I ordered. *"Un cafecito y un pan con bistec, por favor."* The old lady smiled and placed a shot of Cuban coffee in front of me. It was served in a tiny disposable cup, like something you'd put ketchup in.

If ever there was a nectar of the gods, this was it. It's not American coffee, and it certainly isn't your typical Starbucks espresso. Cuban coffee is dark, strong, and bitter. Add a metric fuck-ton of sugar and stir until a rich cream froths the top and you have lightning in a paper cup. It made the waiting easier.

When my sandwich came, I was in heaven. A marinated steak sandwich, screw sauce, because it's meat and it's for tasting. For crunch, it's stuffed with loads of potato sticks. And the bread... Cuban bread is a thing of art. On the outside it looks like French bread except smoother. On the inside, it's a whole other story. It's lighter, fluffier, and soft to the touch, perfect for squeezing on a flat press into a sandwich. It gets stale in two minutes flat if left in the open air, but my sandwich didn't last that long. It tasted so good I knew I wasn't dead anymore. Yeah, a real existential experience.

I popped a cone-shaped paper cup from a dispenser on the wall and filled it from a water jug. I needed to cleanse my palette and digest. Or maybe I was stalling. Having something familiar like this meal was incredibly comforting. I desperately wanted to be in the company of my parents and little sister again. But faced with the possibility, I had no idea what I would tell them.

Mind you, the benefits of being an animist aren't easily explained. It's not something I can chat on the phone about with the extended family in Cuba. My sister never minded, but my parents didn't think the dark arts had any future. In the end, maybe they were right. I had gotten killed, after all.

I gulped down the miniscule amount of water and crushed the cup in my hands. Regret wasn't my style. I was a seat-of-the-pants kinda guy. Live in the moment. And that's what I was now: alive, for the moment.

A famous poet once said, "Seize the day. Put little trust in tomorrow." Well, that's why I was here. I tossed the cup in the *basura*, left my change on the counter as a tip, and headed down the block.

Off Flagler, the businesses gave way to apartments and duplexes, then private housing. Cracked sidewalks and paved driveways, tiny lots with multiple cars out front. My destination snuck up on me and I was at the chain-link fence before I noticed. The house was in bad shape. Yellow paint flaked off the walls. The security bars were faded from the sun. This was a far cry from the Versace Mansion, but it was my home.

The first odd thing I noticed was the "Beware of Dog" sign wired to the fence. We didn't have a dog and there wasn't one in sight. I fought off a frown when I considered my absence. My dad had a bad back and my mom and sister wouldn't be able to fend off a burglar. Without me around, it was likely they got a dog for protection. Even more likely, they just put up the sign in a feeble attempt at security.

The Mustang parked on the street was new too. There was no telling who it belonged to, but it was parked up to the fence like the driver owned the place. My sister could have gotten a new car. I peeked inside. A pair of women's panties hung from the rearview mirror.

Uh, sister and I might need to have a conversation. I shook my head and smiled, then unhinged the gate and approached the door.

It struck me that I didn't have my keys. I patted my pockets out of habit anyway. The front door was open but the metal security door was closed and locked, so I rapped against it loudly.

"Guess who," I said hesitantly, deciding to play this as a light-hearted prank.

Yeah, bad idea. I'm full of those.

A man with an exposed beer belly hanging over his shorts came to the door and gave me the stink eye. "*Que tú quires?*"

"Uh..." I switched to Spanish. "Where's Lydia Suarez? And Oscar?"

The man's face didn't soften at the names of my parents.

"Who?"

"The owners of this house," I said, but I immediately knew I was wrong. The Mustang on the street, the dog sign... I didn't need to see the blank face of this stranger to know that my family didn't live here anymore.

"I don't know who you're talking about," he said gruffly. "This is my house."

I remained quiet, absorbing the news. I think I swayed a little.

Where does a person go when they have no home?

Chapter 8

I was dazed when I left the doorstep. Not sullen, not nostalgic, but straight-up dazed.

The man with the Mustang and rearview-mirror panties was in *my* house, and I wanted to tell him to get out or else I'd make him. I didn't care if he flashed a deed to the property—I had a mind to storm past him and lock myself in my room and blast rock music.

Still reeling from everything else, I did the smart thing and walked away. Maybe it would've been smarter to ask questions, but walking away was as smart as I could handle. Give me some credit. I could always approach later with a cooler head.

With nowhere specific to go, I strolled the old neighborhood, seeing things I recognized, but also seeing plenty of differences. Plenty of cars I had never seen before. A new roof on the Sanchez house. An iron gate on the corner. A missing palm tree.

Slowly I was getting the feeling this wasn't my neighborhood anymore.

The icing on the cake was the brand new stadium where the Orange Bowl used to be. A sleek building in place of the familiar rust bucket. *My* rust bucket. That wasn't the type of thing that changed in a single year.

A parked Fiat next to me chirped as it unlocked. I'd never seen the tiny car before, and I don't mean in the neighborhood. I mean I've never seen the model before. No one was in the car so I turned and kept walking, and that's when I saw the curvy hottie walking my way.

This girl was gorgeous. Supermodel hot, with her own Latina flair. That's not just code for big ass, although hers was serious business. She was short, tan, and had long, straight hair like a styled wig. I couldn't get a good look at her body because she wore loose sweats, but it was obvious from the way her blouse hung that she had a big chest.

The star of the ensemble cast, though, was her face. Plump lips, a Marilyn Monroe style beauty mark above on the left, and deep-brown eyes with matching eyebrows that incited intrigue. I couldn't *not* be fascinated with the girl, and she was dressed down.

She watched me curiously as she approached. I maintained my gait, tried to not look too impressed, and even managed a wink when she was close. That drew a puzzled smile.

I didn't know if that was good or bad.

I continued on, too wrapped up in my own problems to act. Or that's what I like to tell myself. The truth is, I was too chicken to say anything. This girl had the face of a diva. Very intimidating to my former (muscle-less) self. I liked to pretend I was smooth, but nobody was *that* smooth.

"Francisco?" came the singsong voice from behind me. "Is that you?"

I turned quickly, too quickly, with my left hand raised and my right in a fist at my side. A knee-jerk defensive move that made me look like a jerk. I couldn't blame myself for being a little jumpy, but would she? The pretty girl raised an eyebrow, puzzlement becoming shock.

"It *is* you!"

She took some hurried steps my way. I backed up and warded her off with my hand. I didn't know this woman. She saw my reaction and froze in her tracks. The shock on her face transitioned to relief, then fear.

"Who are you?" I demanded, checking the street for any activity.

"You don't recognize me, Cisco?" Her head made a little sweeping motion as she said my name, like women do in movies when they cop an attitude. Except there was no attitude on display, just a little hurt. "It's Milena. Seleste's best friend."

It all came crashing back. My sister and Milena Fuentes were inseparable. And now that she mentioned her name, it was all too obvious. I lowered my guard immediately.

Milena and Seleste were always a little overweight. No one would dare call them fat (especially with me around), but nobody could deny their raw beauty. Milena, especially, had the kind of charming smile that drove men to crazy places. Because I'd always defended them, I think she kind of had a crush on me. But we were eight years apart in age, and I didn't chase high school tail.

But there was a big problem with Milena right now. Namely that she wasn't sixteen years old anymore. The girl in front of me had lost the weight but kept the curves. She'd filled out and walked like a woman, and she didn't look nearly as innocent and shy as I remembered.

This was definitely my little sister's best friend, but not

the same Milena I knew.

"You have boobs now," was all I managed to get out. That's right. Cisco Suarez can be real smooth.

A smile flickered on her face, but she forced it down. "That's the first thing you notice?" Her eyes flashed and narrowed, and it didn't look like she was flirting. She squared herself to me in sudden anger. I didn't know what to expect, so when she slammed both hands into my chest, I figured I got off lucky.

"I went to your funeral, asshole!"

I quickly understood the mixture of pain and anger on her face. The puzzlement made sense. But there was relief as well, like I wasn't the only one who needed answers.

"My funeral..."

She stared at me hard, friendly eyes growing cold. "All this time I thought you were dead. After everything that's happened. And you just show up in the hood and give me a wink?"

"I..." I almost hyperventilated. But I cleared my throat. Shook it off. Got back in control. "I didn't know," I offered weakly.

That gave her pause. She must have seen something on my face. I wish she told me what it was because I had no idea. I was supposed to be calm and in control, with a plan for everything, *Ocean's Eleven* style. Instead, I had no idea how to feel.

"How long have I been dead?" I asked, remembering the thin, flat screens at the hotel and the portable screens at the pool. Even the brand new Fiat ten feet away.

Milena swallowed. Her anger was shaken now, a cocktail of rage and sympathy with a garnish of surprise. "Ten years," she whispered.

My breathing went into overdrive again, which is a stupid expression because overdrive is slower than fifth gear. But I stumbled anyway, worry attacking me from all angles.

Ten. Fucking. Years.

I pinched myself. I double-checked my pulse. Definitely alive, probably not dreaming. I'd been dead for ten fucking years and the world had rolled on without me.

Suddenly light-headed, I caught the ground with my hands and knees. Between gasps of oxygen, which I was pretty sure I still needed, I forced the words out. "My family?"

Milena's mouth opened. Her words, like mine, came hard. Her lips twisted as she debated how to answer.

"What happened to you, Cisco?" she asked softly.

I grunted. In urgency. In warning. In desperation. "My family?" I demanded.

The girl swallowed slowly. "You don't know?" Her hand covered her mouth and her eyes watered. "I went to their funerals too."

Chapter 9

It took me a while to calm down. I didn't want Milena's help. I didn't want to hear anything, really. Her pleas to come inside the house fell on deaf ears. I just wanted to squeeze my head until it didn't hurt anymore.

Eventually something rational took command of my lizard brain. I still refused to go inside and see her grandfather, but I accepted that I needed to take a load off. The passenger seat of her Fiat worked well enough. We sat in the car and caught up.

"It was a couple years after you... died," she said slowly. "Everything spiraled out of control without you, Cisco. It was tough for them. Especially Seleste. She almost didn't graduate high school. Even when she did, she held off going to college."

I listened patiently, quietly, with a tear threatening in my eye. So much for law school. I frowned, sad but sober. In control. Intent on soaking in every last piece of information with a steady head.

"She was just starting to move on," said Milena. "Not forget, you know? But deal. She was getting her shit together and interested in going to school again. Then..."

My sister's best friend rested her head on the steering

wheel. This was tough for her to relive.

"What happened?" I asked sternly.

"Someone broke into your house, Cisco. Your family's house, right down the block. Someone broke into their house and stabbed them to death." She cried again, and I could tell it had been a while since she'd thought of the tragedy. "They said it was a massacre."

If I'd been dead for ten years, that meant my rescue attempt was eight years too late. Some son I was.

"Who did it?" I asked calmly.

"No one knows."

I gritted my teeth. "Why?"

Milena paused, the emotional toll building. "No one knows anything, Cisco. But it scared the whole community. I couldn't live here anymore. I got an apartment, even if it meant leaving my grandfather here all by himself."

"Did you see the bodies?"

The girl turned to me, horror splayed across her face. "They were mutilated, Cisco—"

"Did you see the bodies?" I urged a little too forcefully.

Milena swallowed and shook her head. "They said it was them. Parts of them. But they identified them. The authorities wanted to cremate the remains but, you know, Catholics don't play that."

I nodded. My parents would've been mortified at the thought of cremation. At least their final wishes had been granted. Whatever those were worth. Here I was, back from the dead, master of death itself, and I couldn't tell you a thing about religious salvation. Some necromancer, huh?

My sister wouldn't have cared whether she was cremated. She was like me. On reflection, I guess it was a damn good thing I hadn't been. Otherwise I wouldn't be sitting here right now.

"Where are they?" I whispered. I had to pay my respects. I had to... see for myself.

"Saint Martin's."

I winced. It was a local cemetery in Little Havana. I had a hard time conflating the final resting place of my family with the graveyard I used to bike past while holding my breath. Innocent superstitions rooted deep.

"It's a really nice spot," Milena added after my silence. "Peaceful. Nice to see the family together. All four of you, under a winding oak tree."

"All four of us?"

She was tripped up by the incongruence of the statement. "I guess not really you. But your grave is there, right beside Seleste. Your parents bought all four plots after you died. It was their way of planning to reunite with you one day."

I frowned. They'd be waiting for me instead. Although our deaths overlapped by eight years, I had no memory of that period, no recollection of the afterlife or of being a spirit. I knew my soul existed, that I was more than flesh and bone. I knew it to my very core. All magic was based on that fact, after all. But I had no idea what that side of the world was actually like. Apparently, eight years experience hadn't made me an expert, or even a novice.

Milena interrupted my ruminations. "I can take you there. I have some time before work, actually."

I smiled. Ever thoughtful. It was nice being with someone I had a past connection with, even a weak one, but I didn't know if I could face the truth yet.

"Some other time," I told her.

She nodded like she understood. I twiddled my fingers, wondering where to take the conversation from here. Catching up had lost its allure.

Milena reached into her purse. It was an oversized bag that must have had five changes of clothes in it. She found a tissue and dabbed at her face. The waterworks were done. After a measured silence, she asked, "What happened to you, Cisco?"

I saw the question coming a mile away but still had no answer. I exhaled softly instead.

Milena knew about the spellcraft. She'd never witnessed much of it, but she was best friends with my sister, and I'd shared everything with Seleste. My sister had watched me practice firsthand, and the two didn't keep secrets from each other. Milena knew the deal, but she wasn't involved. I didn't think I should change that.

"I'll tell you when I find out," I answered. I probably wouldn't follow through, but it was semi-honest for now.

She sucked her teeth at me. "Don't even pretend that you're not gonna spill, Cisco."

I smiled. I guess she did have a little attitude after all. "It could be dangerous, Milena. Someone killed me and my family."

Her lips twisted in thought again. "You're still alive at least."

"I'm not so sure."

"So call the cops then."

I scoffed. "It's not that easy. What do I tell them when they ask where I've been the last ten years? 'I'm sorry, officer, I was dead, but I'm all better now.'"

"And you really don't remember anything?"

I shook my head and stared at the dashboard.

Milena leaned back in her seat, studying me. "This is about *brujería*, isn't it?"

I laughed, almost maniacally. Witchcraft. Black magic. It gets a bad rap. People fear it, but there's nothing inherently evil or demonic about it. Power tends to reveal a person's true nature, is all. People don't always like the truth.

Power is a staple of history. Legendary figures immortalized for their mastery in magic, some relegated to fairy tales, others sanitized for history books. Alexander the Great, Merlin, Hitler—they've all been helped along by the occult. The movers and shakers of the world, the special ones, don't fall into their status by accident. There's plenty of hard work, discipline, and knowledge at play.

But I wasn't in the mood for my diatribe. "This is something I need to do myself," I said.

"Oh!" she exclaimed, suddenly excited. "You should see Evan. He can help you."

My best friend. I hadn't even had time to think about him yet. Last I saw, he was a rookie cop for the City of Miami. "What's Evan up to these days?"

She flashed a triumphant look as if she'd solved all my problems. "He's head of some special task force for the city. He's really high up."

I raised my eyebrows. "Yeah?" My buddy had never approved of the spellcraft, but he knew about it.

"For real. You need to tell him what happened. Let me get you his number and address." She dug around in her purse until she plucked out a tiny device with an Apple logo on the back.

"What the hell is that thing?" I asked as she touched the pane of glass. "No buttons?"

She arched an eyebrow. "You sound like my *abuelo*."

Her grandfather. At twenty-four, she was calling me old. "Give me a break," I protested. "I've been dead for ten years. I have no way of knowing what 'the kids' are into these days." I smiled but she didn't find it funny.

"I'm not a kid anymore, either."

"I kinda noticed."

She flashed long lashes at me. "I'm twenty-six. That's older than you were when you died."

I was dumbfounded by the realization. No way to look cool after that. I wondered if dead years counted for anything?

She continued gloating. "You could say I have more life experience than you."

I rolled my eyes. I'd forgotten how much snark Milena dished. She got it from my sister. "You gonna tell me what you're doing with the tricorder in your hand or what?"

She laughed. "You're such a geek. I don't know why I always had such a crush on you."

"Don't blame yourself. You're just a sucker for a nice face."

Her eyes slid up and down my arms. "Well, I'm not the only one who filled out. Death comes with a gym membership, apparently."

I shrugged. It was the one thing I couldn't complain about.

"Anyway," she continued, "I'm checking directions on my *cell phone*. You need one nowadays, although I'm not sure if the carriers offer recently-deceased plans."

"Keep it up," I warned, but I couldn't help smiling. It was nice to live in a world that wasn't so heavy, even if only for a few minutes. "Besides," I countered, "Cisco Suarez has a phone." I lugged the Nokia out of my pocket. The thing wasn't cutting edge when I'd been alive. Next to hers it was an absolute dinosaur. Gigantic, blocky; small, monotone LCD screen.

She laughed hysterically. "Oh my God, Cisco. Why don't you just use tin cans?"

I frowned. My phone had caller ID and a speaker and a microphone. What else did it need?

"Where did you get that thing?" she asked. "The dollar store?"

"It was in my pocket when I woke up," I explained.

Her cheer evaporated and her voice went low. "You mean it's not yours?"

I shrugged. "I guess it's mine. Why else would I have it? I don't remember buying it, though."

"Does it work?"

"Yeah. Someone called me, but they didn't say anything."

She snatched the Nokia from my hands, opened the case, pulled the battery, and tossed the mess of parts outside the window.

"What the hell?" I yelled.

She ignored me and opened her door, got out, and stomped on the phone a few times. "They could be tracking you," she said, returning to her seat.

"What, like with satellites and stuff?"

She shook her head. "It's not paranoid, Cisco. The world has changed a lot in the last ten years. You're gonna get yourself killed if you don't keep up. That's why you need to let people help you."

"Help how?"

She brought up a map display on her phone and showed me directions to Evan's field office.

I nearly drooled on the shiny glass display. "I gotta get me one of those."

"I can't imagine life without one. All the apps you'll ever need."

"You mean you can order mozzarella sticks with that thing?"

Her confused expression turned into boisterous laughter when she realized what I was thinking. "Not appetizers, dummy. Apps. Programs on your phone."

The possibilities streamed through my mind. Maps, websites, games. "You're saying I can get MySpace on that?"

Milena rolled her eyes. "You have a lot of catching up to do."

"Try me," I challenged.

"Okay," she said, a smile playing across her lips. "Let's see. Since you died, Apple became a leading tech company, geek is cool, and they actually make good superhero and James Bond movies now."

I licked my lips. "Hmm, okay. Interesting. Unlikely, even, but definitely not mind-blowing."

"Castro's out of the picture. Fidel, I mean."

I nodded. "I heard something about that."

"We have a black president now."

I resisted the urge to raise my eyebrows. "I admit, that one's a little wow, but inevitable."

She sighed. "Okay Cisco, let me take this down to your level then. They're on the Fifth edition of Dungeons & Dragons, Liam Neeson is a huge action star, and Axl finally released Chinese Democracy."

I threw my hands up to defend against the onslaught. "Okay, okay. I give. You're right. This is a strange new world. I bet everybody's kind and considerate on the internet now."

She stuck out her bottom lip and shook her head.

"Great," I said. "Did they get better at all?"

She thought ruefully for a moment. "People don't say fo shizzle anymore."

"Thank God for small miracles."

She giggled and I followed suit. "This is fun," she said. "And a total coincidence. I visit my *abuelo* twice a week so it's lucky running into you."

"How is the old man?" I asked.

"He watches TV all day. Never leaves the house. But he has his mind and wants to stay put, so I don't tell him otherwise."

I nodded. "What about you? What are you doing?"

She shrugged. "I'm doing okay. I have a condo in Midtown now."

"What's Midtown?"

"You *were* gone a long time. It's a new neighborhood north of Downtown."

"They don't call it Overtown anymore?"

"Further up."

"Little Haiti?"

"No, silly. Not that far. There are lots of shops and new developments there. It's nice. Trust me. A lot nicer than this old neighborhood."

I took a breath. "Whatever you say." But inside I wasn't so indifferent. Milena had managed to get out. I was happy for her.

"Anyway," she said, "take my number too." She scavenged a scrap of paper from her purse and copied it down. She must have everything in there. "Until you get yourself a phone."

"I kinda had one."

She rolled her eyes. "I'll pick up a prepaid for you. Something that doesn't require a contract." She handed me the paper. I now had her Midtown address and cell number along with Evan's office address, all scrawled in glittery pink ink.

"How manly."

"Most men could use some glitter."

I ignored her and focused on the paper. Thinking about the old crew again spun the wheels in my head. My curiosity got the better of me, and I asked a question that was better left alone.

"What about Emily?"

Milena's eyes sagged. Em was my girl. She had been, anyway, right before I died. We weren't engaged or anything like that, but we loved each other. My ten-year absence couldn't have turned out well. I dreaded the answer, but Milena's silence was worse.

"What is it?" I asked frantically. "Did something happen to her too?"

"No, no," she asserted. "Definitely not. Emily's fine. I totally forgot you two were a thing."

I relaxed. I didn't know if I could handle any more bad

news. Then I realized Milena had probably been jealous of Emily. It was silly to think she still might be, though. Her high school crush would be long gone by now.

"What aren't you telling me, Milena?"

She smiled weakly, no trace of mirth on her face. "Well, she's married now. It was a while ago. She probably has kids—I don't know. It's not like we hang out."

I counted to ten. Deep breaths.

It didn't bother me. It really didn't. I'd been dead, and faced with the other horrible alternatives, Em getting shacked up and starting her own family was pretty good news. Not for me, of course. I still loved her. It felt like I'd only seen her a few days ago—a few weeks at most. The fog in my head blurred things. But Emily still felt like mine, whatever the truth was. How could I be jealous of her happiness?

I leaned back in the Fiat. With my knees against the dashboard, I wasn't exactly comfortable, but I tried to relax. I tried to see my resurrection as a second chance.

I was alive, damn it. That had to count for something.

But all I could think of were the mutilated corpses of my family. I'd been long dead, but their blood was newly burned into my brain. Somehow, I knew, this was all my fault.

No one else in my family practiced magic. I was the only one. Not just a black sheep, but into black magic. Spellcraft is neutral, but some of the circles I'd rolled in weren't exactly the most upstanding.

I'd been on to something, I realized. Something that had gotten me and my family killed. Something that could get anyone I knew killed.

I turned to Milena, her pretty face studying me. I didn't know if she was in danger, but I had to be. I needed to keep hidden until I figured out what was going on.

"I need to go," I announced, flipping open the tiny door.

"Wha— Now?" she asked, confused. "Where?"

"I don't know, Milena, but you're not safe around me. No one is." I closed the door and leaned into the open window.

"Can I at least drop you off somewhere?" she offered.

I chewed my lip, wondering at my next destination. "You can do me a favor," I said. "You can not tell anybody else about me."

"Of course," she answered.

I smiled at her. It had been nice catching up. Visiting someone from my old life. To see that some things were still normal. But I knew my life would never be.

"It was good to see you again," I told her, and walked away.

I followed the road, lost in my head. My life would never be the same now, that much I knew. They say everybody dies alone, and that's true, but everybody's also resurrected alone. And that's what I was now. That's what I had to be. A loner.

The Fiat started and pulled alongside me on the street. "Cisco," Milena called out, her voice thick with sympathy. "Are you gonna be okay?"

I kept on trucking. I didn't know what to tell her.

Chapter 10

I kept my next course of action from Milena. What she didn't know couldn't hurt her and all that, but it was more. I was paying Martine a visit, and no one liked Martine.

My sister thought she was spooky. Milena thought the same by proxy. My best friend Evan said I spent too much time with her. Emily *especially* didn't like Martine. According to Em, it's impossible for a guy and a girl to have a platonic relationship. I guess I could see a girlfriend being jealous, but I never did anything with Martine. Not like that. It was strictly spellcraft. And that's exactly what I needed now.

Black magic got me into this mess. Black magic was gonna get me out of it.

I'd taken care of priority number one. Sure, that meant looking out for number one, but it had also meant making a beeline for my family to offer them protection. They didn't need it. They hadn't needed it for a long time.

Now I meant to turn things around. To stop scrambling. Questions had been building for ten years, starting even before the day of my death. Questions in the fog. It was about damn time I got some answers, and one person came to mind to help me. Martine. The girl who'd gotten me into black magic in the first place.

So had she been working a tent at a job fair or what? The answer, like life, is more complicated than that (and doesn't involve a résumé). Time for some background.

I was a normal kid in middle school. A reader more than the playground type. Like all normal kids, I dreamed about being anything but. Still, I didn't decide to be a necromancer just like that. The first step was much more natural and scary. I grew curious about the dead.

My grandfather on my mom's side was the fun one. He always had magic tricks for me, and I'm talking about the cheesy pick-a-card variety. Every single time I saw him, he pulled a silver dollar from behind his ear and gave it to me.

Yes, I know he was supposed to pull it from *my* ear. That's how the trick usually works. But he told me he ate a leprechaun and could pull coins from *his* ears. What can I say? The story wouldn't work if the money came from me. Between you and me, I was a bright kid; I think he worried I'd figure it out if I got close. But I'm getting sidetracked.

When I was eleven, the old man died. My family drove up to Tampa for the funeral. I still remember sitting in the back seat playing with Seleste. She was only three so she had no idea what was going on. Me? It was the first real death I experienced. When we saw him, I knelt by the casket and prayed like a good little boy, but that was where the innocent act stopped. Looking back, I know this sounds weird, but everyone deals with death in different ways. I don't know if it was curiosity or denial, but I checked the old man's ear for that coin.

Honestly, I was shocked it wasn't there.

Even more shocked were my parents. I created a scene

and was scolded the rest of the afternoon. The next day, I got the silent treatment from my parents the entire drive home. But what do you think was waiting for me in first class mail when we arrived at the house?

Before gramps had kicked it, he'd stuffed a silver dollar in an envelope and mailed it off to me. Except it was postmarked after his death. That part resonated with me. From then on, I've believed in a connection between the world of the living and the dead. I knew spirits existed.

Of course, hindsight being twenty-twenty and all that, you and I both know there wasn't anything magical about the envelope. My grandfather hadn't been alive to personally send the coin himself, but it was probably a request to a friend or a lawyer completing the terms of his will. Mundane stuff. A last "got you" from the old man. But I didn't consider that at the time, and that's when it started: my fascination with death and the beyond.

Black magic, well, that's another level entirely. An innocent infatuation through middle school became enabled when I met Martine in high school. She noticed my curiosities and took me on as a sort of lab partner. She'd learned the basics from an uncle or something, and now was free to experiment on her own. Neither of us really knew what we were doing, but it was just enough to get into trouble. We sold some powders and charms. Bush league stuff. Evan and my other friends didn't like Martine but spellcraft was a passion. Evan went off to college. I didn't.

I opted for a different kind of education.

Magic isn't like in the movies. You don't go to school to learn it. Instead, it's pretty much how every culture since the beginning of time portrays it: funneling the power of spirits into action. It takes respect and understanding more than discipline, and some are more naturally gifted than others. Yours truly always thought of himself as a hotshot. And there was a reason for it. I quickly surpassed Martine in ability.

I don't think it made her jealous, but I felt bad. And as with school, I grew bored easily. I didn't want to commit to anything. So I branched out into other patrons and let Martine be the voodoo expert. She was just as hungry as me and got pretty good, always looking for that edge.

In the end, I had a feeling we found it. The edge. And whatever it was, it turned my world upside down. If anyone knew the why and how of that, it would be Martine.

The walk to her place wasn't long. She lived further inland so I moved west on Flagler, taking in the sights. Mostly, the neighborhood hadn't changed. Not really. Some stores had come and gone, the mobile phone companies had different names and logos, but it was the same hood.

After an hour I found the grass alley that led to Martine's house. A few properties were stuck in the middle of the block and had awkward entrances off the alley. It was weird, but it was private. We had liked that back in the day.

Martine's place was situated between two umbrella trees, the same off-white unassuming house I remembered. I watched from a distance to make sure everything was normal. No activity in or around the house. I headed over the step stones leading to the backyard, skirting the garbage cans on the way.

If I knew Martine, and I did, she wouldn't be in the house anyway. She'd be in the shed around back. We called it the cookhouse. It was oversized and had various structural improvements, but it was old. The wood foundation was decayed, but the walls were sturdy, the barn door reinforced. It wasn't a bunker by any means, but there were unassuming wards in the area that warned away curiosity. The death mask statue in the lawn, the wrought ironwork above the door, the brick dust lining the threshold. Nothing to see here but your average den of voodoo.

I paused before the shed. The cookhouse. This was an important place to me and Martine. It was where we practiced. In the middle of a beautiful and sunny Florida day like today? Martine was likely in darkness working on a new powder.

Before I knocked, I spied the crow sitting on the power line above. Martine already knew I was here. That was okay. I trusted the girl. Maybe trust was a strong word, given my predicament. It was possible Martine had gotten me mixed up in this, but she wouldn't do me intentional harm. That much I knew.

I busted out our secret knock on the heavy wooden door: a little hand-rapped Doo Doo Brown. What, you don't know Uncle Luke? Maybe it's a Miami thing. "Guess who," I said with forced nonchalance. Was I overcompensating or what?

I got no answer. A flash of movement drew my eyes to the house. Nothing there, though. The yard was still, the windows empty. I considered the shed for another moment before deciding the house deserved a look. Even voodoo priestesses deserved a break sometimes.

I carefully moved up the concrete steps. The back door was unlocked. That meant Martine was around, moving between the cookhouse and the house. I entered. The laundry room and adjoining kitchen were quiet. The whole house was.

"Martine?" I called out.

I didn't expect an answer this time and didn't get one. A half-full glass of water on the counter caught my notice, though. The contents were still cool. Beside it, a pound of ground meat defrosted in a plastic bag. Nothing disgusting; it was just beef. (Sheesh, necromancers need to eat too.) But it did tell me that someone was around. Today. Now.

My arrival became a cautious search of the house. The living room and Florida room were clear. I winced as I climbed the creaky wooden stairs, but no one heard the noise. I didn't get jumped by a Haitian voodoo gang. Martine and my friends didn't surprise me with a welcome-back-to-life party. The whole house was empty. She wasn't here.

Come to think of it, I hadn't seen her Volvo outside. She must have stepped out for hamburger buns or something. I wiped my brow in relief, wondering why I'd gotten myself so worked up. I returned to the kitchen, opened the fridge, and popped a Corona. A Tupperware container full of rice gave me a great idea.

"Screw hamburgers," I decided aloud. I could start my own welcome-back-to-life party, and I was gonna do it with some of my trademark Cuban cooking. I grabbed a small paring knife and chopped onions, green peppers, and garlic. Then I heated some oil in a pan and tossed the veggies in. For a while I leaned against the counter and waited, enjoying my beer. Just as the *sofrito* was starting to smell good, I got a bad feeling.

I hadn't searched the whole place yet. The house, yes, but not the property. I glanced out the window to the cookhouse and wondered. Something told me not to go out there. To just walk away, forget about Martine, forget about voodoo, and just move on for good. But I didn't listen to that voice. I never did.

I shook up the pan to stir the base and headed outside with my beer, not bothering to close the door behind me. I tried the oversized door to the cookhouse, but it was locked as expected. Locked from the inside. I knew I needed to get in there. For others, with the wards and fortifications, that might be difficult. Not so much for me.

The shed was shaped like a barn, complete with a double-wide door that swung outward. There was about an inch between the bottom of the door and the floor to allow the door to swing over the ground freely. It wasn't much, but it was enough space for me to get through. At least as long as the tree overhead cast its shadow on the entrance.

I stepped on the shadow and phased within it, as I'd done before with the wall in the alley. This time I slipped down into the ground and slid forward.

This kind of movement is limited. It only works along short lengths of shadow and doesn't let me actually go through anything. Not really. But the space I need for passage becomes minimal. Me and my possessions, even the beer in my hand, slid under the door and were inside.

When I phased out again, the faint smell was the first thing to confirm my suspicions. It wasn't strong, but a necromancer gets used to these kinds of things. My boot cracked a piece of glass. It was too dark inside to see, so I let the black seep into my eyes. Dried animals and fish oils weren't all that greeted me. Multiple body parts in varying states of decay were scattered across the cookhouse. Research, I hoped. I mean, a guy's luck needs to kick in at some point, right?

Wrong. In the middle of the cookhouse, splayed out beside an overturned table, was the body of my friend, Martine.

Chapter 11

The shed was a scene from a horror movie.

Multiple bodies were clustered along the walls where they'd been thrown aside. The wood floor was splintered, the furniture toppled. The scattered limbs and heads struck my psyche like daggers. All I could think about was my dead family. Had they been found like this?

The stench of decay was surprisingly weak, but present. I could tell immediately that most of the bodies had been magically preserved. All but one.

Martine rested awkwardly in the center of the cookhouse, her hips caught on the overturned wooden table that was the centerpiece of the workspace. Her shoulder braced against the floor, awash in red. It was a lot of blood, and easily explained: half the girl's neck was missing, like it had just been ripped out.

And Martine—she hadn't been a girl anymore. Ten years older, I reminded myself. Ten years different. I approached hesitantly, afraid to have this new image of her burned into my subconscious. But I needed to see.

I turned her head and grimaced. It was bad. Her mouth was frozen mid-scream. Her eyes were wide and vacant, literally: her eyeballs had been removed.

I turned away. This was done recently, as in hours ago. Her body hadn't started to visually decompose. Barely a smell. The other corpses were another story, but normal. A scene only familiar to a necromancer.

The bodies were Martine's minions. Zombies. And no huckster magic either. They would've been strong, which meant whatever ripped them apart was stronger.

This all but confirmed my suspicions about black magic being at the heart of this mess. Me, my family, Martine—it had gotten us all killed. And now my best lead was gone.

Gone but not forgotten. That's what people say, anyway. In this case, they were right, but I had my own saying. Fight necromancy with necromancy.

The missing eyes were a problem. Somebody had removed them for a reason: so people like me couldn't snoop. I kicked some body parts aside and scanned the floor. Objects were scattered about like Miami had its very first magnitude five. I searched the walls and corners. I picked up a large glass jar of dirt with holes in the lid, shook it up, and examined the contents. I would need it. In fact, the shed was filled with tributes, offerings to aid in black rituals. It would do me some good to stock up.

But first thing was first. I needed to find me some eyeballs.

I know that sounds gross. It is, in a way. But keep in mind, blood magic isn't inherently evil. Death is morbid, but necessary. Some cultures leave their dead out in plain sight and parade them through the streets. My art involves dead things, but that doesn't mean I seek or cause death. Are coroners feared for performing autopsies? No. They get a hit TV show called CSI. I'm a forensic investigator of sorts as well. I just use... alternate methods.

The barn door was shut tight. It budged and jiggled but didn't push open, which was strange because I didn't see anything physically preventing access. No matter. I phased under the door again and adjusted my eyes to the brightness outside.

The crow was still around, except now it was on the far fencepost. For a second I wondered if I was being watched, then the bird dropped to the ground and rustled its beak in the dirt, pecking for food.

I turned to the grass myself, checking for signs of blood, signs that the precious eyes were cast aside. I searched nearby bushes and the path to the street. On my way back, I set down the jar of dirt and checked the garbage cans. They were full and I didn't want to spend a lot of time so I flipped them over.

When I upturned the contents of the second, a large spider scattered from behind the can. I recoiled and let out a sissy yell, slamming my back against the chain-link fence. It was large and furry like a tarantula. Eew.

Yes, I don't bat an eye at dead bodies, but things with more than four legs *gross me out*.

After the waking nightmare scurried off, I inhaled deeply and regained my feet. Using my alligator boot, I continued searching through the trash. It was no use. Whoever had taken the eyes had probably flung them far aside, not placed them neatly in the garbage. Next to a murder rap, I doubt littering even registered.

I strode back to the shed, working my jaw, pondering how best to navigate this setback, when I noticed the crow pecking at its feet again. Something dangled from its beak, halfway down its throat.

"You've got to be shitting me," I muttered.

I stomped toward the black bird, hooting and waving my arms like a madman. It spooked and fluttered to the fence, leaving an eyeball in the grass. The other was still in its mouth.

I lunged at the crow. It took to the air but, in its haste, dropped its meal. I caught the slimy eye and breathed a sigh of relief, but the crow swooped down and caught the hanging optic nerve in its beak. Wings flapped hectically near my ear but I held tight and waved the bird off.

With an angry caw, the crow took to the air, circled a few times, then flew away.

"And stay out," I said. I plucked the second eyeball from the ground and returned to Martine's body.

The fleshy orbs were in bad shape—squished, picked at, half eaten—but they would do. As long as they were fresh, not much else mattered. I popped them back into Martine's empty sockets. She somehow looked worse than she did without them.

I dug around the floor till I found a shattered change jar. I plucked up two quarters and placed them over her mutilated eyes. These weren't normal quarters: they were pre-1965, heavy in silver. You hang around necromancers long enough, you'll find they often work with silver. It's a conduit. The most conductive of all the metals. Scientists like to frame that in terms of electricity and heat, but animists never forget about spirits.

Next, I ripped a strip off the bottom of her blouse and balled it into her open neck cavity. The white fabric drank the blood in. As I waited, I rested my hand on Martine's. I tried to smile, to think of good things, good times, but I couldn't. My mind was all about the investigation. A decent friend of mine, a colleague, was nothing more than evidence to me.

Martine had never outgrown the showy, skulls-and-crossbones phase like I had. Her belt buckle was made of pewter, an oversized disc with a pentacle on top, swimming in a sea of black lacquer. Dominating the center of the five-pointed star was a large skull, angry teeth lacking a bottom jaw. It was my friend's fetish, and I was in need of one. I unclipped her belt and put it on.

It would make my magic stronger, and I absolutely needed to get this next part right.

I pulled the strip of cloth, now saturated with blood, and wrapped it around my head like a blindfold. I rubbed some blood in a grip on the belt buckle and rested my other hand on my friend.

"Here goes nothing, Baron," I said, channeling the voodoo patron Martine had introduced me to.

Seeing the last moments of somebody's life is unnerving, especially through their eyes. All their struggles and fears become a part of you. For a few moments, you *are* them. For a few moments, it is *you* who dies. But it was the best way to get the answers we both deserved.

The moments were silent. My jaw was set.

"Okay, Martine. I'm ready. Tell me what you see."

Then I clamped my hand over her mouth like I was suffocating her.

Chapter 12

I scrape the mallet against the wooden bowl, grinding the delicate orange powder to dust. I'm an expert at this, only I'm not Cisco. I'm Martine, vodoun priestess, speaker for the dead.

The light bathes the room in a warm glow. Hanging oil lamps that Cisco didn't see before. The room is whole now, disorganized but not in disarray. Dried animal husks hang on the walls. Jars of oils and ointments sit on shelves. I am alone with my work, and I see them coming before they know it.

Outside my cookhouse are the brute and his fellow trickster. They should not be here. They are not supposed to come to me.

But I am at home, within my seat of power. I am ready.

I draw the wards away when the man stops at my door. "You may come in," I announce, and the door swings open. "But the anansi is not welcome inside."

The large man at the threshold wears a long jacket with a hood drawn, obscuring his face in shadow. He has the build of an ogre, a football player, a mountain in his own right. He stands as still as the earth as well, facing me, considering my motives.

"Have it your way," he announces in a deep, confident voice. He isn't scared of me, but he should be.

The man steps inside and scans the walls. He takes his time to aggravate me. To set me on edge. I do not disappoint him. "Why are you here?"

He shrugs casually. "We need to talk."

"We do not need to speak in person."

"Oh yes," he says, stepping closer, "we do." The darkness in his hood betrays a glint from the lantern flame.

I peek through the half-open door, seeing the shadow of the pacing trickster. Its unnatural gait sets me on edge, but it obeys and remains outside. "Get on with it, then."

The ogre nods. "We are displeased with you."

"I have done everything you've asked."

"Where is the Horn?" questions the large man.

"The Horn?"

"The Horn of Subjugation," he barks. "Do not play coy any longer. You have been deceiving us. Working with the shadow witch. Subverting our efforts from the beginning."

"Cisco?" I tremble at the name, one I haven't heard in a long time. But he was my only partner. I have no one else now. "What does Cisco have to do with this?"

"He's alive!" booms the man, raining his fist upon the table's wooden surface. The orange powder spills. It could be dangerous but I ignore it. The possibility of a living Francisco Suarez is much more dangerous.

"Impossible."

"It's not," he counters. "Not with powerful black magic. Not with your help."

I desperately search for the man's eyes under the blackness of his hood. I know now what he is here for.

"Resurrection? Such power is beyond me."

The ogre grunts. It sounds like a broken laugh, the noise of a monster. "Not with the Horn."

I shake my head. "The artifact was lost to me. You know this."

The brute doesn't move.

"You must believe me, Asan."

The man in shadow paces across the small cookhouse before turning to face me again. "I did. Once."

Something scurries outside the cookhouse. I ball my hand into a fist and the barn door closes. The man's head turns, but only for a moment. He looks to me again. I know he's smiling, but I can only see a glint of firelight.

"Do not act rashly," I urge. "You are surrounded by allies. Do not turn them into enemies."

"Allies?" he questions. "If I cannot trust you, and you will not help me, then you are a liability. Now more than ever, since he lives."

"And you are sure of this? You are sure he again walks with the living?"

"There is no question. The Bone Saints are tracking him."

I scoff. It is unbelievable. But...

The ogre cocks his head. "Where is the Horn, necromancer? It is your only chance at life."

I step away from the table. His mind is set. I can only hope the trickster runs. "The crow flies true," I say, "ever and only concerned with birdfeed."

The large man grunts again. "Your magicks cannot help you now."

I grip the skull amulet at my waist. We will see about

that.

The wooden floor beneath his feet erupts in a shower of splinters. An undead hand clamps onto each foot. The man pulls away but the grip is strong. He is trapped, a piece of meat waiting to be eaten.

The walls shimmer. Bodies, once unseen, stir to life. My horde. They will have a feast.

The ogre reaches down and grabs both hands. With a powerful tug, he pulls the zombie from the ground. My petite is thin but bolstered by blood. He screams and pulls but cannot get free.

The brute strains and rips his arm off. He throws it at the oncoming horde, then crushes my petite's head with a free hand. The mob closes in on both sides, but the monster is free again.

He strikes like lightning.

Limbs rip asunder. Heads roll. In quick flashes of movement, the ogre takes blows but he withstands them. There is something evil about him. Foreign. Not meant for this land.

I use the commotion to flee, but he sees me and slams me into the table. I tumble to the ground. It takes only a minute for him to cut down my mob and subdue me.

I cough out blood. I'm slow to rise. But I am not done.

The man lumbers my way. I let him grab me, pull me close. He grunts again, but the eerie sound is cut short.

Black liquid dribbles over my hand, cold to the touch. The blade in my fingers is colder still, buried in his belly.

The ogre drops his head, startled by the wound. The hood falls lower over his face. But he is still so strong. "Silver," he muses. "I will use it to inscribe your headstone."

I reach desperately for the orange powder, but it is out of my reach, knocked from the table.

"I will tell you how to get the Horn," I plead quickly. "Let me go, and you will have it. I swear."

He pushes forward into me. I can smell his breath.

"You have told the same lies for a decade. I am sick of them." He pushes closer still. "And I am so thirsty."

I press away but he holds firm and leans in. The hood falls away and I see a flash of metal teeth, shining in the weak light. They sink into me, tearing away my flesh. Devouring me.

My struggles stop. My thoughts slow. He drinks my essence, and I know that I'm slipping away.

Chapter 13

I ripped the blood-caked blindfold from my face and rasped on the floor, too weak to stand. I had expected someone powerful, but not like that. Martine had been a decent bokor, with ten more years of skill than I'd seen before. She'd even learned a bit of glamour. All that, and that thing had just cut her down like an afterthought.

Here's the thing about necromancers: they're not very durable. Death magic is about insight and control. A straight-up fight with a bruiser was better had at a distance. With an army in between.

Asan, this thing—whatever it was—had magic in its bones. It moved too fast to be human. The black blood hinted at a Nether creature. A fae. But it was unfamiliar to me. Incredibly stout. Incredibly ruthless.

And it was looking for me.

Good money he was the one who'd called at the Versace Mansion. This creature was on the hunt, and it knew about the cookhouse. It wasn't safe here.

I used the table to help myself up, stomping the fatigue from my wobbly legs. Experiencing Martine's death was a shock to my system. It wouldn't have any lasting physical effects but I had some funk to shake off. The bigger picture had more troubling repercussions.

According to their exchange, Martine and I had found something ten years ago. An artifact called the Horn of Subjugation. (Yeah, scary things have scary names.) The fog of my death blocked it from memory, but Martine had known about it.

I shook my head and gave my friend one last glance. She'd been working with them. At some point, anyway. In over her head. Maybe I'd played a part, but more likely I'd been played. And when, ostensibly, the proverbial shit had hit the fan, I was a liability because I was a free agent.

Amazingly, whatever had gotten me killed continued to elude the ogre ten years later. What did Martine say about the Horn? A crow flies true, always seeking birdfeed? A riddle? One last ploy to stay alive? Maybe she had only promised to help him to save her neck. If so, it hadn't done my family any good. And the ogre, Asan, knew: if I'd gotten to Martine now, it would all come out. He knew I was coming, so he killed her, just hours after I was resurrected.

That's why he'd taken the eyes. He knew I'd be right here, right now. He wanted to stop me from finding out about the Horn.

That meant this was probably a trap.

The door was still warded shut even though Asan was gone. He wasn't in here now, I was sure of that. So why'd he take the trouble of locking the shed?

As in Martine's vision, I heard scurrying outside. Fingers of light blazed through the cracks in the structure, and I realized now why the oil lamps were gone.

The cookhouse was on fire.

I looked around for anything worth saving. Any tokens

I'd need in the coming days. Most of the sacraments were smashed and scattered. Besides, the shed began filling up with smoke. I slipped low, into the shadow, and dashed under the door.

And ran headlong into a brick wall.

Not a real brick wall, mind you, but that's what it felt like. The shadow outside had cleared away. Had I trapped myself? Had the sun moved? I figured it was the fire. The licking flames would kill any constancy of shadow that could carry me.

It started getting hot inside. I could try slipping into shadow and remaining stationary, but that would only work until the fire ate inside the structure. We weren't there yet, but it would be soon. I was lucky they hadn't lined this place with oil, but that would've tipped their hand.

Okay, so I had time for a shadow manifestation. I was under darkness and the screwiness from the Death Sight was gone.

I marched right up to the barn door and summoned Opiyel, the Shadow Dog. I needed him to give me everything he had, because this wasn't a normal wooden door. I wasn't adept at hand-to-hand combat, but I didn't need to be with this kind of punch. I drew my fist back and tugged at the black energy surrounding me. My forearm became bathed in a black cushion, like the wake of a meteor meeting the atmosphere on descent. Then I hammered the barn door as hard as I could.

It shook on its hinges but held firm.

I narrowed my eyes. These weren't Martine's wards any longer. They were something strong, meant to withstand force, physical and ethereal. They knew I'd have magic. Did they know about the Shadow Dog?

The heat continued to increase. It hurt, but the smoke would get to me before the fire. I ripped another piece from Martine's blouse to tie over my face, then saw the breathing mask she wore when mixing her powders. It was a thick, burlap rag commonly used in voodoo rituals. I wrapped it around my nose and mouth like a Wild West outlaw. Immediately, my lungs cleared. I took in a breath not unlike a crisp beach breeze. With the amount of smoke building inside, that meant the mask was enchanted. Maybe I had never given Martine enough credit for her skill set. More powerful than a novice, but not powerful enough to save herself.

I was one to talk. Maybe I should wait until I got out of this mess before passing judgment.

My boot scraped over orange powder and sent a few sparks in the air. I remembered the stuff from Martine's final moments. She'd been prepping a new batch when Asan interrupted her. Maybe I could use it.

I withdrew the ceremonial knife and turned to the mutilated bodies against the walls. They wouldn't do. They'd been dead much too long.

Good thing I had a fresh corpse to work with.

"Sorry, girl," I said, turning to Martine. "Looks like I need your blood one last time."

The blade sliced her stomach open cleanly. I salvaged the spilled orange powder from the floor and scooped it into her open belly. Then I swiped some fish hooks from the wall and used them as crude staples to close her wound.

Many necromantic spells require ritual. Raising Martine as an automaton would've taken much too long—time that I didn't have—but that wasn't my goal here. Whatever brute strength a zombie could muster, my shadow magic should match. No, I needed something stronger than a punch.

I dragged Martine's body to the barn door. In minutes, the blood and powder mixture would ignite my friend like a bomb and blow everything to kingdom come.

Me too, if I stuck around for it.

I moved to the far wall, shifted into the shadow, and planned my next moves. I was safe here. Although magically activated, this would be a physical blast that couldn't touch me. Within seconds I'd be free. But someone had lit the shed on fire. Someone would doubtless be watching from the outside to make sure I succumbed to their trap.

And I wasn't gonna let that fucker get away.

I waited patiently. This kind of bomb didn't have a digital timer or a countdown. It could blow in a second or a minute, and when it did, I'd be ready. I allowed the darkness to slip from my eyes and blinked away the tears. I'd be bathed in sunlight when the shed blew. No sense being blinded afterward.

Before the blast, a piece of ceiling tore away and collapsed on the floor.

The room flooded with light, both from the fire and the sun. It ripped me back into the physical world against my will. No more shadow, no more sanctuary. Sparks rained from above. The rafter on the ground burned brightly.

I considered my options. It wasn't as simple as ducking under a table. With the sun above and the flames at ground level, any useful darkness in the shed flickered away.

I ran to the broken floorboards and reached for the exposed dirt underneath, shoveling handfuls into the fire. It sputtered and the corners of the room darkened. I kept shoveling, knowing I had only seconds to live.

Another rafter fell and fire erupted beside me. This plan was screwed. I couldn't put it out in time. With only a moment to spare, I stared into the hole as I dug. The hole the zombie had sprung from. Martine's petite. There was enough space underground for me. I lowered myself in, barely squeezing past walls of soil.

I heard ripping flesh and smelled searing meat. The room shook. My palm faced the top of the hole, blue energy sealing me in. Blinding light engulfed me and everything went silent, like someone pressed the mute button. The shield protected me from the blast and the fire, but it couldn't handle anything heavy. If a rafter landed on me, I was done for.

The rafters landed everywhere in the backyard *except* inside the cookhouse.

Large pieces of wood crashed into the bushes and trees and grass around me. My hearing came back, but it was just ringing. I dragged myself from the hole and checked the damage. The only piece of the shed that still stood was the warded door in its frame. Lines of bright red stretched across it, flickering like old neon tubes. It was a web that held the door shut—once invisible, now straining and weak from the force of the explosion.

That was some strong magic.

The ringing in my ears lessened and I shook off the daze. Licking flames snapped and hissed in the wind. A huddled mass floundered beside the house. Whatever it was, the blast had blown it against the wall. The torso struggled to get up, but it wasn't a human torso.

It was the same tarantula that had been hiding behind the garbage cans. Only now it was two feet tall.

"Fucking spiders," I muttered.

Chapter 14

It all made sense now. Asan had a companion. Martine had called it anansi. Only that wasn't a name, it was a type of being from the Nether.

The Nether is under us. Everywhere. Just a secret doorway away, it's a world of twisted, grotesque creatures. Anansi are trickster spiders from Africa, or at least the part of the Nether that maps to Africa. They're cunning foes that can shift in size and shape. No doubt the baboon spider had set the trap to kill me, watching in anticipation as I almost burned to death.

It had just found out I wasn't easy prey.

It skittered away to the side of the house, running for the front. The walkway was still well-shadowed beneath trees. I gummed up the ground. The giant spider's eight legs had trouble pushing through.

I checked the yard for other surprises. The anansi was just a pet. Where was the master?

The combination of explosion, fire, and smoke had cleared out the yard. The birds were gone, as well as the squirrels and insects. No sign of Asan. It was just me and the anansi. After the type of day I'd had, that suited me just fine.

The giant tarantula was almost clear of the shadow. I

chased it down the side path. In defense, it brushed its furry back legs at me. Hair filled the air like a cloud of spores, flying toward me. I threw up my shield and hunched behind it, avoiding the brunt of the attack. The floating hairs weaved through the air in odd patterns, going around the blue energy protecting me and backtracking after they passed. Scores of tiny barbs cut into my skin. I shut my eyes, thankful that I still wore the voodoo toxin mask so I wouldn't breathe in the needles.

I set my jaw and attempted to inch forward, but it was too much. The spider hair slashed at my arms and face. I backed into the yard and ducked around the corner, away from the deadly cloud. The damn thing was covering its escape.

I ran into the open back door of the house. The kitchen was filled with black smoke, and not from the shed fire. The peppers and onions were burning. I rushed through the house and out the front door, beating the slowed spider to the driveway. I jumped in its path just as it found daylight. The anansi screeched and sprayed me with saliva.

Great. The spider could make noise too. All that was left to realize my deepest fears was for it to crawl into my ear and lay eggs.

It reared up like a horse and doubled in size in the process. The anansi slammed its two front legs down hard. The ground shook as I sidestepped the blows. The spider swiped articulated legs at me. Several catlike claws slashed uncomfortably close to my face.

This thing was big and strong now. Absent a giant can of bug spray, I wasn't sure how to kill it.

I channeled the dog collar. Opiyel. It took extra effort in

the sunlight, but a tentacle of shadow lashed out from the side path and curled around the spider's back leg. The darkness tugged the anansi back into the shade, where I was stronger.

I charged. Large fangs extended like switchblades from its mouth, revealing dripping digestive juices. I lunged forward into the shadow and brought it around my fist, then connected a haymaker with whatever was the equivalent of a spider jaw.

The anansi literally flipped, pulling a full rotation in the air before latching sideways onto the house. Eight sets of claws raked lines over the concrete and ripped into the side door beside the garbage cans.

The effort of the punch had required dissolving the shadow tentacle. Shadow charming is intricate and requires concentration. Manifestations are pretty much a one-at-a-time operation. Now that I was done boxing, the tentacle returned.

This time, the feeler wrapped around the metal garbage can. I lifted it and slammed it down on the tarantula, my version of a rock and a hard place. The metal crumpled like a soda can and fell away. The anansi barely hissed.

It looked like the squishing tactic wasn't gonna work. Maybe there was a giant magnifying glass around.

Again I raised the garbage can. The shadow tentacle crushed it further, compressing it into a solid wrecking ball. Before it came down, the spider smashed open the window on the top half of the side door, shrank down a couple sizes, and crawled inside.

I growled and let the cannonball drop. My tentacle lashed out, just barely hitching onto a spider leg before it disappeared inside. I tugged hard, fighting the beast's strength, but it wasn't caught off guard this time and held its ground. I grunted and moved closer, straining against it. Suddenly, the tentacle ripped backward with the leg, except it wasn't attached to the spider anymore.

Eew. I released it and the appendage twitched by itself on the floor. Gross.

On the door, thin strands covering the window caught the light, then faded out to nothing. More invisible webbing, holding the door closed and blocking the broken window. But that couldn't slow me here.

I slipped into the shadow and phased forward, past the magical barrier and into the house. It was smokier now. I repositioned the burlap mask, still hanging around my neck, over my nose again. That didn't do anything for my eyes, though. It was tough to see. I did notice the smoke detector on the ceiling, its battery wire hanging, disconnected. I let out a wry chuckle. Classic animist precaution.

The anansi scrambled to the kitchen, going for the back door. Hot on its many heels, I shot around the corner, giving little consideration to how the trickster had earned its name.

In the heat of pursuit, I ran straight for the door, not noticing the anansi waiting in the corner. My legs seized up mid-run, constricting and causing me to fall forward. I caught myself on the counter beside the stove and spun around, aware of my mistake.

The baboon spider was tiny again. Almost unnoticeable. I could have run right by it. But the anansi didn't want me to get away either.

Around my knees were several loops of shining white

line, disappearing from sight but still every bit as solid. Elbows resting on the counter, I struggled to free my legs.

The anansi had other plans. It grew. Two feet. Three feet. The spider expanded in size until its presence in the kitchen was almost comical. The giant creature took cautious steps toward me on eight furry legs. (Well, seven now.) Its fangs were appendages as well, and two little feelers jutted out behind them. Imagining its intentions sickened me. If the anansi had its way, and enough time, it would suck me dry, not eating me but drinking me, crushing my flesh and bone into dust like I was a big ol' smoothie.

I wasn't gonna go like that.

The enormous spider unfolded two huge fangs and lunged at me.

My shield was worthless here. I threw up my forearm. One of the crushing mandibles caught it and a fang whizzed by my ear and tore my mask away. Damn those things were long. The anansi scratched at me but I warded it off with my arm. It might not be able to devour me through the tattoo, but I only had so much strength to keep it at bay. I was in a bit of a bind and needed a new trick.

Shadow magic is limited in sunlight, but sometimes the absence of shadow is even worse. Outside, the tentacle had reached into the sun and dragged the anansi to darkness, but that construct had to originate somewhere. A strong, solid shadow is necessary to source my magic. It's where Opiyel thrives.

Well-lit, modern interiors, like kitchens? I'm kinda boned. Which meant I needed to get creative, if less subtle.

The anansi released my arm and reared for another bite.

I grabbed the frying pan off the burner and swung. Hot oil seared into spider skin. A sickening smell of burnt Cuban food and sizzling hairs joined the black smoke.

I coughed and the spider shrieked, coming for me again.

The cast-iron pan knocked a fang away, but the damage was minimal. The spider jutted a front leg at me next. I ducked below the attack and my face stopped short of the flames on the gas burner.

Fire. Fire kills spiders, right?

The pan had spilled its contents but was still lined with enough oil to ignite. I swept it over the burner—

The anansi knocked the pan from my hands with a well-timed swing. The cast iron clattered to the tiles behind the spider. And my legs were still tied.

The creature almost laughed, if that was possible, and spread its two front legs over me. Mandibles wiggled with minds of their own. Digestive juices pooled at their razor points. A set of spider eyes blinked, save the two that were injured by oil.

The anansi struck like a cobra, and from my repertoire of clever maneuvers, I went for duck-into-a-ball-and-scream. Hey, getting the job done is more important than looking cool. The mandibles slammed into the stove top above me, brushing the open fire. The tarantula's entire face, already soaked in cooking oil, burst into flames.

The anansi's screeches, horrible before, were now death-curdling. My stomach shriveled into a knot. I rolled across the floor as the giant spider thrashed in the relatively small space, knocking plants and spices from the walls and banging into cabinets. But the death throes didn't last long. If there's one sure way to kill a spider, to almost make them explode, it's with fire. Ten seconds, twenty tops, and I was covered in anansi guts.

Some *sofrito*, huh?

Still on the floor, I tried the ceremonial knife on the invisible bindings. Surprisingly, it cut through with ease. Coughing from the smoke, I crawled out the back door and watched my friend's house burn. The explosion of the shed had been loud and sudden but, from the street, contained and invisible. It was possible the authorities would overlook it. Now, with an entire house in flames, they'd come rushing.

I wasn't sure what people would find. Corpses. Martine. Giant spider bits. Hopefully it would all burn away. But there was one thing I could prevent them from finding for sure: me.

I went down the path with the garbage cans and grimaced at the severed spider leg. At least it wasn't moving anymore. Using a plastic bag from the scattered trash pile, I hefted the leg and shoved it through the window. Somehow I managed that with my eyes closed.

Fire spilled into the hallway and began erasing evidence that I was ever there. The flames seemed to steal my happy memories of the place, not to mention anything that might've been useful. My boot kicked the oversized jar of dirt as I stepped away. I sighed, picked it up, and moved on. There was nothing else for me here.

Chapter 15

Of all the people I knew, Martine was the one that could've helped me. Watching her last moments of life only confirmed that. I bet she'd known exactly how I died, why I died, and what happened to my family. Assuming cooperation, a few minutes with her would've filled in all my blanks.

I hadn't come away completely empty-handed though, and I'm not just talking about the jar of dirt I stashed on a side street and the enchanted cloth around my neck. I had information now. A Nether creature named Asan was hunting me. An artifact called the Horn of Subjugation was involved. Naturally, the former would kill for the latter.

At the same time, the death sight had introduced doubts. Asan was capable of murdering me and my family, but I'd figured those for Haitian jobs. I also doubted Martine's loyalty, once a solid partner, now a possible (and dead) traitor. Were the Bone Saints mixed up in their plot? I wondered if Asan was a Bone Saint himself, but Haiti was the New World. The pet anansi suggested Old World roots.

Sure, my understanding of the situation wasn't a field of rolling flowers, but I wasn't lost in the woods anymore either. My info wasn't great but it was a starting point. And hey, I'd almost been dissolved and devoured over the course of several hours. Just being alive was cause for optimism.

Still, I was left with few people to turn to. I couldn't trust anyone hooked into the magic scene, not anymore. And I couldn't risk the lives of my friends by being seen with them. But my absence hadn't prevented Martine's death. The mere threat of my turning up was enough to have her killed. What if my other friends were in a similar position? As long as I didn't carelessly lead anyone to their doorsteps, didn't I have an obligation to check on them?

One name kept tumbling around my head, prompted by Milena's glittery ink: Evan Cross.

Normally, I'd leave my best friend out of this. Spellcraft was not his cup of joe. But his position as a police officer could come in handy. If not for clutch assists, what were best friends for?

I've known Evan Cross since elementary school. Back when I was normal, he likes to joke. There's truth to the humor. Back then, we were just kids. We played with action figures and went on bike rides. Kid stuff. Then Evan and I grew apart. He played sports. I played RPGs. He exercised, and I exercised my imagination. By the time high school rolled around, Evan was the quarterback of the football team and I was a full-blown animist. Go figure.

It's amazing we remained friends through it all. True, he dislikes my craft, but he has a good heart. He ignores what he disagrees with and sees me as the same eight-year-old he used to BMX race with.

After he returned to Miami with his criminology degree, Evan breezed through the police academy and aced his field training. I knew him as a rookie, but he was too smart for patrol. News of his promotion was no surprise. Head of a special task force? Well, maybe just a little bit.

When the bus dropped me off in Downtown Miami, I checked my six. I couldn't shake the eerie feeling that I was followed. Hey, it's not paranoid if it's true. Not only were the Bone Saints after me, but Asan as well. And the last thing I wanted to do was endanger my friend.

I found Evan's field office without incident. It was an unassuming building without signs or markings announcing the police affiliation. Evan was more legit than I thought.

You might think it's a dumb move to walk right into a police station after the kind of day I'd had. I don't entirely disagree. Usually, I'm a planner. Things don't always *go* as planned, and sometimes it's more stressful keeping a plan together as it falls apart, but I like to be in control. To see all the angles. I wanna know what someone's going to say before asking the question. To know how things will play out before setting my pieces on the board. For example, it would be nice to know if I'm walking into a trickster spider trap. And, in this case, that there's not a warrant out for my arrest, before I submit myself to the police.

But desperate times, and all that.

Besides, I trusted Evan. He probably had a new best friend by now, but I didn't. He'd see that. He'd do the right thing.

I opened the door and marched in, expecting to give a fake name to a front desk officer. Instead I was greeted by several cluttered workstations. The layout of the office didn't waste any real estate. Just enough space for the staff to work effectively and comfortably, but no more. High-tech computers (to me anyway) dotted the main room. Everything from equipment, files, and personal items found a proper place. Thankfully, the actual detectives were absent.

Two doors loomed against the far wall, one open and one closed. I approached slowly, wondering if I was trespassing at this point. The name placard on the closed door read, "Sergeant Ronaldo Garcia." When I got close enough to the open door to check the name, Evan Cross looked up at me from behind his desk.

"What are you—" he started, pausing just as suddenly. His eyes widened and his mouth hovered open, trying to speak but failing.

I smiled. "Who'd you have to blow to get this office?"

The bad joke barely registered on his face. Evan stood up. "Cisco?"

I tried to come up with an equally sophisticated punch line, but sometimes perfection is best left alone. I just shrugged.

"Holy shit!" boomed my best friend. "You're alive, you son of a bitch!" He hurried around the desk, gave me a hug, then drew back to look at me. "I can't believe it."

My friend had short, dirty-blond hair and what could only be described as a cop's face. He was taller than me, and I wasn't short. Thinner, but well-muscled. The white shoes, white pants, and polo combination didn't scream tough guy. The double shoulder holster with twin Colt Diamondbacks did.

"Jesus," I muttered. "You look like Steve McQueen."

Evan laughed. "Thanks."

"Don't worry. It's mostly about the bad-ass-in-charge

persona, not the looks."

"You're no spring chicken yourself," he said, eyeing me over. "You've lost some of that boyish charm in your face. But man, you've been working out."

"I'm not sure I recognize myself anymore."

He cocked his head. "You look tough."

"It's just a facade."

Evan nodded. "You're back," he repeated, and excitement slowly turned into an awkward frown. "But how?"

"That's what I'm here to find out."

Evan blinked, checked the main room, then shut his office door. He knew *about* magic. He didn't practice, but he knew *I* did. Just because he didn't have the stomach for it didn't mean he refused to believe.

"I've never heard of resurrection magic before," he said, keeping a distance from me now.

"Me neither, except that it's impossible."

"Impossible," Evan agreed.

"Exactly. *Totally* and *utterly* impossible."

Evan watched me uneasily. "Right." He backed up and sat on top of his desk without taking his eyes off me. After a minute of silence, I shook my head and sat in one of the chairs facing the desk.

"Relax, Evan. It's me. I swear. Why don't you pour me a shot of whiskey from the bottle I know is in one of your desk drawers?"

He half smiled, paralyzed for a second, but the suggestion of something familiar and normal, a drink with a friend, shook him loose. He returned to his seat and pulled a sealed bottle of whiskey and two rocks glasses from the bottom drawer.

Aside from beer to take the edge off, I wasn't much of a drinker. Maybe I didn't like losing control. Evan often encouraged me to man up and drink something that would put hair on my chest. There was no way I was gonna give him the ammunition to call me out today. Not when he was the one crapping his pants.

He poured two shots and added soda water to each, then passed mine over. I tried a sip and bit back the saltiness of it. Evan took his in two gulps, so I followed suit. It was only after the burn in my throat calmed that Evan spoke.

"You're supposed to be dead, Cisco. Your blood was everywhere. I've seen the crime scene photos."

I slid the empty glass on the desk. He gestured to the bottle and I shook my head.

"I don't know what to say," I confessed. "I woke up today in a dumpster in South Beach. Next thing I know, the Bone Saints are trying to kill me. *Again*, apparently, since they claimed to have done it already. Oh, and by the way, it's ten fucking years later."

"Can you ID them?" he asked, leaning forward. "Can you ID the one who killed you?"

"I was hoping you could tell me."

Evan leaned his forehead into his hands. "Fuck."

"Are you telling me you don't know?"

"No one knows, Cisco. It was a big story. It got a lot of play in a slow news period. We put out requests to the media for information, but you know how tight-lipped the magic community is. They don't say shit."

"Were they looked into?"

"I don't know, man. I pointed the detectives to that

voodoo friend of yours, tried to find answers on my own, but I was a scrub back then. I never got anywhere. Neither did they." I stared at him, upset at his ineffectiveness. He saw my expression and held a finger up like he had an idea. "But with you back, maybe we can make headway."

I raised a skeptical eyebrow. "What kind of headway?"

"The detectives weren't qualified for something like this, right? So they tried, but by now your file's sitting in an unsolved pile in a dusty box somewhere. But you can give us new leads. Your testimony alone is enough to get your case re-prioritized."

I shook my head.

Evan kept going. "It'll be easy, Cisco. I'll personally do everything I can to push this—"

"You don't get it," I said, raising my voice. Sometimes you have to do that to get him to stop. "I'm dead. I've been dead for ten years. I can't magically reappear and file a police report. 'Yes, officer. That's the man who killed me. But don't worry. I got better.' No one's ever going to be accused of this in a court of law." I hissed in frustration. Some bright idea. "Besides, my death took a toll on me. I don't remember anything that happened."

My friend went sullen when the reality set in. He shook his head. "I wish I'd known you were alive," he added.

"I wasn't. But I am now. I don't know what happened but I'm gonna get answers. People are going to pay for what they did."

Evan threw his hands over his ears. "Whoa, don't tell me that, man. I'm a cop."

I jolted to my feet. "Where were the cops when my family was killed? My little sister..." Tears came to my eyes but I forced them back. Dwelling on Seleste and my parents wouldn't leave me in the right state of mind.

"Don't blame me for that. I'm outclassed here. What did the voodoo bitch say?"

"Martine," I corrected. "She's dead. Killed hours ago by a man she called Asan. A man who was looking for me."

"Dead?" The surprise was evident on Evan's face.

"Yes, because she would've talked to me. I'm being hunted, Evan. Martine and I got into something. That's why I need to stay underground."

Evan Cross kept shaking his head as if denial could help. "I told you she was trouble, Cisco. I always told you she'd get you into trouble."

"Skip the speech," I warned. "I need answers, not more lectures on spellcraft."

"Why not? Because I'm right? I told you not to play around with that stuff since day one. Remember in school when you used to draw pentagrams and listen to death metal and wear all black?"

"That was just a phase," I said, slightly embarrassed.

"It was black magic, Cisco. Once you started playing with roadkill, you officially lost the right to call it a phase."

"That's different. The early stuff was teenager bullshit. I was a kid, man. But practicing was real. It's not devil magic, and it surprisingly doesn't dictate your choices in music."

Evan scoffed. "Make jokes all you want. Nobody liked it. Nobody liked you hooking up with Martine either."

I rolled my eyes. "Jesus, you sound like Emily now."

He stopped short and jutted his chin out. Whatever my girlfriend believed, Evan knew it wasn't true. My friend shook his head and took a measured breath. "Cisco, the point is that nobody thought what you were doing was safe. You need to own that."

Normally I would've snapped at him for the self-righteous act, but Em was still on my mind. Four years together. Out of my reach now. The last thing I wanted was to put her in danger.

Evan frowned. He hadn't liked Emily a whole lot at first, but I think that was because he thought she broke our crew up. After he got to know her, he understood why I was into her. Beautiful, Australian, she had a lot of experience traveling and knew about varied cultures. Both of us shunned higher education as useless. Maybe it works for other people, but for us it felt like thirteenth and fourteenth grade. One step above day care. We stopped focusing on class and focused on each other, always talking about traveling the world.

"Milena said she's happy now," I chanced.

Evan raised an eyebrow. I wasn't even sure he knew who Milena was. My friend rubbed the back of his head and winced. "Look," he said weakly, "I'm not gonna hide this from you. You're my friend, and I'm just gonna be upfront about this, even if it hurts. Okay?"

My heart stopped.

Evan said, "Emily's my wife now."

Chapter 16

"That's a bad joke," I said to my best friend.

Evan Cross shrugged firmly. "You were gone five years, brother. Emily went out with a couple different guys in that span, real douche bags if you ask me. I always looked out for her, though. You know that. Next thing you know, both of us are single, commiserating, and—"

"I get the picture," I snapped, before he finished the thought. Milena had said Emily was married, but she left out the part about it being to my best friend. I was stunned.

"I... This... How..." I fell back into my seat.

"I'm really sorry to tell you that," he said. "There was a small part of me that thought, if you knew, you'd be happy for us." The bastard even sounded sincere.

Look, I know ten years is a long time. If they held out for five, they weren't dancing on my grave or anything. And I truly couldn't blame Emily for moving on. But with my best friend? It felt unnecessary. Like I'd lost both of them in one fell blow. Life was throwing me yet another beating. Cisco Suarez, the dead horse.

"Let's just change the subject," I said, trying to outpace my self-loathing. "Onward, not backward."

Evan Cross nodded and sat back, but he wasn't relaxed.

His jaw was tight. His shoulders were tense. Mine were too. I avoided eye contact as much as possible.

"Look at you," I said in a lighter tone, trying to be happy for him. He was my friend, damn it. "You got your own office. The nameplate on the door says Lieutenant. You've done okay."

He nodded. "I command my own unit. The DROP team."

"DROP?"

"As in DROP the bad guys."

"Maybe you should DROP the acronym."

His face went sour but he shook it off. "District Risk Overview and Prevention. Miami's divided into five districts, with five city commissioners. This gig's a political appointment."

"Sounds kinda like you have five bosses."

"That part's not great," he admitted. "But it's big-picture stuff. The commissioners are concerned with long-term improvements to their districts. That's where the DROP team comes in. We analyze crime trends from the top down, look for underlying motivators for crime, and choke it out at the source. We're specially reserved for the long view."

Emily must be proud. "Sounds fancy."

He shrugged. "Eh, I'm practically a politician now. I get a call, work up an analysis, and send the boys out. Meantime, I'm sitting on my ass. Perks of old age, huh?"

I kept checking out his office so I wouldn't need to look at him. "I wouldn't know."

He smiled. "Come on, buddy. Whether you've been alive or dead for the last ten years, you aren't twenty-four anymore."

I couldn't disagree.

Evan stiffened. "Look, man, I'll help however I can. You know that. But I don't mess around in your circles. I don't understand the rituals that go on out there and I don't want to. My task force is purely mundane. That will slow me down. What I can do is get you gang intel."

My eyes zeroed in on his. "The Bone Saints."

He nodded. "My sergeant came from the gang unit, so I'm plugged into the scene. And what I don't know, I can find out."

"Let's hear what you do."

He nodded, eager to get down to business. "The Bone Saints have been making the news lately. A power struggle at the top. Elevated violence on the street. There's not a lot of intel on their new leader because he only recently came into power. The old boss was assassinated last year in a very public shoot-out. That's the official word." Evan leaned in and crossed his hands together. "It's clear to people like us that magic's involved."

"Tell me about it."

"The Saints are into all that voodoo shit, like you and Martine. Jules Baptiste supposedly had a falling out with his lieutenants. I thought he'd be around forever but they got him. That triggered a power play. Several other deaths followed, anyone from top leadership to low level peddlers—all street scum in my book."

I nodded, attempting to categorize everything I heard into easy buckets. Threat, ancillary, or worth looking into. "Who took over?"

"His name's Laurent Baptiste. And before you ask if

that's a common Haitian last name, they're related. He's the younger brother of the old guard, like Fidel and Raul. You heard about that, right? We got Bin Laden but needed to wait for Fidel to retire. Unbelievable.

"Anyway, from what I understand, Laurent Baptiste has majority support now and the takeover is complete. The guy's creepier than his brother. Paints his face and carries a snake around, and encourages his crew to do the same."

"All the bokors do that stuff," I said. He looked puzzled so I explained. "The Haitian necromancers, the bokors, they have a flair for the dramatic. The Bone Saints always did that."

Evan eyed me, surprised I knew that much. "Well, from what I've seen, there's a lot more face paint out there."

"That means they brought in more talent."

"I wouldn't doubt it," he said. "The Bone Saints have been more organized under his leadership. More of a long-term problem. Not just drugs but tax scams and stuff. Baptiste is a control freak in every sense of the word. If his guys are trying to kill you, it's definitely by his order."

Sheesh, I didn't even know the guy. His brother, the previous leader, probably hadn't been in power ten years ago. How could a dead man get mixed up in an internal gang beef?

"What's the African connection?" I asked.

Evan raised his eyebrows. "African?"

"I was almost killed by an African trickster spider today. I burned it down in Martine's house."

"Holy shit, Cisco. I don't want to know about that."

"Forget it then. It's dead. But it makes me wonder how the Haitians are connected to the Old World."

My friend looked at me like I was stupid. He leaned forward and whispered, "They're black."

I shook my head dismissively. "Thanks, jackass. I was hoping for something a little more concrete."

"Hey," he said, shrugging. "You're the expert, but voodoo, Santería, all that saint stuff came over from Africa with the slave trade. It's all the same crap."

"Maybe to the uninitiated," I said. "Think about how different Los Angeles and New York are, and they're in the same country. Africa's a gigantic continent."

"Whatever," he said. "You're the expert."

He said it sarcastically, as if I'd made a mistake and was backtracking with an unnecessary explanation. I didn't bother getting into it with him and moved on.

"What about me? How'd I die?"

Evan paused, going circumspect on me. "You really don't know?"

"I don't remember my death or the days leading up to it. I don't remember getting mixed up in anything, or even being scared. It's like, yesterday was a random day, only today's ten years later, and all I've got to show for it is a bad hangover."

"You are the worst material witness ever, you know that?" Evan shook his head and grew solemn. "We found your blood, man. Buckets of the stuff. Even though your body was never recovered, there was too much blood loss for survival. Everybody said it was impossible. Zero percent chance. And since the crime scene was on Star Island, we figured you were dumped into the Bay or the Atlantic."

The body of water between the island of Miami Beach and mainland Miami is called Biscayne Bay. Some islands lie off the MacArthur Causeway in between. Star Island is one of them. It's billed as the home of the stars. Puff Daddy, Shaq, Gloria Estefan. Real swank places.

"What was I doing there?"

Evan shrugged. "We don't know. The homeowners at the time were on extended vacation in Germany. They were cleared. We couldn't place anybody else at the residence. The property was on the market and a sign was out front, but the economy's been in the shitter since you've been gone. No one was buying or watching the house. We think squatters were involved."

I sighed. More like DROP the ball. Evan noticed my lack of satisfaction and became defensive.

"Listen, Cisco. The room was a mess. A pentagram was drawn on the floor with your blood. Judging by the smears, your body was once in the center of it. There were candles and dust and—"

"What kind of dust?"

"I don't know. I'm sure it was analyzed, but it didn't lead anywhere. The point is, we're out of our depth with this occult stuff."

I nodded in agreement. It was going to be the hard way then. "I need access to the property."

"Cisco, the evidence is long gone."

Forensics are one thing, black magic's another. After ten years, detecting trace Intrinsics wouldn't be a walk in the park, but given enough time and channeling, I could find something. I *had* to find something.

"I want the address," I said, leaving no room in my tone for debate.

"I don't have it. I don't remember addresses from years

ago."

"Then get me the file."

Evan rubbed the heels of his palms on his forehead. I could see him working through the logistics of getting me the case file. Going against procedure, asking favors, sticking his neck out.

"You owe me this, Evan. You can't sit on your ass forever."

He snorted. "No one sat on their ass. This was out of my hands. I say 'we' only to refer to the City of Miami, but I wasn't allowed anywhere near your case. I tried in the early days and got reprimanded for it. It was over by that point. I couldn't do anything for you." He was angry, but it didn't look like it was at me. He put his head on the desk. "I wish I'd known you were alive, man. Damn it. I wish I'd known you were alive."

I shifted uncomfortably. Wondered what this was like for the people whose lives I was interrupting. Maybe everything was silky smooth before ol' Cisco came back to town. Maybe the only thing I would do is scratch and tear and burn everything I touched.

I kinda liked the sound of that.

With a lull in the conversation, I re-examined the absurdity of my predicament. The police couldn't help me, Martine was dead, Em wasn't around to give me a pep talk. For maybe the first time in my life, I was on my own.

"What about my family?" I finally asked. "Tell me you have something there."

The same lost look continued to plaster his face. "I don't know what to tell you. There was a lot of blood, but the murders were years apart from yours. The scene was different. A massacre. No signs of ritual. The murders aren't officially linked."

I frowned. The desperation hurt. It physically hurt. Being dead was painless, being alive torture. The absence of information, the futility of the police investigations, the lost time—they were all needles biting into me, twisting deeper.

"What if they're not dead?" I asked.

Evan's face hardened. "Cisco..."

"I'm serious. Everybody thought I was done for. We both know damn well that the killings are related."

"We don't know that."

"Bullshit we don't. If I came back, maybe they did too."

My friend's forehead knotted. He was trying to be patient, but it came across as condescending. "Cisco, they were butchered. Hacked into pieces."

"You saw the bodies?"

His lips tightened and he nodded slowly. "I'm sorry, man. It was them. I don't know shit about magic, but nothing could bring what I saw back."

I nearly convulsed. Hope was important, even when it was hopeless. Holding on to that faint, stupid glimmer of a chance that my family was still alive gave me something to fight for. Maybe I was fooling myself. Maybe I should have stayed dead.

"What open leads *do* you have?" I asked stubbornly.

"You tell me," snapped Evan, losing his cool. "You come in here after ten years and make me feel like shit when you were the one mixed up in it."

"I didn't do anything. Don't put it on me like that."

He raised his voice. "Who had it in for you? Who wanted to destroy everyone you loved?" I grumbled and turned away, but that only emboldened him. "I told you not to mess with black magic, man. You never listened. Not then. Not now."

"Now?" I returned. "What other option do I have *now*?"

"How about being happy you're still alive? I want you to move on and figure out how to *stay* alive. Your family's been dead eight years. Digging them up won't do you any good."

"Oh, the hell with this," I spat. "You think I can walk away from this? Whoever killed me killed my family. Solving any of the murders gets me one step closer to ripping that bastard's heart out."

"You're living again, Cisco. Don't you see that? You're living, and you can't live for revenge."

I laughed coldly. "That's exactly what I'm gonna do. But it's not only about vengeance. Martine was murdered today. Who's next? I need to stop them. I'm the only one who can. If it's not me, then who?"

Evan squirmed in frustration but didn't have an answer for me. "So you're gonna go messing with black magic again. That's a great idea, Einstein. See how many more people get killed."

"It's not the magic," I said. "It's the people. Somebody needs to pay. My family's gone, Evan. You can throw me and Martine under the bus if you want, but my family didn't deserve what happened. No one ever brought them justice."

My friend could be a self-righteous bastard when he wanted to, but he knew how to pick his battles. He kept his mouth shut while I fumed.

I shook my head. Words couldn't help anyway. Nothing could.

I let out all my steam in a great big exhalation.

"Unbelievable," I said, smiling because there was nothing else to do. "My family and I were murdered, years ago, and everyone else went right on living."

Evan grimaced weakly. "That's what people do, Cisco."

No. Not when Cisco Suarez was dead. I locked eyes with him. "And what did *you* do, Evan? Besides 'take care' of my girlfriend?" It was a low blow, but I took the shot I had.

"I looked, man. You wouldn't believe the depths I went looking." Evan paused and held a far-away stare. "It cost me a lot."

I didn't care about his departmental reprimands. I was his best friend, damn it. My voice softened. "How could you turn up empty, Evan?"

He shook his head sadly. "I never had enough gas in the tank."

We both stared at his desk. A little stand had an outward-facing stack of business cards. Lieutenant Evan Cross. DROP team Coordinator. Maybe I was riding him a little hard. I couldn't guess what the days and years after my death were like. He'd probably gone through it with me and then all over again with my family. He hadn't been friends with Seleste, but my parents had cooked him meals and encouraged his education. I'm sure he remembered them fondly.

Of course Evan would have done what he could for me and mine. That wasn't in question. But he said it himself: he was outclassed here. I couldn't blame him for not being an animist.

He saw the determination on my face. I saw his worry. Maybe he hadn't yet realized things could never be the same, but I knew. I was way ahead of him.

After a minute, Evan relented, as I knew he would. "I don't have the case files," he said.

I didn't miss a beat. "You need to get them to me. There might be a clue. Something that would be missed by the police. Something that only an animist would see."

"They don't just loan these files out."

"You're not a scrub anymore, Evan. Use your political connections. No one needs to know the files will leave your hands."

He bit his lip but nodded.

I took to my feet before he could change his mind. My head spun. I was drained from the heavy conversation. From just being alive.

He scrambled to stand before I left. "We should catch up more," he said, snatching a business card and jotting his address on the back. "Why don't you come by the house for dinner tonight? Eight o'clock. You can see Emily." He paused awkwardly. We both did. "You should talk to her. She needs to know."

"Yeah," I muttered, taking the card. "Maybe." But we both knew that wasn't happening.

Chapter 17

Sometimes life punches you in the gut. A couple times, if you're unlucky. Once in a while it goes so far as to kick you when you're down and curb-stomp your head for good measure. Since I'd already been dead once, I figured fate was just trying to cover the spread.

But that's okay. I can deal with adversity. I get back up. There's nothing magic about that. As a kid I was a scrapper. Now, with my magic and my muscles, I could certainly manage.

The walk back to Little Havana would take a while, and the sun was getting low in the sky. I needed to hitch a ride. I considered my options and checked the streets just in time to see a Haitian round the corner a couple blocks back.

I hurried into an alley and masked myself with shadow. I didn't know for a fact that I was being followed, but this was twice in one day that I'd gotten the itch. Maybe parading around town on foot was a bad idea. Wheels. I needed a taxi or something.

I gave the man time to pass me but he never did. Eventually I peeked out and didn't see him. My nerves must have been acting up. When I noticed how fast the sun was falling, I cursed. It was getting late. My gut told me to wait.

Play it safe. But I only had one chance at this today. I was desperate, and I needed to beat the sun.

Screw it. The coast was clear. I continued briskly down the sidewalk. Have I mentioned I was desperate?

As I hiked down the street, a 1970s Monte Carlo with peeling brown paint pulled alongside the curb and parked. An old Cuban man got out and waddled to a crowded cafe window without bothering to close the door or kill the engine. He must have really wanted a *café con leche*.

I understood the impulse but had higher priorities now. As I passed his car, I checked my six again. No Haitians in sight. Without missing a beat, I slipped into the Monte Carlo and gassed it. I didn't peel out or cut off traffic. No, the trick is to look like you own it. Like you belong. So I used my blinker and waited for a car to pass and waved at an old lady crossing the street. And before you knew it, I was a mile away.

The new wheels were slick. I like big cars and it's hard to beat anything the seventies put out. I returned to Little Havana and recovered the large jar of dirt I'd stashed in an alley. By the time I parked and approached the iron gates of Saint Martin's Cemetery, the sun was just readying to set.

Here I was, the dead visiting the dead. Was it irony or a homecoming? There's a reason cemeteries close before sunset, and it doesn't take a necromancer to explain why. The main office was locked up. The gates were shut. No doubt the staff took the permanent residents here seriously. That meant it was just me. And just in time for visiting hours.

I circled the perimeter to a spot where a large tree cast a shadow over the gate. Phasing in was a simple matter.

Finding my family's graves was more difficult. I wandered as the minutes passed. The sun dropped below the horizon. That officially kicked off twilight.

In the wake of the sun, I was left in a bright afterglow of fading atmosphere. Even though the sun was below the horizon, rays of light reflected around the curvature of the Earth. The lack of a direct light source, however, meant the shadows all around me disappeared. In case it's not obvious, my shadow magic is weakest during these moments. Fortunately, this strange marriage of night and day has the reverse effect on necromancy.

Soon enough I saw the winding oak tree Milena had mentioned. At this time of day, it was beautiful. I approached the grouping of rectangular headstones laid flat on the ground. Oscar, Lydia, Seleste, and Francisco. The Suarez family. The perfect subject of an *Unsolved Mysteries* knockoff.

I dropped to my knees, placing the jar of dirt with holes in the lid beside me. I should say something. Pray maybe. Anything to get over the emptiness I felt. My parents and my sister were buried here, but seeing my own name etched in stone was the real mindfuck.

Francisco Suarez. He walks alone but always has a home.

I dropped my head. Sounded like my mother, the poet. I'd always been the black sheep of the family. Walking alone was a reference to me branching out, and probably to my spirit in the afterlife as well. But why ignore the literal interpretation? Here I was. Alone.

As far as a home, well, always is a long time. Home's forever gone. Even this grave, my resting place, had an empty coffin (if they even bothered to put one down there at all).

The story with the rest of my family was tragic too. My parents had purchased this family plot when I was killed. They cried, prayed, and buried my memory. No one could say the same for them. There were no epitaphs below their names in stone. I wondered why Milena or someone else from the neighborhood hadn't taken the initiative, but I couldn't blame them. It was the responsibility of family.

Twilight doesn't last long. Just till the remaining light from the sun fades and everything goes dark. Thirty minutes maybe. With that in mind, I got to work. I dug into the grass with my hands.

I know it's morbid, but that's what I do. Besides, I was supposed to be dead and buried here too. If I was alive, there was a chance my family was as well. Even if Evan wouldn't believe me. I needed closure and all that.

But I wasn't doing what you think I was. People dig graves in movies all the time, but I guaran-fucking-tee you the scene skips over the actual digging. Can you imagine clearing out six feet of dirt with a shovel? I can't. Here's a fact: the cemetery staff does it with machines. If you ever wondered why murder victims get discovered in shallow graves, it's because digging sucks. Luckily, I had a different aim.

With only a cup-sized hole over each grave, I unscrewed the lid of the jar. The dirt in here was softer and much easier to claw through. I pulled out a clump, shook it off, and held a squirming earthworm between my fingers.

The little guy was casually active, like he'd just had his whole world ripped away but was thinking about a nap. I placed him on the ground before me and collected three of his friends. Then I withdrew the ceremonial knife, wishing I'd bothered to sterilize it since its last use, and pricked the tip of my finger.

From top to bottom, I traced a line of blood across the center of my lips. Then I picked up a single worm, cupped it to my mouth, and whispered. He went in door number one, topped with loose soil from the jar. I repeated the ritual for the other graves.

This is what I mean about necromancy requiring patience and ritual. This spell takes a day to complete and only works during twilight. What I had done with Martine's body was a quick hit. An opportunistic spell on a fresh corpse to glimpse a window of death. The spellcraft I now worked needed time because I was after something much older.

Yes, this was much easier than digging—more low key as well—but it would take a day for the worms to do their work. I would have to return tomorrow. Which meant one more day of hiding before I could take action. One more day of shadows.

A raspy caw scraped the air. I glanced up and saw a crow pass overhead. A low growl behind me warned that I wouldn't be hiding after all. I wasn't alone in Saint Martin's anymore.

Chapter 18

Still on my knees, I turned and saw the zombie pit bull from South Beach scampering my way. I gripped Martine's belt buckle and established a link to the dog. When I made eye contact, the zombie slowed and became less aggressive. Something prevented me from gaining full control, though. That should've been a piece of cake with the skull fetish.

Regardless, the dog wasn't the problem. I could keep it from attacking me easily enough. What had me worried was who the dog had led to me.

You see, I'd been outplayed. When I'd taken the dog's collar in the morning, it licked me. If the pet was attuned to tracking, I'd be pretty easy to find as long as I was in the neighborhood. It likely took the bokor some time to track down his pet and prep it to tail me. Good thing I'd left South Beach shortly after, but it was only a matter of time before the Bone Saints caught up with me somewhere else in Miami. Chances are that Haitian had clocked me downtown, called the cavalry, and tracked me here. All because of a lick.

Hey, cut me some slack. I'm still a little rusty.

I checked the sky but didn't see the crow anywhere. The graveyard was otherwise empty until the pit bull's master turned the corner of the office building with two flunkies carrying automatic pistols.

The group looked different from this morning. More prepared, maybe. More determined. Or maybe it was just their makeover. All three had pulled their nice duds from the closet. Jet-black cargo pants and shiny, patent-leather boots. The two gunmen wore tight camouflage shirts. The bokor had some kind of tan ceremonial robe that looped around his arms and left much of his chest exposed, more tattoo than skin. The etchings glowed a pale green in the dying light.

All three men had white skulls painted on their faces, eyes and nose left as hollow, black cavities. The bokor had a silver hoop through his nostrils, a stud through his upper nose, and long hanging earrings. Matching silver gauntlets armored his fingers, more ornate than protective.

I guess they were bringing out the big guns tonight.

Still, this wasn't nearly the same fight it had been in the morning. I wasn't the same confused fawn. I had my fetishes now. I'd learned a few things. And I was ten orders more pissed off.

I grabbed a handful of the dirt I'd exhumed from the graves and slowly stood, realizing my momentary disadvantage. It was still twilight, which meant some of my stronger shadow magic was neutralized. Judging by the light left in the sky, that problem would be resolved in a few minutes. I just needed to buy time.

"I don't like being followed," I growled, trying to hold them at bay with my temper. The pit bull cowered but the men continued their approach. The two gunmen split out to my flanks. They watched me with practiced precision, if not knowing what I was capable of, at least familiar with the unpredictability of magic. With their faces painted, maybe they knew a little themselves.

Blood. Without shadow, I needed blood to fight this gang off. With a fist of dirt in one hand, I reached for my knife with the other.

The bokor snapped his silver fingers at me and the pit bull yelped. It charged me, ignoring my attempts to pacify it. I readied my shield but didn't need it; the gunmen were content to watch. They were, however, enough to distract me. The dog was on me in no time. Too fast for me to draw my knife.

The zombie lunged, snapping powerful jaws on my extended right hand and clamping down. Some of its dog collar, now on my wrist, helped armor my arm. It wasn't enough. I grunted as the teeth pierced my skin. This was no love bite.

My natural instinct was to pull away. Doing so ripped my flesh even more and didn't get me any less stuck. The men laughed as they watched me struggle with the animal. That pissed me off. Cisco Suarez wasn't a sideshow. I fought the panic away, then improvised.

I hooked my left arm around the pit bull in a head lock, pressing my body close to keep it from yanking my wrist back and forth like a chew toy. The dog opened its jaw to bite my face. Instead, I shoved my right hand deeper into its mouth, forcing it to bite down or choke. New scrapes opened on my wrist. The ball of dirt in my fist was now dripping with my blood.

Blood that I needed for my spell.

I released as much of the graveyard soil as I could, right

down the pit bull's throat. It gagged on the blood and dirt but, let's face it, zombies don't need to breathe. As the dog grappled violently, I leaned in and whispered in its ear.

"Shhh," I soothed.

And then the dog went to sleep.

The mirth on the bokor's face immediately vanished when his pet slumped to the ground. You know how they say you can sleep when you're dead? It's true. Sleep for the dead is permanent. Whatever magic animated the animal's corpse was dispelled.

"Sidney!" screamed the bokor, and—I shit you not— there was sentiment in his voice.

Some necromancers grow attached to their loyal minions. I've never had that much fondness for them. Death to me is clear-cut. A corpse is an empty husk without a soul. After death, there's nothing left to treasure, but don't tell the fine staff of Saint Martin's.

The bokor obviously didn't see things my way. He thrust both armored hands above his head to ready an attack. Then a piercing whistle cut through the twilight.

"That will be enough," boomed a voice from across the cemetery.

Two figures approached from the far end of the lawn. They strolled with the patience of lovers in the park. The man wore a tuxedo and top hat. As he passed several headstones he nodded as if acquainted with the occupants. His escort was a woman as tall as he was, with ropey and muscled arms. The gunman nearest them slung his weapon over his shoulder as they passed and smiled.

During the long silence, darkness fell and encompassed the cemetery. The shadow washed over me like a comfortable fur cloak.

"Who the hell are you supposed to be?" I demanded in a gruff voice.

Skulls shone in the night. Two sets of exposed teeth grinned wide, one painted on his lips, and the other yellowed from the cigar clamped between them.

"Don't you recognize me, *blanc*?" he asked, amused. "I'm the man who killed you."

Chapter 19

My face flushed at the revelation. I knew I'd be face-to-face with my killer at some point, but I hadn't expected him to introduce himself. I forced a cool exterior but fumbled over what to say.

The man in the top hat spread his hands in peace. "Let me introduce myself," he said in a thick Haitian accent. "My name is Laurent Baptiste."

My eyes narrowed. "The leader of the Bone Saints."

"Naturally."

Laurent took a hard pull on his cigar and watched me with interest. His hat was adorned with feathers and a wooden cross. His tuxedo was worn with age. The paint on his face was simpler than the others. More traditional. Less menacing. Possibly to counter that, he had a real-life snake wrapped around his neck.

I could feel the power oozing off him, empty and cold. This man wasn't just a bokor. He was a houngan. A high priest.

I ran my eyes over his getup. "Kind of a walking cliche, don't you think?"

I joked, but I knew the reason for the top hat and tux. It's the traditional dress of the Haitian dead. Houngans, as religious figures, are often expected to mimic the effect.

"What brings the Bone Saints to my neck of the woods?" I asked.

"There are many saints here, *blanc*," Laurent replied. "But the Baron is the greatest."

I snorted. He was talking about his patron. Orishas, totems, gods. All the same thing. Around Miami, between the Cubans and the Haitians, you hear the word "saint" thrown around a lot.

That might be confusing without a bit of history.

Christianity, traditionally, has not looked kindly on pagan religions. They're like oil and water (although stakes and fire might be more accurate). So what happens when people who worship many gods are conquered and told they can only worship one? Easy. They smile and nod. They find a way to venerate the many in secret. Except the best secrets are kept in broad daylight. In this case, in church, in full public view of their oppressors. The trick is to call one spirit Saint Peter, another Saint Matthew, and so on. Aliases for gods. Soon enough, they're surrounded with creepy statuettes and paintings. Saints, get it? They keep The Church happy while continuing the same ceremonies they've practiced for hundreds of years.

That's why the irony of the cemetery's name wasn't lost on me. Saint Martin is the syncretized version of the High Baron of voodoo. The Baron fueled my magic, and Martine's, and Baptiste's. If there was voodoo around, the Baron was involved. The difference was, Laurent was a houngan. To him, this was something closer to religion.

"Tell me the truth," I said. "You wear that snake just to freak people out." It was kind of working.

Laurent smiled, but I recognized the scorn in his eyes. He hated me. He'd hated me enough to kill me, and I'd never even met him.

"Shut your mouth," said the staunch woman at his side. She was dressed plainly and would've blended in with normal folk, except her sneer and buzz cut made it clear she was tough as nails. "You will speak to Laurent Baptiste with respect," she warned, waving her bo staff in the air menacingly. "And you may live longer."

I wiped a bloody hand on my tank top. "Living's not my problem," I said, eyeing her wooden weapon. She didn't actually know how to swing that unwieldy thing, did she?

Laurent huffed impatiently. "Why are you here?"

Although the gunmen kept their distance, the bokor converged on us. His body tattoos glowed brightly now that it was fully dark. "We should just get it over with, Baptiste."

The gang leader raised his hand. "Silence, Jean-Louis Chevalier. I would know his answer." Baptiste turned back to me. "What is it? You are looking to exhume some allies to defend yourself? To commune with my enemies?"

I stared at their blank faces. They didn't know. They didn't know my family was here. I wondered if they knew who I was.

"Something like that," I said. The bokor raised an eyebrow as he worked it out. "You guys and your names," I said, changing the subject. I layered on the fakest French accent that would make Pepé Le Pew proud and mocked them. "Laurent Baptiste. Jean-Louis Chevalier. Even your names are full of themselves." The bodyguard fumed at my continuing disrespect. "What about you? What's your name?"

She would've shot lasers from her eyes if she could. "Max."

I raised my eyebrows. "That's it? No last name heavy on the drawl? Like Pierre or Narcisse?"

"Just Max." She ground her teeth.

"Enough of this," boomed Laurent. "How are you still alive? I saw you die with my own eyes." The man leaned in to me and whispered. "And believe me: I am an expert on death."

I didn't doubt him. Remember what I said about animists who specialize in one magic being more powerful at it? That was this guy in a nutshell. An elder houngan who channeled the High Baron. To him I was just a dabbler, albeit a talented one.

The High Baron is similar to the other voodoo barons, of which there are many. Death, disease, pestilence, curses. Voodoo is poison, powder, and potions. But the High Baron creeps into domains that the others can't touch. Life. He offers healing properties. That kind of magic is exceedingly difficult, and nothing that I can touch. It is, after all, much easier to rend something apart than to mend it. I figured a houngan like this could shed light on my situation, even if coming back from the dead was supposed to be impossible.

But his question revealed his ignorance. This man may have killed me, but he sure as hell hadn't brought me back.

"Forget about why I'm alive," I said. "We're gonna talk about why you killed me."

Laurent smiled. "This is not a negotiation, *blanc*. For your sins, you will die tonight. Confess, tell me all that you know, and I will ease you over to the shadow world peacefully."

The shadow world. The Murk. The land of spirits. No matter what you call it, it never sounds appealing.

Max and Chevalier circled me.

I opened and closed my fist, squeezing blood from my wounds, working it over my palm. "Would you believe I have a case of selective amnesia?"

He snorted. "Who is your master?" he demanded.

For all his power, this dude was seriously misinformed. "What master? Shit, who's yours?"

He didn't miss a beat. "I serve the spirits."

"Yeah? What do they tell you about me?"

He grumbled and repeated his question. "Who is your master?"

"I have no master," I answered coldly.

Max's staff came down, but I was ready for it. My forearm caught the downward blow just above my head in a flash of blue.

Chevalier swiped at me with a silver-clawed hand. I side-stepped the attack and caught his wrist. My grip tightened and the blood on my palm turned. It bubbled and darkened and the bokor screamed.

I readied my attack on Laurent, but I hadn't expected Max to be so fast. She flipped the staff around, swinging the bottom at me instead of the top. The wood came in under my defenses and rapped me in the side. I fell backward and released Chevalier.

Back on the dirt, I rolled away from my attackers. They both suddenly stepped away. In a second, I saw why.

Laurent dumped a pouch of white powder into his palm, put it to his mouth, and blew. The particles flew everywhere, but mostly in my direction. I phased into the shadow of the night and slid forward, right between the houngan's legs. The powder blew away harmlessly in the wind.

I materialized behind Laurent and readied a punch to his kidney. The shadow drew in around my fist and I struck, but once again I underestimated his bodyguard's speed. Her staff came down hard and knocked my strike down, nearly breaking my wrist in the process.

She pulled her weapon back and jabbed at my chest. I hopped backward and avoided contact. Unfortunately, I moved too far from the group and became an easy target for the gunmen. One fired my way.

Bullets, meet pure, unadulterated energy.

The energy of my shield flared strangely. The familiar blue flash was there, but small orange sparks spiked out where the bullets contacted my magic. They felt like hail against my shield, each one noticeably sapping my energy.

I don't like surprises. Rather than deal with the problem, I jumped back into the fray with Max. That forced the gunman to cease firing. Unfortunately, it gave the bodyguard an opening.

She came at me fast. My Norse arm tattoo caught her first strike, but she spun in a circle and attacked me from the other angle. Spoiler alert: I don't have the same protection on my right arm. I waved my hand and a string of shadow flew up from the dirt behind her. It caught the tip of her staff before it slammed into me, halting it mid-air. Max almost lost her grip on the weapon as she continued forward.

Before she could recover, I stepped into her and grabbed the staff myself. I gave it a yank toward me and Max, already off balance, was pulled closer. In my short opening, I gave her a solid knee to the crotch.

She doubled over to the floor. Nothing magic about that.

I swung the staff in an arc around me, fending off Laurent. Oh God—he had the snake in his hands. What was he doing with that thing? Better than a spider, I figured.

Chevalier had pulled back, either to recover from my decay attack or to work up one of his. I swung my staff defensively again and realized my immediate threat was the closest flunky. He trained his machine pistol on me.

I chucked the staff at him. It wasn't a damaging blow, but it hit him and kept him from shooting me. Before he had me in his sights again, I wrapped my right arm around Max's neck and yanked her to her feet. Using her as a body shield, I charged the gunman. He couldn't get a clear shot and hesitated.

Checkmate, asshole.

"Shoot them both!" ordered Laurent.

Maybe I spoke too soon. The pistol erupted into automatic fire. Max struggled in my grip but I held strong. I ducked behind her and threw up my shield to protect my face. Max didn't fare so well. While her upper body was protected with mine, she twitched several times as bullets tore into her legs and stomach.

Maybe a second too late for Max, but just in time for me. I shoved the broken bodyguard at the flunky and grabbed his gun. He didn't let go, and for a moment the three of us fumbled awkwardly at each other.

Then the other gunman opened fire.

I ducked, pulling the machine pistol with me, but the

bastard still wouldn't let go. I spun around to position myself behind them and the gunfire kept coming. The flunky tied up with me gurgled and slackened. I spun around and drew the gun up, a loose arm still hanging from it. I wrapped my finger around the dying man's finger and pulled the trigger like a two-man job. The shots were wild at first, but I steadied my aim and cut down the other gunman.

Chevalier ran toward his fallen comrade to go for the weapon. I fired at him and he shied away like a frightened cat, taking cover behind a tree. Then I trained the pistol on Laurent.

I must have looked like a madman. My right arm was covered in blood, holding a gun that was still in the grip of a dead man. I was crouched and Max lay over my back, wrapped up with the flunky. It was all worth it for the priceless expression on Laurent Baptiste's face. For the first time, he was speechless.

I shook the pistol loose, found a spare magazine on my dead friend, and reloaded the weapon. I crawled out from under Max and stood. She fell to the floor and groaned.

Somehow, she was still breathing.

Max lifted herself on her elbows and coughed. Feathers and cotton, like the stuffing of a pillow, ejected from her mouth. She rasped heavily. It was a dry sound, but that didn't mean she wasn't bleeding. A hole in her neck leaked dark blood and more stuffing.

"What the actual fuck?" I said, turning to the houngan. "She's not a zombie."

"Isn't she?" asked Laurent. He was clearly nervous. Probably stalling and considering his options. I looked around but Chevalier was nowhere in sight. That meant zero options in my book.

"I'd know if she was dead."

The head of the Bone Saints smiled. "There are many kinds of death, *blanc*. And there are many kinds of zombies."

"Yeah, yeah, yeah. I'm tired of this game." I stomped toward the man, the pistol aimed squarely at his face. "I know a little about death too, houngan, and unless you want to meet it, you'd better start talking."

Chapter 20

Laurent Baptiste scanned the cemetery grounds. Two dead men, one gasping woman, and a rotting dog were the sum evidence of foul play. Chevalier the bokor was strangely absent.

"No one left to help you," I said to the frowning gang leader.

He calmly ignored the threat, instead choosing to be impressed. "Now I understand why they chose you."

"Who?"

He shrugged. "That is the question I posed you, no?"

I slammed the butt of the pistol into the side of his head, knocking his top hat off. He grimaced and rubbed the sore spot. The houngan's hands were painted white as well, skinny bones of ivory against his black skin. He opened those hands in peace, pointed to his jacket, and slowly reached in. I bobbed the gun slowly in warning, but he only pulled out a cigar, bit off the end, and spit out paper. I could only assume his first had gotten lost in the scuffle.

He also withdrew a butane lighter. It was a chrome number with a skull on it—something you might pick up at Hot Topic. Hey, we're necromancers. Skulls are kind of our universal symbol. There's a giant one on my belt buckle, so

I can't poke fun.

I kept my finger on the trigger in case this was a trick, but all Laurent did was light the cigar and return the lighter to his pocket.

"This is what we're gonna do," I started. "I'm gonna ask questions. The first time you lie to me, I blow your head off. Got it?"

The man frowned again. I could tell he understood, but he was taking his position entirely too calmly. That kinda freaked me out.

"Did you send that spider after me?"

He puffed on his cigar and narrowed his eyes. "No."

"What about Asan? You know who he is?"

"No."

My teeth ground in frustration. Not because he said he didn't know anything, but because I believed him. "I'll give you an easy one, then. You said you killed me..."

Laurent pointed to my chest. "Stopped your heart cold."

"How?"

The man chuckled. "How indeed? You were not easy to take down. Not easy to *track* down, for that matter. It took the better part of a year."

"You looked for me for a year?" I wasn't into Bone Saints business. It didn't make sense that they'd care about me that much.

"Yes. And when we found you, we came at you silently. We hit you hard from all sides."

"Why? What did I do to you? What did my family do?"

The head of the Bone Saints raised his eyebrows but remained silent.

"What did my family do to you?" I repeated.

I thought I saw worry creep into his face. "I don't know."

I squeezed the trigger slightly. Almost too much. I spoke softly but sternly, leaving no question as to my intent. "Why did you kill my family?"

Laurent Baptiste took a long pull on his cigar. He could see the possibility of not living past this night. For the first time he actually considered his death.

"I did not kill your family," he said.

I fired the machine pistol. A few bullets screamed past the man's ears and rapped against tree leaves in the distance. Laurent recoiled from the deafening noise. One hand grasped his ear, but the other reached for something on his waist. A charm.

I slammed my weapon into the bones of his hand, pulling shadow into the blow. A sharp crack announced the break. At the same time, I heaved my shoulder into his sternum. Laurent fell backward to the grass, landing next to his newly lit cigar.

"The next shots won't be a warning," I said. "Don't lie to me."

The Haitian leader coughed but answered as fast as he could. "I do not lie about this," he pleaded. "I do not know your family. I do not even know your identity. How could I kill them?"

He sat up, patting the ground for his cigar. I put my alligator boot on it and ground it into the dirt. Laurent sighed and resigned himself to a faraway look.

He didn't know my family. That's what I'd thought when he asked why I was at the cemetery. It seemed true. And the expression on his face. He hadn't expected me to ask about my family.

"Forget them," I said, starting over. "Why do you want me dead? Why'd you kill me?"

Laurent shook his head. "Is this a joke, *blanc*? After everything you've done, you ask me that?" He tried to stand but I pushed him down, keeping him on his knees. He scoffed. "Yes, we wanted you dead. You were so strong. You killed too many of us, but I got you. I put my hand on your heart and stopped it for good. I cut the rat's head and swallowed it. I drank his blood and poured it into your wounds so that your heart would never beat again."

Eew. He put the blood from that sewer rat in my body? Time to update my vaccinations for hep, tetanus, and the plague. But something about Laurent's story didn't fit my narrative. It didn't make sense but I was too wired to unravel why.

"I dispelled it," he explained. "Powerful magic. It weakened me to do it, but I was triumphant. It no longer had a hold on you."

Laurent was rambling now. "What magic?" I asked, shaking.

"You should not be standing here."

"What magic are you talking about?"

"You were meant to die in that dumpster, *blanc*. To pay for what you've done."

I stumbled back a step. I wasn't sure what he was going on about, but I'd figured out what didn't make sense about his story. I'd found the incongruence.

"That's not right," I said. "The dumpster was this morning. I died on Star Island ten years ago. South Beach was where I came back to life, not where I was killed."

Laurent's jaw hung open for a spell before widening into

a double-toothed grin. "Ah," he said. "Do you not remember? Do you truly not know?" He returned to his feet. I didn't stop him this time.

"Know what?" I demanded, holding the gun to his head. My hand shook.

"You think you know about death, *blanc*, but you are a child. There are many kinds of death. We only know what the spirits tell us. Baron Samedi whispers in my ear." He nodded, coming to a conclusion. "Yes, it should not surprise me that you do not know the truth."

I beckoned with the pistol for him to continue.

Laurent recovered his cigar from the ground. He ripped the ruined end from it and relit it. "These are expensive. You should know. They're Cuban, like you."

"Keep talking."

He puffed on the stogie until it had a good burn going. "I didn't kill you ten years ago, *blanc*. I killed you yesterday. Or at least, I thought I did."

I sighed, relieved to straighten out one fact. "Okay. Then who killed me ten years ago?"

"I do not know this thing. But in our line of work, would you not see the value in doing so?"

"I need a reason," I barked.

"I do not know the reason. Perhaps you should ask your master."

"I don't—"

I cut myself off, indignation fading to panic. What did he mean? It couldn't be. But...

"Why did you try to kill me?" I asked.

Laurent laughed warmly. It was a lustrous bellow that curdled my skin. "I have done what any man in my position would have. Killing you was retaliation for your sins."

My mind raced. I thought about Martine working with Asan. The ritual on Star Island. The Horn of Subjugation.

"I haven't done anything," I uselessly protested.

"It is not your fault, *blanc*. Zombies serve the will of their masters, not their own."

And with a shudder, everything clicked into place. *He walks alone.*

I didn't remember the last ten years—not because I was in a box underground, but because I had been the walking dead.

Chapter 21

"That's impossible," I screamed, head spinning.

Laurent bellowed some more. "Impressive, yes. Impossible? Hardly."

All the little mysteries of the day flooded my brain, pooling into rational explanations. The Haitians were pissed at me for something I must have done but didn't remember. The new tattoos on my skin were protection for a pet. Protection I'd used as a thrall, which explained my familiarity with them, my muscle memory. The dark aura. The strange resistant qualities my body exhibited. It was all explained away in a single stroke.

Someone hadn't just killed me ten years ago. They'd taken me. Consumed me. Commanded me. The Bone Saints had a beef with me, sure, but the one they really wanted was my master.

"But I'm not dead," I reasoned. "Right now... I'm alive."

Laurent nodded. "It would appear that way. But as the Baron teaches, there are many kinds of death." He motioned to Max, his bodyguard. I jumped when I saw her standing.

I twirled the gun on her. She didn't look healthy, but she didn't look dying. Laurent's magic was robust. He was a true voodoo high priest, and even then he could only guess at what happened to me.

That left the obvious question: Who was my master?

No way it was Martine. Friendship aside, she simply hadn't been powerful enough. The full blame had to land on Asan. He'd been the one who called me on the cell phone, right after I went rogue. He was tracking me down. Hunting his lost pet.

I turned back to Laurent. "You're telling the truth."

He puffed his cigar. "I am rather fond of my head. I'd prefer to keep it intact." He eyed my weapon as he spoke.

I lowered it. "Then you see I'm not a threat to you anymore. We can both go our own ways in peace."

The man's entire face smiled; eyelids hugged together and twin sets of teeth flashed. He nodded and plucked his top hat from the ground. As he placed it on his head, the houngan stepped away and watched me with intent eyes.

It was unnerving.

"Wait a minute," I said, noticing his accoutrements. "What happened to your snake?"

His smile never wavered, but his gaze strayed to a point behind me.

Suddenly, from behind the houngan, a bright spotlight flared to life. I ignored it and spun around. The snake behind me reared up, tensile strength evident on its mottled black and brown scales. My instinct was to phase out, and suddenly the spotlight fit into the picture. Cisco Suarez wasn't escaping into the shadow this time.

The snake struck. It seemed impossibly fast, but I managed to jam my left forearm in its path. The snake's wide jaws clamped around my armor tattoo, fangs reaching past the protected area. Latching down, puncturing my skin. I tried to shake it off but it held strong.

Instead of pressing his advantage, Laurent backed away further. I couldn't make sense of it until the gunfire opened up again. I should've seen it coming but thirty pounds of snake is a helluva distraction.

The bokor held the other machine pistol in one hand and the spotlight in the other, making extensive use of the spray-and-pray method. Good thing he got more practice at the graveyard than the gun range, otherwise I'd already be dead.

I swung my arm forward, still weighed down by the snake. My palm opened and a blue semi-sphere materialized before me. The barrage of slugs pounded against it, once again flaring orange. I sensed the difficulty again. Each bullet sapped my effort. Each collision made me wince.

I returned fire at the bokor. I didn't hit him, but I suppressed the spotlight. Chevalier ducked behind a tree and the beam of light flashed wildly at the sky.

Max's staff cracked down on my gunhand, jolting the pistol free. Just as well; it was nearly empty. She readied another blow. Without the spotlight trained on me, I entered the shadow. I fell away from the world, becoming the darkness, slipping along the ground before snapping back. The bodyguard's blow slammed into the grass a few yards from me.

Unfortunately, the damn snake was still latched to my arm.

The spotlight trained on me again. I ran away. Chevalier and Max followed, but the bullets were much faster. They rang against my shield, the force pummeling my arm. One or two flew in under my guard, grazing my strengthened skin. I dropped to the ground and curled into a ball, now immobile but behind full cover.

The snake chewed at my arm, refusing to admit it was too small for the task. Its fangs squeezed against the edge of my Norse tattoo, unable to secure a full grip but probably pumping me full of poison regardless. Maybe it thought it would eat me. The snake was either overly confident or had done this sort of thing too many times to count. I didn't care to find out.

After a quick reload, another barrage of automatic fire came my way. Pinned down, I was an easy target. Not only that, the rounds were beginning to physically hurt. I grunted as each orange spark seared my skin. I struggled to pull the snake away as my magic slowly failed. Pieces of blue energy flaked away until, in one blinding flash, my shield cracked.

Multiple collisions peppered my outstretched arm. The snake took a few bullets and fell away. I groaned and forced my eyes to focus on the flashlight.

Maybe I couldn't call up shadow where I was, but it was pretty damned dark behind Chevalier.

A thick tentacle shot up and grabbed the bokor around the waist. I would've snapped him in half if I had the strength. As it was, I settled for yanking him to the ground. He dropped the flashlight and fell, but not before one of his bullets found its mark.

My chest erupted in a gout of blood. No shield, no resistance. The bullet cleanly pierced my flesh and I felt like I'd been punched in my rib cage.

Max's head swiveled to the bokor and then back to me.

With him down, no longer firing, she was clear to rush ahead.

I was hurt bad, but there was plenty of time for that later. Since I hadn't been shot in the legs, I decided it best to use them. I ran.

I ran hard and fast. Neither of us were especially quick. I guess we both had enough holes in us to slow us down. I skirted the grounds, the three of them on my heels, using the shadows to my advantage. But I was tiring and in no condition to fight anymore.

Just as I thought my lungs would burst, I came upon the iron gates, cornered by Max. I smiled in relief and phased through. The bodyguard jumped and caught the top iron bar with outstretched hands. Impressive. I drew in the shadow and it sputtered weakly. As Max heaved herself up, I swung my fist between the bars and clocked her in the chest. She tumbled to the ground. I didn't stick around to see if she got back up.

I was back on the road in the stolen Monte Carlo in no time. My body was going numb, but as long as I felt my legs I was stepping on that gas. Putting distance between me and the voodoo crowd was the only way I'd make it through the night.

Laurent had turned on me. He'd been telling the truth and had every reason to believe the same of me. Instead he tried to finish me. That meant he would never back down, no matter what happened.

But there were no more undead pit bulls to pick up my scent. The Bone Saints wouldn't be able to find me anymore if I stayed out of sight. That was the smart play. I couldn't take on that many animists (and whatever Max was) at once.

Whatever Max was. What the hell was I? An automaton, filled with stuffing too? I checked the bullet hole in my chest. Nope, just heaps of blood. What a relief.

Cisco Suarez, the undead zombie thrall. That explained the neat muscles. Ten years of hard labor will do that. But I wasn't just any zombie. I was still alive. Maybe I was thirty-four, not twenty-four. Maybe I was a new man, more mature, free of my old ego and know-it-all attitude. Or maybe I was lightheaded and on the verge of passing out.

Baptiste had sworn that he stopped my heart. That implied there was one inside me to stop. That much was comforting, but with every beat of that heart, the stain on my tank top spread.

Chapter 22

I needed to see Emily. If I was going to die—again—I
wanted to be with her this time.

The Monte Carlo cruised to Brickell. The area was
different than how I remembered. Snazzed up. New
buildings, lots of restaurants and restorations. A buzz of
activity infecting the air.

I didn't really know where I was going, though. Miami's
an easy place to get around in. The roads are lined up in a
standard grid system, with streets going east/west and
avenues north/south. Brickell changed that, angling the
roads to line up with the diagonal coast. I needed to pull
over several times to get my bearings. Once I almost
nodded off.

The hole in my chest leaked bright blood. My hand did
an admirable job of plugging the flow, but I was more
worried about my insides. The bullet had pierced the top of
my chest, above my heart, I thought—I hoped. I could
breathe okay. With any luck, my lungs were still intact.

"What am I doing?" I berated myself for stopping again.
At least I was sure I hadn't been followed.

I studied Evan's business card for the tenth time, now
bent and covered in blood. Second Court. In between

Second and Third Avenue. I headed further down the street and finally saw the small road. It was a dead end set against I-95. A quaint little area, if a bit polluted by highway noise.

The house I pulled in front of was anything but quaint. It was a two-story McMansion on a block of small, Spanish-roofed houses. The building had boring, modern lines. Vinyl windows, newly planted palm trees, even a red-bricked driveway leading to the garage. A shiny yellow Corvette, a model I'd never seen before, was parked outside the garage.

I turned off the headlights but left the car running, contemplating the house with mixed feelings. Evan wasn't rich, but he'd done nicely for himself.

"What am I doing?" I repeated, forcing down the pain. I was tired of it all. Of staunching the blood. Of gritting my teeth and pretending I wasn't beat to all hell. I shifted in the driver's seat and noticed my left arm, more covered in blotchy black bruises than not. I'd acted like I was bulletproof, and I might die because of it.

But I had a dinner date with my best friend and the love of my life. I'd been robbed of saying goodbye the first go around. That wasn't going to happen again.

I saw Emily through the large dining-room window. She was beautiful. The indoor lights reflected off her pale skin and bathed her in a warm glow. She was a little older than I remembered, of course, but even more fabulous, like she had come into her own. She wore a simple dress that she made extravagant. She walked with her usual bounce. While she might have put on a few pounds, her long blonde hair and smile were exactly as I remembered.

It scared the shit out of me.

Was I here for me or for her? Would it do her good to see me? Like this?

I didn't have any right to be here...

I could tell Emily that I'd fucked up. That I'd been cocky. That I was sorry. I could tell her that Martine and I had uncovered an ancient necromantic artifact and a Nether creature had turned me into a zombie for ten years to find it. Or maybe sticking to sorry would be best.

The crazy part? I couldn't mention Martine at all. Emily would look more kindly on the zombie servitude than the thought of me hanging around with Martine.

What I did know was that Evan and Emily weren't in danger because of me. The Bone Saints didn't know who I was. Evan and Emily had no knowledge of the Horn or anything occult. No animists would barge through their doors. They were fine with or without me.

So it was me I was doing this for.

I checked the car's clock. Still a half hour till eight. I was early. Not that I'm big on dinner party etiquette, but I used the excuse to stall going inside. It was enough to watch her for a while.

Emily placed three plates on the table beside three linen napkins and three crystal glasses. Breaking out the good china for me. It looked wonderfully domestic, like a glimpse into the future I would never have.

Not the future. The past. Emily was my past. She was still alive. Happy. I was grateful for that. A part of me thought that going inside would be a step. A beginning. I could pick up the pieces of my old life.

But pieces were all I had. My life was a box of mismatched puzzle pieces, five-thousand count. Putting them together was easier said than done, and I was growing more frustrated with each failure. Sooner or later, I wouldn't be solving the puzzle anymore—I'd be flinging the box across the room.

Evan Cross entered the dining room and placed a bottle of wine on the table. Never saw either of them as wine drinkers, but they had a cultured image now. Picturing Emily as a wine connoisseur made me smile. Her husband placed his arms around her and they kissed. My smile vanished.

It sickened me to see them embrace. I mean, I knew they were married, but give me a break here. The knowledge was barely a few hours old and I hadn't even thought about them kissing or... worse. It was a lot to process.

Evan stroked Emily's hair and looked into her eyes. They talked and laughed. The voyeur in me wished I could read lips. Emily waved her hands around, becoming more animated. Maybe they would have a spat and get divorced by dinner time. But Evan reined her in, took a breath, and calmly explained something to her. Em turned white and went all serious. She glanced around and I could see her word "Now?"

Evan nodded and lifted her chin when she tried to look away. She was stunned. Apparently she had just found out who the surprise dinner guest was.

They spoke for ten minutes. Fifteen. A range of emotions from shock to accusation to sadness played across her face. I almost wanted to storm in and end the show. Or to start it, really. But I couldn't. After a while, Evan retired back to the kitchen, and Emily put her hand to her mouth.

I don't know why. I froze. I felt vulnerable just as she

did. I thought she could feel me, sense me just outside the window, staring at her like I was a shy high school kid. But she didn't know. She didn't look for me. Instead, she turned to a mirror hanging on the wall and fixed her makeup and hair.

That was flattering at least.

I coughed, checking my palm for blood. None yet. But I was still fading. Weak. At first I hadn't thought I'd make it here. Now it looked like I had time to spare.

Emily left the dining room and I smiled at her bounce. This didn't seem like a bad place to die. I waited in the car for a few more minutes, dozing off.

After some time, Emily returned. Her eyes were red. She'd been crying but she was strong. She always had more fortitude than I ever did. She was taking this news like a champ.

When she placed a fourth place setting on the table, I admit I was a little slow to catch on. Emily called out and her daughter approached the table.

That threw me for a loop.

What was I here for? What did I want from her, now, after ten years? Emily was a mother. A different person with a different life. Something I would never have.

There wasn't a single thing I could offer her.

And what was I supposed to do? Drink beers with my best friend while the two of them laughed at all their private jokes? No thanks.

That was supposed to be my life in there. That was supposed to be my future.

I shifted the Monte Carlo into drive. Homecoming was overrated.

Chapter 23

I floored the gas pedal, concerned only with leaving. It wasn't for another few minutes, when the adrenaline wore off, that I realized my mistake. I had nowhere to go. I wasn't so sure I could make it anywhere either. The car still had half a tank, but I was running on fumes.

My entire left arm was stiff. Between Max's bo staff, a hexed snake, and a number of bullets, it had been pelted worse than a punching bag. My right arm was better off, but crusted with blood and dog spit. The hole in my chest? That was the doozy. A shallow wound (as far as gaping holes go) but the bleeding refused to stop. So much for resistant skin.

I couldn't keep going like this. I drove through the north end of Brickell, passing new storefronts left and right. After a major revitalization, I didn't recognize the area anymore. Luckily, there was one place that hadn't changed. A little tattoo parlor snuggled up to the Miami River. The joint looked exactly the same as it did ten years ago: run down and empty. Like me.

There were no spots so I parked illegally, halfway on the sidewalk. Tow me. See if I care.

It was still fairly early, but Kasper (the owner) wasn't

exactly the paragon of business acumen. His hours aren't what I would call scheduled. Since he lives in the back of the shop, his workday consists of drinking and growling irritably at anyone who enters. The growling is worse some evenings and his regulars know when to stay away. Since all the lights inside were off save for the red neon, tonight looked like one of those nights.

Perfect, I thought, and went inside.

Kasper's shop is the opposite of impressive. It gives tattoo parlors a bad name. Etchings in color and black and white fill reams of paper, taped and stapled to the walls. Symbols and designs scrawl across the ceiling and doors. Buckets and supplies rest on chairs and counters instead of shelves and drawers. Most of the curtains are half disintegrated. Of course, since we're talking about a crazy, Norwegian biker, the walls are adorned with badass medieval implements too. A Viking helmet with protruding horns. A large hammer. A block of wood from a boat. Some things never change.

Kasper is an old friend, but that might be an overstatement. He's famous in the magical community for his ink. Not only is he a damn fine artist, but he's a grade-A scribe as well. Sigils and runes are a form of enchantment, a whole animist vocation unto itself. Most people see graffiti and tattoos as scribbles, and they're right often enough—but not always. In Kasper's tattoo parlor, you'll find sigils up the wazoo. The hum of their power delicately buzzed in the air, impressive to anyone familiar with magic.

"Kasper?" I announced, betting good odds he was in a respectable stupor already. I nodded to myself when he didn't answer. It was expected.

I went to the back office. "Guess who?" I pushed the door open and frowned at the empty sofa. I guess some things do change.

I wandered back to the main room, getting a bad feeling. The three tattoo stations appeared recently used. For all the clutter, the shop was a dump, but not abandoned. It was strange for no one to be around when—

The floor flashed red. Not the whole thing, just the bit that I stepped on. A red hexagon, like a stop sign, glowed on the dirty cement floor. It wasn't a circle of power—not really—but it sure froze me in place real good.

"Gotcha!" came a sharp voice behind me.

I tried to step aside but my feet were glued in place. There was movement behind me. I rotated my hips to spin around just in time to hear the clack-clack of a slide-action rifle.

I slipped into shadow, not even sure it would work. It did. A round blasted the floor where I'd been standing. I slid backwards and under, past the man with the gun.

Materializing right behind him was easy. Pulling the manifestation of shadow into my fist wasn't. It wasn't the low-lit, red neon lighting, it was me. I didn't have much strength left, so I had to make this one count.

I belted my attacker in the small of his back. A flash of blue smacked my hand away. He didn't budge a bit, and I suddenly realized who I was fighting.

"Wait," I said. "It's me! Cisco."

Kasper turned with determination. He wasn't what you'd call quick, but he knocked me on the head with the rifle just the same.

I fell on my back as my friend readied another round in

the chamber. I kicked my foot up at the last second and jerked the rifle as it fired. The bullet ate into the ceiling and rained down chunks of tile dust.

Kasper came at me again, this time with a kick. Still vulnerable on the ground, I pulled my foot back and stomped him in the gut.

More blue flashed. Pain shot through my leg. I slid away to get a good look at the old man. My shadow sight revealed his face, haggard as always, with a white beard covering half his chest. He was skinny except for a round beer belly. A full bodysuit of tattoos covered his shirtless torso and arms. There were even some on his face. With my magical sight, the scrawls glowed an azure blue. The bastard was protected with tats that put mine to shame.

He swung the empty rifle down now, trying to crush my head. My forearm blocked the blow in my practiced fashion. Unfortunately, while the armor held, Kasper was stronger than me. Not for nothing, but that was saying something with his scrawny frame. With each end of his weapon in his grip, he forced the barrel down on my neck.

"It's me," I repeated, before the rifle pressed against my larynx and squeezed me to the floor.

Kasper's face was inches from mine as he hefted his full weight on me. The same old man I knew, except his eyes were wild with rage.

I'd seen those eyes once, in the reflection in a car window. My eyes when I had first woken up this morning. It wasn't rage he was feeling. It was fear.

I pushed weakly against the barrel of the weapon, unable to free my airway. It was a struggle I was losing. My knuckles went white, my face red. My blackened left arm was almost entirely numb now, and the scabs on my right had reopened. I was a mess.

I fought. I fought as hard as I could. I grew light-headed. About to pass out. Then the rifle snapped into three pieces.

Kasper stumbled forward and righted himself. I drew in air and recovered my senses. We looked at each other, both confused by what happened.

My metallurgy had never cracked anything that strong before.

The biker jumped to his feet and ran for the back hallway. Most people would figure he was bailing, but I knew Kasper would never surrender his parlor. Down the hallway, I spied his true goal: a honking-big battle-axe hanging on the wall.

I wasn't gonna try an encore performance of my metal trick. I was pretty tapped so I went for something easy. I slid into the shadow again and beat Kasper to his prize, solidifying between him and the weapon, ready for his next attack.

It was an interesting one. The old man stopped short and flicked the light switch on the wall. There went my shadows.

I shook the black tears from my eyes and held up my arm. "Kasper! Would you fucking cut it out, you dumb redneck? It's me!"

My friend flinched, indecision taking over. He stood wired, in a stance of readiness, but in moments he relaxed. Kasper scratched his beard in contemplation. "Cisco?"

"Yes!" I screamed. I stumbled against the wall for support.

"Oh, why didn't you just say so?"

Chapter 24

"*Coño tú madre*," I muttered under my breath.

"No, no," lectured Kasper, wrapping my arm over his shoulder. "Don't you start with that Spanish nonsense. And I'm not a redneck. I'm from Norway." The biker effortlessly dragged me to an ink station. He swept the junk off his chair and laid me down. When he pulled up his stool, I suddenly felt like I was about to get a root canal.

"What do you expect?" I complained. "We're buddies and you tried to kill me."

He shrugged. "Don't sweat the details, Cisco. Hell, I thought you were trying to kill *me*." Kasper surveyed the damage to his shop and shook his head. "That ceiling's gonna leak."

I snapped my fingers weakly in his face. "Focus, old man. I'm the one doing the leaking."

Kasper studied me carefully. "You weren't followed, were you?"

"Just me."

The scribe moved to the wall and dug through his cabinets. So he did use those things.

"I realize I was a zombie for ten years," I said.

"Was?"

"Yes, as in past tense. But even if I still was, why the ambush? Why'd you think I would kill you?"

He frowned as he collected supplies. "You weren't just any zombie, broham. You were a hitter. A one-man death squad. An undead who used magic. Do you know how fucking rare that is?"

My brow furrowed. "Actually, I do. I'm a necromancer, remember?"

Kasper returned to the chair and shoved a bunch of gauze in my chest wound. The height of medical science. "You built a scary rep over the years, broham. Nobody wants to fuck with you. And I mean *nobody*."

"Tell that to the Bone Saints."

"That's different. You've been in open war with them. You killed their leader. The new one's kinda pissed at you."

"Baptiste," I said, still digesting the news. "His brother. I've met him."

"And you're still alive? I hear he's one bad SOB."

I shrugged. "I could've iced him. At least, I got that impression. But he's always surrounded by help." I frowned. "At least that explains the animosity." Kasper laughed as if I'd made a joke.

I closed my eyes. A zombie hit man with black magic. Slip into the shadows, sneak up on a target, and take him out. A year ago I'd done that to Laurent Baptiste's brother. He'd never forgive me for it. After hunting me for months he'd finally cornered me in South Beach and somehow got to me. Except, that wasn't me. My body, sure, but not my mind. I was a thrall. And for some reason, the real me returned. Only now I was a notorious killer. Hated and feared in equal measure.

I always said I wanted to be famous.

"Laurent was telling the truth then," I mused. "He said he wasn't the one who turned me. He said he had no knowledge of my death ten years ago."

Kasper fished around for metal tools and I kept my eyes closed. Baptiste wasn't important. The bigger picture was the story of my servitude. Asan and the Horn.

"So Baptiste's just another victim," I reasoned. "He doesn't know who my master was. He can't help me. But if I was hitting the Haitians, finding whoever turned me is as simple as finding their enemies."

Kasper grunted. "Good luck. The voodoo gangs all take bites from each other. Then you got the street dealers that don't know magic, although I guess you can rule them out. Still, there's a lot of bad blood between the Biscayne gangs. Especially lately. Now you have Nigerians and Puerto Ricans in the mix too. The area's a grab bag of criminals."

"Except no one wants to be grabbed." I grew solemn and tried to puzzle out my situation. The more I thought about it, the bigger the problem became.

Kasper must have been doing the same. He scoffed. "You're not supposed to be back, broham. That's why I attacked you. No one has the kind of voodoo power to live through what happened to you." He cocked his head slightly. "I mean, besides you, maybe."

I laughed and opened my eyes to a small pair of tweezers. "I was a quick study, Kasper, but let's not kid ourselves." We were talking withered-old-man-studying-in-an-ancient-tower kind of powerful. Movies. Fiction. Not real life.

I grunted as Kasper dug the bullet from my chest. "This

slug lodged into your rib bone," he said. "Lucky son of a—" The biker frowned and examined the bullet. He went over to the sink and washed it off.

"What about Martine?" I asked. "How powerful was she?"

Kasper returned with a needle and thread. "You mean that black girly you used to hawk potions with? I haven't heard a peep from her in ages."

"She's dead."

He paused with the needle above my chest and stared at me.

"It wasn't me," I assured him.

The old man nodded and then, without warning, went to work with the needle. It wasn't my skin he started with, but the torn flesh inside. I ground my jaw tight, suddenly not in the mood for conversation.

Kasper was a field medic in the final years of Vietnam. That puts him in his mid sixties now, though he could pass for younger. Always handy with needles and knives and flesh, when the war ended he turned his skills to more artistic endeavors. He knows his stuff, and not just the medical part. After I was stitched up, he traced a rune over the wound with a gold paint pen.

"That should keep it sealed and clean," he said. "Though I'm not really sure you need it."

It was exhausting to speak so I settled for a quizzical look.

He tapped my stomach. "It looks like you're no stranger to being shot. You've got grazes and bruising along your arm too. Except it looks like you've been playing with paintballs instead of bullets. What kind of healing you running?"

"Don't know." I tried to sit up but Kasper pushed me down. Just as well since I was still in pain. "I was gonna ask you," I continued. I opened my left palm to display the tattoo. "You know who inked these?"

Kasper traced the arrow on my arm with his finger, then studied the snowflake on my hand. "Excellent shading," he said. "Strong lines. Must be a good-looking guy."

I raised an eyebrow.

"You know," he said. "A suave motherfucker. A badass who knows his shit."

I pulled my hand away. "*You* did these?"

He shrugged and flashed a guilty face.

"First of all: Good looking? Suave? Have you checked a mirror lately? Secondly, what the fricking heck?"

"How the hell you think I knew about you?" he asked. "Becoming a zombie hit man wasn't in your obituary. You came in with a guy five, ten years ago. It was you only it wasn't. No jokes. No beer. You were the blandest dude ever. Speaking of which, you want a beer?"

"No," I snapped. "I mean, yes. But we need to focus."

"I know, I know." Kasper disappeared into his office and returned with two brown bottles.

"You got a Corona?"

"I don't drink that piss anymore. This is a stout. You'll like it. Tastes like Cuban coffee." He flipped the caps off and handed me one. I took a chug. Much thicker than I was used to. In my state, it was hard to down.

"You sure you don't have a Corona?"

"Hey, broham. Beer's changed a lot in ten years. Everyone's doing microbrew now. Even in this town."

"Fine," I said, taking another swig and sitting up in the chair. "Tell me what you know. From the beginning."

Old Kasper nodded resolutely and organized his tattoo equipment. He pulled a table over and stacked it with ink, a needle, sanitary wipes, and his beer. Then he plunked onto a stool and examined his handiwork on my palm.

"This is the Helm of Awe, an old Viking symbol of protection. A simplified one, anyway. It's hard to ink. Even harder to use." He studied the tattoo from different angles. "It looks like shit now."

"It's worse than that. The shield shattered completely."

He nodded and produced the bullet he'd pulled from my chest. "Two things. First is this."

He dropped the slug in my free hand. It wasn't a silver bullet or anything, just a regular round nose. It was slightly disfigured from hitting the bone but still intact. The etchings were clear, tiny inscriptions along the bullet. The Bone Saints were using magic bullets against me.

"You do these too?" I asked snidely.

"No way, Jose. I'm strictly a defense contractor, broham. If a lone operator like me got into the weapons game, somebody would smoke my white ass. I stick to the big D and everybody's friendly. It's not as profitable but I live to spend my money."

"Or drink it."

Kasper smiled and chugged his beer. "Life's about experiences, not things."

I knew he wasn't having a joke at my expense, but his friendly advice didn't help. I didn't have experiences *or* things. Just a large void where my life was supposed to be.

Kasper killed off his bottle of stout and let out a deep

burp. "Whatever healing or armor you're working is great against bullets. Not invincible, of course. Nothing is. But a hell of a lot better than the average bear. These enchanted rounds are gonna give you trouble. They're magic-piercing. They'll take a toll on you, but the Helm should've held out. Mind if I have your beer?"

Kasper was going for it before I shook my head. When he put the bottle down, he picked up his needle. "You really shouldn't have alcohol right now anyway."

The biker stuck the needle in my palm, again without warning. This time I was ready for it. Believe me, a tattoo on the palm is nothing compared to a bullet in the chest. I listened as Kasper continued.

"You should recolor every five years or so. These are the originals I drew way back when. Just like a muscle or your mind, you need to keep it in shape. You've been hitting the gym but ignoring your ink."

I nodded, admiring his handiwork. "Which you're supposed to be telling me about."

He laughed. "Yeah. You'll have to excuse me. I get... philosophical when I drink." Kasper cleared his throat and spoke in his grumbly voice, sounding both captivating and aggravated at the same time. "So when was it? Nine years ago? Ten? I don't know, but you were taken out by then. I even stuck my neck out and asked around. KIA, broham. That's what the street said. Now, in your line of work, a missing corpse is a curious thing, but I figured they burned you."

I clenched my jaw. "They should have."

He nodded. "Looks that way. Anyhow, sometime later, you came in with a scary fella. Big. African. Looked real familiar with wetwork. He didn't talk much and I was fine with that. You didn't either and that creeped me out."

"Was he Haitian?"

"I don't think so. I'd bet a beer he was from the motherland. Something about him was too foreign, like he didn't fit in here."

"Animist?"

"I couldn't tell, but he made my skin crawl."

"Sounds like the one who killed Martine. Goes by Asan, I think, but I guess you didn't get his name."

"You're guessing right. That's not how I operate."

A full name or background would help since I hadn't seen his face. But Kasper had. He'd seen him up close and personal and didn't think he was Haitian. Couple that with the anansi back at the cookhouse and the African front made a lot of sense. Competition for the Bone Saints, probably. More black on black crime. Except I'd been the trigger man.

Now that Kasper was on a roll, he kept going. "The big man gave me the specs and enough money to keep it quiet. I did my thing. Slowly. You know how long these took to ink? Months of weekly sessions. He wanted a lot of power in them, and you could handle it." Kasper sighed and shook his head. "You know, I tried talking to you when he went out back. You weren't having it. I knew you were in trouble, but I thought it was a new circle you rolled in. I thought maybe you were doing me a favor by keeping me at arm's length. It wasn't until another couple of years that I realized how bad you got it."

Bad was right. I was taken to the shop to get a tweaked engine. A shiny, late-model zombie, with all the bells and whistles. The pride of someone's stable.

"I can't remember it," was all I said.

Kasper finished the recolor in silence. He moved on to the line along my forearm, strengthening the edges, sharpening the tips of the arrow. His work looked cleaner and meaner than before. Maybe it was what I needed.

At some point I dozed off, but it couldn't have been long. A beer's worth. Maybe three in Kasper's case. Waking up again felt wrong, like my body belonged to a screaming toddler who wasn't having it. I tried to ignore Kasper but he was insistent.

"I can't have you dying in my shop, Cisco." Friends.

I yawned and checked his work. "If you believe it, I actually feel better somehow."

He shook his head. "No healing magic, my ass. You figure out what they did to you, you stand to make a lot of money."

"All for ten easy payments of your immortal soul."

He tried to smile but held off laughing. Kasper was serious now. An awkward silence filled the shop. He wanted to say something but didn't know how, and I wanted to say something but didn't know what. Kasper had been a borderline friend back in the day. Maybe I couldn't even call him that much today. The pre-nap joviality was gone. Now Kasper was all business. Tying up loose ends. Nothing more.

He stood. "Listen, uh, you got a place to stay, broham?"

And there it was. We were done here. There'd be no crashing on his couch. No hiding out in his tattoo parlor. No more Cuban coffee stouts. The old man had done me a solid, but it was time to move on.

"I'm not sure," I admitted. "Anything would be an improvement after waking up in a dumpster."

He nodded but didn't ask questions. I could tell he didn't want any more answers. He already knew enough to be in danger.

My feet were wobbly when I first got up but they found their strength. I stretched my tank top back over my head; it was a torn, bloody, stained mess. The seconds ticked away, and I had to think fast.

Evan's house kept popping into my head. Despite the black magic lectures, I was pretty sure I could count on him. My best friend was the obvious solution. He wouldn't even mind that I'd stood them up for dinner.

But I couldn't face Emily. Not yet. I'd rather live on the street, and my old solution of dying wasn't working out. For reasons that were slowly coming into focus, I was feeling better.

I reached into my pocket and pulled out a fold of bills. "How much do I owe you?"

"Screw that, Cisco."

I counted out thirty-seven bucks. A tad under his usual fee. Folded in the wad of bills was a note with Milena's pink handwriting. And her address.

"You got a computer I can look someone up in?" I asked.

"Sure do." Kasper pulled out a flat phone. Large, thin, and all glass. Within a few minutes he mapped out Midtown for me.

"I gotta get me one of those," I said in awe. The future is now.

Kasper rapped me on the shoulder. "On the run and all you think about is getting a hot piece of snatch."

"Hey, she's my sister's friend." I frowned. "Was."

The biker flitted about nervously. "Shit. I'm an asshole. Sorry I brought it up."

So he'd heard about my family being killed too. "Forget it. You're doing too much already. I owe you."

He shook his head firmly. "No way. This one's on the house, broham. For old time's sake."

"You know I hate charity," I told him. "I gotta pay you back somehow."

My friend looked me in the eye. No hint of levity, philosophy, or his usual self. "You can pay me back by staying away from me and my shop. You're in the big time now, Cisco, and that's way out of my league. I don't want you coming 'round here again. If that recolor doesn't protect you, nothing will."

Welcome: worn out. Kasper opened the door to the street. I waited for a minute and watched a car pass, and my friend couldn't look me in the eye. I couldn't blame him. After I hit the sidewalk, I said, "It's just as well. There's no Corona here anyway."

Kasper forced a smile. Then he shut the door and bolted it behind me.

Chapter 25

My stolen car was still parked on the sidewalk, but the rear windshield had been smashed with a brick. Karmic justice for the illegal parking job. Except karma had hit the wrong guy. At some point the *abuelo* I stole the car from was gonna get it back. I felt bad about that, but there was nothing I could do. I was already full up on karmic payback.

This time I got on I-95 and drove north. It was finally getting late so traffic was light. Before I knew it, I exited into a neighborhood I'd never seen before: Midtown Miami, a ritzy stretch of new construction.

Milena hadn't been kidding when she said she was living okay. Don't get me wrong—she wasn't rich. But these were swank condos in high rises, clean streets, shopping strips, and fancy restaurants. In my book, that was living.

I parked down the block from her building, a large tower of glass. The marbled lobby was impressive, but security wasn't. I strolled right past the front desk without a word. I've learned the look on your face can be as good as a key: appear like you belong and people don't ask questions.

One elevator and eighteen floors later, I knocked on her door. Milena opened up wearing a long black T-shirt. It worked as a dress because of her short frame, but hung a little too high on her wide hips and barely covered her underwear.

Holy moly. If I'd felt dead a second ago, I was fully alive now.

"Cisco?" she asked in a domestic voice. Not sleepy—it was too early for that—but relaxed.

"Hey you."

"*Ay dios mío!*" she said, noticing my once-white tank top. Where there wasn't dried blood, there was dirt and yellow stains of unknown origin, and plenty of rips and holes to boot. She pulled me inside the condo. "Are you okay?"

"You alone?" I asked, looking around nervously.

She nodded. "Let me get a look at you."

"No," I said. Milena ignored my protests and pulled my shirt off. I think she actually ripped it even more. "What happened to you?"

"I'm fine," I stressed. "At least *some* of that blood's not mine. And the scratches and bruises just look bad."

Milena had to check for herself, but even a stitched bullet wound doesn't look too scary. She nodded, concerned but satisfied. As her excitement wore off, she arched an eyebrow. Instead of worrying about my health, I got the impression she was checking me out. I couldn't blame her. I was the same Cisco Suarez she remembered except beefed up. I suddenly realized she was a hot girl and we were both half naked. I turned away.

"I've got nowhere else to go," I said, dejected. It hurt to say it. More than I thought it would. I mean, I knew I was pretty much homeless, but saying it out loud hit me hard. So much had changed in ten years. I didn't have a place in this world anymore.

"You can crash here," she said without a hint of trepidation. "As long as you need."

I shook my head. "I can't do that to you. I just need one night on your couch. One more day to figure things out."

I grabbed my shirt from her and tried to fold it. It didn't cooperate. On the third attempt, I just tossed it on the floor. The large living room had a high ceiling and a spacious balcony. The place was organized and my ratty clothes— hell my entire presence—felt like a violation.

"Nice place you got here, Milena. You can afford this on your own?"

She smiled coyly and nodded.

Seleste and Milena were always destined for bright futures. I was stupid enough to think I was too, but that's different. Seleste and Milena were great students. Smart kids. Everything a parent (or grandparent in her case) would ever want.

"You really made it, huh?" I asked with an impressed smile. Milena shot me a puzzled look. "You and Seleste always had big dreams." She turned away suddenly. It hit me too. "At least one of you made it," I amended. Cisco Suarez, the downer.

I wandered to the couch. My face tightened and I fought against the urge to cry. To give in. Manly pride fighting a not-so-manly battle. I sat down to buy myself time to recover.

It was me that had robbed Seleste of her dream. All her promise, ripped away in a puff of black magic.

Milena didn't say anything for a while. Then she sat beside me and hooked her arm around my shoulders. I flinched at her touch. At first. It wasn't that I didn't like it—

I just wasn't used to it. It was strange to me, to have connections in this world. Part old, part new. But it meant something. Human beings are meant for contact. I truly believe that.

"Sometimes," began Milena in a wistful voice, "the details don't matter. The past. The things we do. The random things that happen." She sighed. It was obvious she thought about Seleste whenever I was around. I hated that I brought her that pain. "Cisco, whatever happened, whatever you did—it's okay. I can see you struggling but... it's okay."

I turned away again. What did she know? But I realized *I* was the one who didn't know how to be human anymore. In death, I'd abandoned family and friends. Mom and Dad and Seleste died too. It was Milena that had to deal with that, not me. She'd been the one who needed to move on and make hard decisions.

I used to think I was smarter than everybody else. Better even. I wasn't weird, they were buffoons. I was a natural at spellcraft, which only reinforced those beliefs. And it distanced me from my family. No matter how powerful or practiced I'd become, I couldn't save them. I couldn't save myself.

I would have given it all to have them back. My magic. My life, even. Just if they could live.

Tears welled in my eyes. I wiped my face and clenched my jaw, silently scolding myself. I didn't have time for weakness. It took all my concentration to bottle my emotions. It was a stupid moment, and I hated it, but I won out.

Milena noticed my brooding and hugged me. She didn't ask questions. She just waited with me in silence. It was comfortable. It felt like friendship. It felt like trust. And I found precious little of that these days.

The tension eased from my muscles. I wasn't wired anymore. I was still sore (there was plenty of that to go around) but relaxed. I lifted my arm and wrapped it around Milena to hug her back, and I suddenly felt self-conscious. I shouldn't have, but I did.

Here I was, with a hot girl, but it didn't feel right. I was too worried about what Em would think. How ridiculous was that? Emily was married with a daughter. I guess old hang-ups are the worst kinds.

I pulled away from the embrace. Milena sat up, slightly embarrassed, then stood abruptly. I almost said something but didn't. She disappeared down the hall, and I was relieved when she returned. She handed me a blanket and pillow and smiled at me without judgment.

It was a good look. I needed that kind of support right now. I smiled back, then lowered my eyes over her form. Her voluptuous body came with a much smaller waist than I'd remembered. The bottom of her T-shirt was caught on her hip, and we simultaneously realized she was standing there flashing me her underwear. She immediately tugged the hem down.

"Sorry," I said.

She waved me off. "No problem." Her words were quick, spoken before I'd finished apologizing.

I straightened in my seat, wanting to change the subject but having a hard time looking her in the eye. Judging by the way she shifted on her legs, she was having similar thoughts.

"You know," I said. "I saw Emily today."

Sometimes I say the dumbest things.

Milena sat down, surprisingly compassionate. "I'm sorry. I should've told you who she was married to. I just couldn't bring myself to do it after telling you about your family."

"It's not a big deal. I get it."

She nodded but I could tell she still felt bad. "Did you visit Saint Martin's?"

I pointed to the stitches on my chest. "That's where I got this."

She leaned in and pressed me down into the cushions. Her fingers traced Kasper's golden mark on the wound. "Magic?"

"Not mine," I answered groggily.

She silently ran her fingers up and down my chest. "Maybe you should show me some time."

I couldn't be sure, but Milena was bordering on flirty. It wasn't the smoothest move on my part, but exactly two seconds later I passed out.

Hey, gimme a break. How many days have you gotten shot, been bitten by an undead pit bull, trapped by a giant spider, and hunted by a Haitian voodoo gang—all after waking up in a dumpster after getting killed the night before? Sometimes I swear my life is a *Twilight Zone* episode. Even better: For all I knew, I was living and dying every day, repeating an endless *Groundhog Day* loop. My own personal flavor of hell.

Milena had said that details didn't matter sometimes, but she was wrong. Details were what I needed. I knew that I'd been a zombie, but what kind? Serving what cause? What exactly had happened to me? And would I still be alive when I woke up?

The questions all faded away under Milena's caress, and I dreamt of many things, both living and dead.

Chapter 26

I woke up the next day, cold as a corpse, buried under a thick blanket. Milena must've kept her AC set to arctic. I was lying lengthwise on the couch, which would've been more comfortable had it been more than a glorified loveseat. My head and legs arched over the armrests and I think there was a remote lodged into my back.

It was the most comfortable I'd been in days.

"Just in time for breakfast," said Milena in a chipper voice that hurt my ears.

I pulled the blanket away. She was behind the bar in the kitchen. I sat up, excited for bacon and omelets and biscuits. Two frozen waffles popped out of the toaster.

She glanced over her shoulder and saw my expression, then dialed her enthusiasm back a notch. "Sorry. I don't do cooking. All these nice appliances and I have no idea what to do with them."

"That's a shame," I said. "I was beginning to think you were the perfect date." I stretched to my feet and shook off the cowboy boots I still wore, then made a beeline for the kitchen. "There's nothing to a standard Cuban breakfast. Toast, a pound of butter, and a five-egg omelet."

She flicked an eyebrow. "Why not pour quick-dry

cement in your arteries while you're at it?"

I rounded the corner of the bar and got a full look at Milena's backside. I froze. Her clothes weren't loose fitting anymore. A black tube top exposed her shoulders and jean shorts hugged her butt. She was showing a lot of tanned skin and it all looked good. Milena wasn't just cute or hot, she was a straight-up bombshell. Her clothes squeezed her impossibly small waist and wide hips. She had an hourglass figure like I hadn't seen before. And a butt like nobody's business.

When she turned around, my jaw literally dropped. "You have boobs."

She rolled her eyes. "You already did that bit yesterday."

"Yeah, but I actually have visual confirmation today."

I wasn't kidding. It's not that the shirt was especially low cut, it's that her ladies were generously portioned. They filled out the tube top and then some.

"Bought and paid for," she said, pressing them together and squeezing them up. She was torturing me now. Service with a smile. When I didn't retort, she laughed and bounced away with her waffles. "The kitchen's all yours, hotshot." She'd worn that getup on purpose. Maybe she wanted me to forget about Emily.

"You're seriously gonna eat that?" I asked.

"I don't have time for anything else. I need to work soon."

"Sure," I said, trying to play off my disappointment. "I need to get out of here too."

"You don't have to—"

"I should."

The food was just a distraction, I realized. A way to

forget. No way was I gonna sit down and have a normal breakfast. (Never mind the fact that Milena didn't even stock real butter.) I dug in the freezer for waffles too. If you can't beat 'em, join 'em.

We finished our meal without conversation. I put my game face on. Milena didn't try to cheer me up. She knew what I was thinking. What I had to do. Hell, she'd probably help if she could.

"Do I have time for a quick shower?" I asked.

"Quick."

I didn't waste any time.

When I got out, I studied my wounds in the mirror. The scrapes on my arms didn't hurt anymore. The bruising had faded considerably. The stitches in my chest were peachy, but still some pain there. I wasn't exactly Wolverine or the Hulk, but considering I was upright, I was impressed.

Milena knocked and said she left something for me. Wrapped in the towel, I opened the door. She wasn't there but she'd left a plastic bag with clothes in it. I closed the door and went through the contents, surprised that everything still had price tags. She must've woken up early and gone shopping for me.

A brand new tank top, white, stylish. New jeans with a few strategic scuffs—a far cry from the damage on my current ones. She'd even stocked me with several pairs of socks and underwear. As I dressed, each piece of clothing effected a surprising change in my mood. I wasn't wearing a dead man's clothes anymore. Even better, I felt normal.

I found Milena in the living room, proud of herself.

"This is the exact same outfit I wore yesterday," I told her.

She shrugged. "It looks good on you. Sorry I didn't replace the boots. I forgot to check the size."

I chuckled and shook my head. "I never would've guessed I'd be wearing alligator boots and wife beaters."

"To be honest, you kinda rock them now." She gave me a wink. "Now come here you big dummy." I joined her on the couch and she handed me a small phone. "This is a burner. Anonymous. Prepaid minutes. It's disposable, so if you think someone's tracking the number, toss it."

"They can track these?"

"Trust me. It's a different world now."

I checked it out. It wasn't nearly as nice as her phone. It was fatter with a thicker frame, but it ran all the basic apps I needed. She showed me them and the screen she'd set up for me. She even listed her own number in the contacts under "M." I added Evan's info using the same unbreakable cipher.

While I toyed with the device, Milena got ready for work. Eventually, she grabbed a paper shopping bag with fancy handles and I walked her out. It wasn't until the elevator that I peeked inside.

"Um, Milena, why do you have thongs and stripper heels in your bag?"

She reflexively yanked it away, then sighed as she realized it was pointless. "Exotic dancer heels."

I chuckled at the joke but her face was deadpan. She wasn't kidding.

"You're a—"

"Shut up!" she yelled as the elevator door opened. An old couple recoiled, aghast at the volume. Milena stormed past them, her flip-flops snapping across the lobby floor.

"Tourette's," I explained to the elderly couple. I gave them a cartoony shrug to really sell it, then raced outside and caught up with Milena. "Look," I said. "I'm sorry. It's not my place to judge."

"You're damn right."

I nodded. "And I get it. Paying for law school or whatever, right? Like you said, the details don't matter."

She halted mid stride on the sidewalk. I almost ran into her. "Those are the wrong details, Cisco. I'm not going to law school. I'm not going to any school. Dancing is what I do to pay my bills. It's how I live. It's how I got out of Little Havana."

"But," I fumbled, not wanting to offend her but having to ask. "You and Seleste were always such good students..."

"Yeah, well, shit didn't exactly go as planned. Did it?" Her eyes flared and she spun away from me.

I followed again. "But can't you find something better?"

"Better how?" Still stomping. No eye contact.

"I... I don't know, Milena. Something a little more... A little less..."

She stopped again and flashed angry eyes at me. "More respectable? Less sleazy? Screw you, Cisco. What happened to no judgment?" She stormed away again.

"I didn't mean it like that," I said, but we both knew I had. I continued after her, feeling like an asshole. After a couple blocks, I spoke up. "What are you doing? Walking?"

"Yes," she answered. "It's only a few more blocks. Parking costs money and they give me a ride home. It's better than some customer copying down my license plate."

I nodded, and I saw it. The savvy. The toughness. What had happened to me and Seleste was forever a part of her.

Everyone's damaged in some way. That's what life does to a newborn. It slowly gives and takes indiscriminately, piling on and stripping away like so many coats of paint. People are just the remnants, the left behinds. And everything considered, Milena was doing very well for herself.

"Listen," I pleaded. "Just stop one second. I don't want you to leave like this."

She slowed, huffed, and turned to me. Her eyes were daggers at the ready, but I knew I was safe.

"I didn't mean anything by it," I said. "Just took me by surprise is all. Honest."

Milena pressed her full lips together and frowned. Then she threw me a bone and nodded.

"You need a ride at least?" I asked.

"I'm fine," she said. "You've got more to worry about. Call me sometime, okay?"

I waved the phone toward her. "I will."

Real smooth, I was. Handled that revelation with all the grace of a cat with its head caught in a bag. I watched Milena walk another two blocks with a bit more bounce in her step. She put some extra shake in her ass just to taunt me. You see? She could be mean too.

I trudged back to my car and found it missing. Guess it wasn't my car anymore. Found and towed by now. The police must have come and gone. Better them finding it empty than with me behind the wheel.

I still had a few bucks for a taxi. I flagged one down, sat in the back, and dialed Evan.

"We missed you last night," he said when I announced myself.

"You told Emily?"

He took a breath. "I did. You're gonna need to see her."

I chewed my lip instead of responding. Then I changed the subject. "You didn't tell me about the infighting in Little Haiti."

"What infighting?"

"The voodoo gangs going at each other." I mulled it over. "The African connection."

"What're you talking about, Cisco? There aren't any African gangs in Miami."

I frowned. He was probably right. What did I know? But there were small populations scattered throughout the city. I thought of the anansi, the unfamiliar voodoo, and Kasper's information. I took a stab in the dark. "What about the Nigerians?"

Evan skipped a breath. "The who— How do you know about them?"

"Someone's taking out the Haitians, vying for control of Biscayne Boulevard. Remember their leader that was taken out with magic? That was me. A hit man. A thrall."

"You did that?"

"The world according to Laurent Baptiste."

"Jesus, Cisco. You talked to Baptiste?"

"Are you just gonna repeat everything I say in the form of a question? I told you I was getting to the bottom of this. What did you think that meant? Hallmark cards?"

Evan didn't make a sound, but I could practically hear him thinking it over. He knew something he hadn't told me.

"Okay," he conceded. "We need to talk. Just... not over the phone. Let's meet somewhere. Bayfront Park. You know the fountain?"

"Come on, Evan. I grew up here."

"Can you be there in half an hour?"

"I'm close enough." I hung up the phone.

I wasn't sure if this was bad, but it wasn't good. Evan had held out on me. I'd originally asked him about an African connection and he'd been mum. Now, the second I mentioned Nigerians, he wanted a covert meeting in a public place. There was something I didn't see yet.

"Hey," I called to the driver, knocking on the plastic between us. He turned down the music and looked at me through the mirror. "You get any of that?"

The driver was a black dude wearing a fisherman's hat. He pointed to the speakers. "I couldn't hear."

"Right," I said, not pressing the issue. "Looks like I have a change of plans."

Chapter 27

My destination was a straight shot down Biscayne Boulevard in light traffic. The taxi pulled to the curb alongside the park without a lot of time to spare. The fare almost tapped me out. I paid the cabbie and asked him to wait anyway.

"Money first."

"What?"

"I saw what you had left. Don't ask me to wait if you can't pay."

I sighed and scrounged back in my pocket. "Here's my last four bucks."

He nodded and accepted the scrunched bills. "That gets you ten minutes."

I slammed the door and wished I still had the Monte Carlo. Not dealing with this was worth the risk of getting arrested. I shook it off and reminded myself that it was a new day with new possibilities.

Bayfront Park, surprise surprise, is a park that sits in front of the Bay. I suppose the naming committee skipped out early that day to watch a movie or something, job well done. The park isn't much besides grass and palm trees sliced with intersecting lengths of wide sidewalks, but it works as a public space. It's mostly known for fireworks, free concerts, and guys selling *arepas* out of little carts. In the daytime, without an event going on, things were more laid back. Quiet, almost, but enough people and daylight to keep things reasonable. Easy visibility in all directions.

In a plaza by the waterside, Evan Cross leaned against a railing that circled a large fountain. It was plain as far as fountains went. A bowl of concrete that sprayed and swallowed water. A fountain next to the ocean. I never understood the point. A few pedestrians were scattered nearby, but most were lounging closer to the Bay.

No good shadows in sight, of course.

"You afraid of something?" I asked when I came upon my friend.

He turned, trying to act casual. He wore light clothes again, tan this time, but the effect was marred by the black bulletproof jacket he wore on top with the word "DROP" across the back. His twin guns were holstered as well.

"Don't be dramatic, Cisco. It's just a vest."

"If I was gonna attack you, the vest wouldn't help."

"Exactly," he said. "So it's not for you."

I nodded in a way that told him I wasn't so sure. I scanned the waterside again and caught a couple men watching me.

Evan smiled and shook my hand. "Got yourself cleaned up, I see. Where're you staying?"

"Don't worry about it," I answered, checking the perimeter of the park. "Why are we surrounded by cops?"

My friend's smile froze in place, then drained into a sigh. "Sorry about that. They won't move in unless I tell them to."

"What the crap, Evan? Is this why you wanted to meet in

broad daylight?"

He stepped toward me with his police officer braggadocio. "You're the one who just admitted to operating as a hit man for ten years."

"*Slaving* as a *zombie* hit man," I corrected. "As in, not my choice. I was dead and under compulsion."

"Then what the hell are you now?"

I turned my back to him and checked the field. No one advanced in SWAT formation. I wasn't sure how much to trust Evan. The feeling was probably mutual. Maybe the units were just a backup plan.

I laughed it off. "Fucking Frank Bullitt here. You always did watch too many movies."

"We waited for you last night," Evan said softly. "It was the only thing we could talk about." I didn't answer and he spun me around by the shoulder. "We're friends, man."

Sometimes, even when things are really obvious, it's still jarring to hear them out loud. I considered him, and I could tell he meant it. But he *had* held out on me.

"I'm Cisco, bro. The same Cisco. I don't know about the last ten years, but I know about now."

He smiled again, dissolving some of the tension between us.

"Is anyone listening to us?" I asked.

He shook his head.

"Good. Do you have my case file?"

He chewed his lip. "I couldn't get it yet."

"I'm serious about that file, Evan. I might need it to get somewhere with this."

"I know. I told you I'd try. I need time."

I nodded. He could've been humoring me. "Then tell

me about the Nigerian gang."

Evan ran his hands through his short hair. "There's no gang. They don't have the numbers for street power."

"So how do they make moves in Little Haiti?"

"By working *with* the other gangs. The Nigerians are either higher level players or independent contractors on the bottom rung of the ladder. They either are the muscle, or they pay for it."

"Pay who?"

"That's the thing," he said. "They have associations with the Haitians. The Saints. Smaller gangs like the Westies and 71st Street Hoods. They wouldn't be taking out their allies."

I grunted. I thought Evan had more imagination than this. "Maybe they're only friends in public. The Nigerians don't have the numbers for all-out war, so they talk business and send outside players to do their dirty work. People like me. It's death anonymous."

He shook his head slowly. "I don't know. What put you on this Nigerian kick anyway?"

"We don't get too many West African spider tricksters in these parts. And whatever voodoo I've been hexed with didn't come from any of the Haitian death barons."

"But—"

"I'm telling you, Evan, if there's Nigerian activity, it's a worthwhile lead. If I find out there's a connection and you knew about it..."

He put his hands up in a mixture of apology and indignation. "Don't go down that road, Cisco. This is you and me we're talking about. But there is something."

I checked the park. Everyone seemed miles away but I

leaned in anyway.

"There's a meeting today," he confided. "That's why I wanted to talk to you."

"What kind of meeting?"

"The Saints are having a sit down with a particular Nigerian businessman." Evan saw the excitement on my face and waved it away. "He's not a gangster, Cisco. He's a community leader. He runs a nonprofit promoting unity and culture."

"And happens to be meeting with known criminals in public."

Evan was ready with an explanation. "Baptiste isn't just a criminal. He runs legitimate businesses up and down the Boulevard. That means legitimate businessmen sometimes interact with him."

"But you know better about Baptiste."

"Everybody does. We know what he is but we can't arrest him. He plays off his family history and needing to overcome the obstacles of minority culture. He's an unlikely success story. The public eats it up."

"What about his esteemed Nigerian business partner?"

"Namadi Obazuaye. He's not a bad guy. He does outreach with the city commissioners and police."

"The commissioners?" I fumed. "As in, your boss? Do you fucking work for this guy?"

"He's legitimate, Cisco. The commissioners work with community leaders. When they need police details, the DROP team is the first in line for the overtime."

"I can't believe it. You actually *do* work for these guys." I got a bad taste in my mouth and bared my teeth. DROP the real police work to score political points. "These are the facts, 'Lieutenant.' Namadi has heavy West African ties in this city. He's associating with a voodoo gang that's been under fire, by myself no less. We're all tied up in this somehow."

"There are other facts you're ignoring. Like all the good Namadi has done for the poor neighborhoods of the city. All the redevelopment projects he's taken on."

I hissed. "Redevelopment isn't noble. It's profitable."

I knew Evan was hearing me, but his face was stiff. An impassive mask of disbelief. Maybe he didn't want to believe he'd been close to a bad guy. Maybe he discounted my opinion because I wasn't a detective. Maybe he needed more convincing.

"Stop being so stubborn and open your eyes," I snapped. Some of the undercover officers watching us tensed.

Evan Cross hooked his hands on his hips and laughed. "I can't believe this. It's high school all over again. You can only see things from your perspective. Nothing else matters to you."

"You know I'm right."

"Do I? You've never even met Namadi but you have him pegged. Meanwhile, I'm the one doing everything wrong." Evan pounded a finger in my chest. "You're reckless, egotistical, and overconfident. And now you're running around Miami like an outlaw."

I hissed at him. "Stop exaggerating."

Evan turned away and shook his head, like a father sick of disciplining his kid. "There was a shoot-out at Saint Martin's last night."

I frowned. "Lots of people shoot guns in Miami."

"At night in a closed cemetery? The same one that your

sister and parents are buried at?" He rested his elbows on the railing and hitched a foot on the bottom rung. "What are you doing, Cisco?"

I narrowed my eyes, about to snap back at him, but I realized he probably saw the same defensive mask on my face that I saw on his. I stared at my red boots for a minute, then sighed and leaned beside him. I crossed my arms and watched the perimeter. "They followed me. I dealt with it."

"Dealt with it how? You didn't kill Baptiste, did you?"

I shook my head.

"Then you only made it worse."

I clenched my jaw. Yesterday, I'd been behind the eight ball. Scrambling and on the run the entire day. But today was mine. The Bone Saints didn't know where I was anymore. They'd assume they were safe at a sit-down behind gang security.

"Why today?" I posited. "Have you asked yourself that? How long has this meeting been planned?"

"I don't know," Evan admitted. "The gang unit picked it up last night."

"After my run-in with the Saints?"

Evan Cross frowned and nodded.

"The meeting's about me."

My friend remained silent. A last-second emergency meeting late at night? The timing was too coincidental for Evan to deny the plausibility of my theory. He rapped his fingers in irritation on the railing, over and over. I finally saw the work conflict. Evan could be working for a corrupt politician for all I knew. His job could be on the line.

Evan pulled a white envelope from his back pocket. "You should stay away from them, Cisco. The Bone Saints are street scum. Low-level wannabes. Adding another player to your list of enemies will decrease your chances of living. Namadi Obazuaye doesn't have the firepower of the gangs, but he has enough resources and connections to make your life hell."

"And if he already has? What if he used his resources and West African connections to make me his personal hit man for the last decade? If that was him, should I still leave him be?"

Evan nervously clapped the envelope between his hands.

I shook my head in disappointment. "What would you have me do, buddy? What's in that envelope?"

He handed it to me. "I spoke with Emily about this. You weren't there to discuss it, but she agreed. We got some cash together for you."

I opened it, rifled my finger over the fat stack of cash, and chuckled. "This isn't a payoff, is it?"

Evan's face was serious. "Get out of town, Cisco. Don't tell anyone where you're going. Not me or Emily or anyone else you've spoken to. You didn't deserve what happened to you. None of your family did. But maybe you can enjoy the rest of your life."

I cocked my head and backed away.

"The streets should be clear for the day," he continued. "The Saints will be busy at the sit-down. It's the best chance you have of leaving town unimpeded. Just disappear."

I snorted, incredulous. "Not gonna happen, tough guy. And I don't need your blood money."

"That's not what it is. Jesus, what kind of person do you think I am? That's some personal money that my wife and I put together because we care about you. Get some food.

Buy some normal shoes."

"Hey, don't diss the boots. They're growing on me."

He rolled his eyes. "Just get out of town, Cisco. And keep the money. It comes with no strings attached."

I slid the wad into my back pocket. "Fine. I'll take the money, but I won't take your advice. I'm staying and I'm going to that meeting. And fuck you if you won't help me."

Evan's face twisted in anger. "You can't keep doing this, man. Emily *just* heard about your return last night. If you charge into Little Haiti with a bullheaded plan and get yourself killed again, it's not fair to her."

"It might wrap things up nicely for you though," I reasoned.

"That's not fair!" His emotion all poured out at once. No more mask. I swear, my friend almost decked me. I probably deserved it. It was a cheap shot. To Evan's credit, he didn't retaliate with one of his own.

"The Bone Saints base down in a block-wide series of tenement buildings. It's their turf and it's locked down. You'll never get in and out alive."

"Maybe not without your help."

Evan expressed his displeasure. "I could check if the gang unit is running surveillance."

"Do they have someone inside?"

"In the gang? No. But maybe I could get you some intel. Lie low until then. Don't do anything stupid."

I didn't like it. It sounded more like a stalling tactic than anything else. I held my phone out for him. "You can start with the address."

Evan ran his eyes over the Bay and sighed. He grabbed my phone and punched in an address.

"You really can't help more than that?" I asked as I took back the phone.

"Get involved? Personally?" He looked me right in the eyes. "No way."

I didn't hide my disappointment. "I've been dead, Evan. I've got an excuse. What have you been doing for the last ten years?"

His hands went to his hips again. Facing his demons was business as usual. "You said it yourself, Cisco. You were killed, resurrected. That's impossible. No one should be able to do that. You can't beat whoever you're up against. What chance do I have?"

I didn't answer, but I was pretty sure his Colt Diamondbacks wouldn't help.

"I have a family now," he maintained. "I can't make a widow of my wife or an orphan of my kids. Shit, man. That's the best-case scenario. I saw what happened to your family." His voice was a whisper now. "It was horrible."

I laughed in contempt. In disgust. I was sick of the pile-on. It wasn't an appropriate reaction, but I didn't care. Maybe I was going crazy. I backed away from my friend.

"If your team's around Little Haiti later," I said, "tell them to DROP to the ground and keep their heads down 'cause I'm coming for blood." I spun in my cowboy boots and started to leave.

"Wait," called Evan, wincing. He opened the back of his shirt and pulled a manila envelope from his waistband. "I had a feeling you'd say something like that."

I grabbed the new envelope. This one was too big for money. "What's in this one?"

"Your personal items. We found them dumped at the

crime scene where you were killed. Your sister originally kept them until..." Evan cleared his throat. "Anyway, I'm not sure why I held on to them, but I figured they shouldn't fall into the wrong hands. Just in case."

I nodded absentmindedly and ripped the seal open. More links to my past. To who I used to be. The manila envelope was filled with old spellcraft tokens. Fetishes, powders, tributes. The implements of black magic.

Chapter 28

I banged the taxi's trunk as it pulled away from the curb. The driver jumped and slammed the brakes, then shook his head when he saw me. I slid into the backseat with a smile and laid a clean hundred in his hand. His eyes widened.

"Can you get me to Little Haiti?"

"Oh," he said in a mocking voice (but still taking the money). "Why would you assume I know where Little Haiti is?" He judged me through the rearview mirror.

"Um... Because you're a taxi driver?"

He smiled. "Just messing with you. Forty minutes."

"Take Biscayne. I wanna hit some stops on the way."

He nodded and pulled onto the Boulevard.

I rested back in the seat and closed my eyes. The Haitians and Nigerians weren't meeting for another few hours. I had plenty of time to decide on a plan, but one thing I wasn't doing was waiting for Evan's intel. Knowing him, he'd never get back to me and hope I missed my appointment.

Not today. Today was Cisco Suarez Day. Sunny and full of hope. I was tired of being the one chased around. It was high time I did the chasing.

The manila envelope crumpled in my grip. I checked the

contents again. A straw mask, large enough to cover the top of my face. It had cut-out eye holes. Long strands of straw ran along the bottom edge like a beard. The mask was a single-use component that would definitely come in handy today.

I also found my belt pouch, a rectangular nylon bag that cinched to my waist, useful for holding fetishes and favors. Inside were small candles, matches, pre-1965 quarters, and other common spellcraft tokens.

The last item in the envelope was a silver dog whistle. It felt familiar between my lips, and I wondered how I'd gone without it for so long. The whistle is a fetish, not an artifact. A focus for my spellcraft, devoid of any inherent magic of its own. It's really just a plain old whistle, only worth the weight of its hollowed silver tube. But we've talked about silver's importance to necromancy before. It's a holy metal. A purifier. The skull buckle was pewter so I needed the whistle too. This fetish alone did more to heighten my power than anything else in the envelope.

A black cat darted across the double northbound lanes ahead of us. The taxi swerved but the animal tried to beat us across the street. The car overtook the cat with a sickening bump.

"Aw hell," exclaimed the driver. He cruised forward at ten miles per hour, checking his mirrors.

"Stop," I said. The street was empty. It was worth checking.

"What?"

"Stop the car."

He did and we both looked back. The black lump in the road didn't move. I bet the cat didn't think much of Cisco

Suarez Day. Sunny and full of hope my ass.

I scrunched my nose. "Is hitting a black cat bad luck or good luck?"

"Stupid stray," complained the man. "It came out of nowhere."

I nodded in sympathy and opened the car door.

"Where are you going?"

I approached the animal, slowing as I neared. I didn't see any blood. We'd hit it at a low speed, but that wasn't much consolation to the cat. A solid knock on the head with a bumper would do it in. I kneeled beside it and squinted. No collar. No movement. It looked fine, but it was dead.

Without thinking, I returned the whistle to my lips. This was curious timing, right after recovering my fetish and all. Using my knife, I slit my fingertip and rubbed the cat's head, then blew into the whistle. There was no sound, at least not to human ears. I checked the cat, but nothing happened. Like I said, I was rusty.

A car blazed by in the neighboring lane and laid on its horn. More vehicles followed. I wasn't in a good spot for this. I scooped up the dead animal and returned to the taxi. The driver didn't look happy.

"What are you, a crazy person? You're not bringing that in here."

I opened my mouth to insist. Before I could, a piercing meow startled us both.

The cat cuddled in my arms; bright green eyes stared up at me. It surprised me a little, but I regained my cool and slid into the back seat.

"It's fine," I said. "You barely nicked it. I'll take it to a vet."

Cars piled up behind the taxi as a new wave of traffic hit. The man shrugged, already bored, and drove on.

I leaned back and studied the animal in my lap. It appeared to be a perfectly healthy cat, but you and I know better. Twenty seconds ago, it had been dead. Now it licked blood from my finger. I'd never done that so easily before.

After some time, I directed the driver to pull up to a store. I left the cat in the car, fitted the nylon pouch to my belt, and got ready to do some shopping.

With magic, preparation is everything.

The most powerful spells are not immediate. They require practice, prep, and patience. Animists have plenty of quick hits in them, but the serious stuff is planned. It involves groundwork.

Most people, when planning something covert, might opt to shop at a military supply store. Some might go high tech and acquire spy equipment. Me? I hit up the local 7-11.

Stuff inside was mostly how I remembered it. (Except for the quesadilla dog slammers. I'd have to try those some time.) For now I stocked up on plastic lighters, knock-off sunglasses, and other incidental items I'd need in Little Haiti. I passed an aisle with cheap baseball caps and picked one that read "I Heart Miami" with sunbeams coming from the heart. That was part of a disguise. I grabbed kitty treats because a hungry zombie is a bad zombie. Oh, and I scored a raspberry butterscotch Slurpee because *I hadn't had a Slurpee in ten years*. (Who was I kidding? I got the quesadilla dog slammers too.)

I returned to the car ready to go. The taxi driver informed me that the cat had been yapping at a dog outside the car. Everything looked kosher now so I just shrugged.

As we continued on our way, I silently considered my predicament.

The Bone Saints wanted me dead because I'd assassinated the old Baptiste. Now they were unknowingly meeting the businessman who'd likely ordered the hit. On top of that, I was now alive—a problem from both ends because the new Baptiste hadn't forgiven me and Namadi Obazuaye would see me as a loose end. If the truth got out, maybe they'd kill each other for me, but to get to them, I'd need to surround myself with an entire gang of voodoo practitioners on their home turf.

In other words, this was gonna be a hell of a party.

Chapter 29

Little Haiti was nicer than I'd assumed. Smallish houses mostly, very residential, with a strip of businesses on Second Avenue. No buildings higher than two stories, which gave a lot of space to the high Miami sky.

I had the taxi circle the block. I knew it was the right place when we passed the herbalist shop across the street. A large awning loomed over the doorway, various flowers and grasses hanging from it like curtains. From the outside the shop had an ominous look. An enclosed cavern that housed the unknown. It kept the riffraff out, I was sure. Only animists like me knew the real value of the sacraments on sale.

As Evan had mentioned, the block we circled wasn't just a single address or unit. It was more like a compound. A series of two-story concrete tract apartment buildings planted themselves in an open field of grass, taking up almost an entire city block. The units were blocky abominations born of nineteen-eighties squalor, dressed with the original, faded pink paint. The property looked more like a run-down school than anything else, but I assumed it to be project housing. A strong metal fence, painted green and twice as tall as me, ran along the exterior sidewalk and surrounded the wide block.

Welcome to Bone Saints headquarters.

As we passed, a high school kid with an obvious gun in his pocket entered a side gate. He nodded at the guard who opened the way and they bumped fists. A few others in the field took note of the entry. None of the people were residents; they were hired help. Scouts wandered the property. Wide fields of green grass between the buildings provided easy sight lines. In the broad daylight, the combination of open space and low buildings didn't give me much shadow to work with.

Luckily, while the compound ran right up to the street on three edges of the block, the fourth was lined with residential housing. Small, old, dilapidated houses—sure—but hopefully gang-free. They had small backyards that bordered the green security fence. I figured that was my best bet.

I thanked the taxi driver, picked up my cat and other belongings, and let him keep the change. He must've been familiar with the area because he sped off in a hurry.

I picked the least-habitable house—no cars out front, no movement or sounds within, windows and doors shuttered—and made my way to the backyard. Low palms and bushes concealed me as I confirmed the house was empty. I checked a metal shed in the back along the neighbor's chain-link fence. It was missing a door and didn't have anything of worth inside. Since the shed faced the yard from the side, it provided cover against nosy neighbors, as well as offering a perfect view of the green metal fence and the Bone Saints beyond.

I ducked inside and went to work. Standard stuff, at first.

Incantations on the sunglasses. Tightening up the bindings of the straw mask. I fed the cat some nibbles and tested out basic commands on it. Sit. Lie down. Jump. Cisco Suarez was an everyday cat whisperer.

After everything was set, it was still a little early. I decided to scout the property a little better. I set the black cat loose in the backyard, sat on my haunches, and closed my eyes.

Unkempt grass brushes my whiskers. I choose each step with caution but glide smoothly over the ground. Smoothly between the metal bars that wall off larger things.

I opened my eyes and peeked from my cover. The cat continued moving on its own, which was normal. But something was off. I was rusty still. He was hard to drive, more like a horse than a car, being urged to steer rather than responding to the turn of a wheel. I'd need to strengthen my necromantic muscles another time. For now, my little operation was running along smoothly.

Let's address the obvious concern: You might think it stupid to spy on a bunch of bokors with a zombie cat, but these animists were wholly unfamiliar with my magic. Martine had taught me their ways. Bokors all channel one of the Barons of Death. Their patrons are famous in these parts. But they're not the only patrons of death.

There are all kinds of zombies. All kinds of death. That's what Baptiste had said, and he was right. Haitian voodoo is a patchwork art, a hand-me-down of African origin. When the slaves had been carried away from their homeland, they lost their foundations, churches, artifacts—even their holy ones. They had to rise up and work with what they had. Improvise. What resulted was a different kind of magic.

More immediate but less polished.

Spellcraft arises from need. It's another tool in the belt of a free-willed populace. The man makes the magic, not the other way around. Neither is inherently good or evil to start. Motivations are where things get complicated. Motivation is birthed by need.

That's why you can't assume the Haitians have the corner on death magic, with voodoo and all. Death is everywhere. Every culture since the beginning of time has revered and feared death, and anything treated with that much respect is bound to be tied to powerful magic.

Opiyel is a Taíno zemi, a god of the indigenous Arawak people of the Caribbean (notably including Cuba and Florida). The dog spirit was believed to guide dead spirits to the afterlife, what animists know as the Murk or the Shadow World. Besides myself, I didn't know of anyone whose patron was Opiyel, the Shadow Dog.

So I guided the dead cat, hoping it would be enough to trick even experienced bokors for a while.

Some men laugh up ahead. I skirt them and smell a dog with them.

A Rottweiler on a leash. It smelled alive, as did everyone else. Better to avoid them anyway.

I trot directly toward the animal, curious.

What? No. Go the other way.

The dog grows excited and comes for me, but the man holds him back.

I opened my eyes again. What the hell was the cat doing? Instead of avoiding attention it was attracting it. The scouts watched as the cat tried to sniff the dogs butt. The Rottweiler wasn't too keen on the idea and kept spinning around to face the smaller animal. The two Saints laughed at the show.

Without warning, the dog growled. The owner yanked him away but the Rottweiler was determined and pushed back. His handler strained. Then the cat made a loud yap that, if it wasn't a cat, I could only describe as a bark. The Rottweiler backed away, tail tucked between its legs. The Haitians traded their laughs for bemusement.

Man this was risky. First the cat came back to life way too easily, now it was too difficult to control. In the distance, out of mind, nobody would suspect the cat of much. But this display? Anyone skilled in voodoo might recognize him for a thrall.

I closed my eyes and urged the cat back on task.

Bored with the animal, I prance away. Toward a central structure.

Each building was composed of four apartments: two top, two bottom. Concrete steps lined opposite walls, giving each residence its own entryway. The cat climbed a set of stairs to the top, hopped onto a windowsill, then leapt to the roof.

Nothing spies me up here. I look down on them all. The dogs. The people with the guns. The parked cars. A few men perch atop other buildings, like me, but I am small enough to escape their notice. I am invisible to everyone. That is the best way to watch.

This was a great spot for intelligence. A cat's-eye-view of the grounds. Significantly more than I could manage from the outskirts.

There was a lot of activity in the yard. Security was tight. Spotters on the roofs, streets, and entrances. Some of them were just kids. Most of them were armed. To me, the hullabaloo signaled a big event. The Haitians were taking this meeting with Namadi seriously.

The same kid I'd seen on the sidewalk earlier was let out again by the same gate. He stalked along the property and turned the corner, patrolling the block.

At the same time, a guard swung a long gate open. A white Hummer limo turned into the lot and the gate closed behind it. It surprised me to see Namadi in just the one vehicle. Evan had made it sound like the guy would have an entourage.

Then again, maybe Namadi trusted the Haitians. Even if he wanted them out of the way, they sure as hell didn't know that. He was their guest of honor. Their show, their security.

It was past noon, the sun still high in the sky. Daytime wasn't ideal for my operations, but I wasn't the one setting the schedule. I needed to work with what was in front of me, and right now I watched Namadi Obazuaye and a single bodyguard escorted up the steps and inside one of the buildings. The chance was too good to pass up.

I let the cat watch, moved back to the front yard of the property I was hiding on, and ensconced myself in the bushes. What little shadow existed hugged me close until I became as black as it. Then I waited.

The patrolling scout rounded the corner. He wasn't much. A high school kid with baggy shorts. After he passed, I crept up behind him and reached for the pistol squeezed into his waistband. By the time he turned around, the gun was in my hand and pointed between his eyes.

His eyes widened in panic. "Don't shoot," said the kid.

I cocked my head, working through his islander accent.

"Don't shoot," I repeated, in exactly the same cadence.

His eyebrow twitched. "What the fuck, *nèg?*"

I held the gun steady. "What the fuck, *nèg?*" I was getting the hang of it.

The kid, confused and wetting his pants, turned to run. I brought the pistol down on the back of his head. Put him out cold in one try. Then I snatched him up and dragged him to the shed.

Chapter 30

Before you judge me, I didn't kill the boy. He was alive and I didn't intend to change that. Getting knocked out might just be the best thing that happened to him. He'd skip whatever trouble came next. I wished I had the same luxury.

Despite my prep work, I didn't have anything to tie him up with. Keeping him alive was a risk, but I figured things wouldn't stay quiet for long anyway.

I lit a beeswax candle with my 7-11 lighter. I pulled a few strands of straw from my mask, wet them with my tongue, and held them against the flame to work up a good smoke. Smoke was like shadow: evanescent, malleable, and without form. I let some wax drip to the concrete foundation of the shed and pressed the candle to it so it stood up on its own. I held the straw mask over my eyes and put the I-Heart-Miami cap on, brim forward and pulled low enough to hold the top of the mask to my face. Now it was a hands-free model.

I moved to the darkest corner of the shed and put my hands over my face, blocking the candlelight—creating shadow. Then I focused on the unconscious kid's face and became him.

I didn't change at all. Physically, mentally, it was still me.

But to any observers, I would now look like the scout. They would see his body, his clothes, and all the other things they normally did. All I had to do was wear the mask.

There were some caveats. The illusion only lasted as long as the candle did. Fitted to the concrete floor with dried wax, within the confines of a shed, the flame was safe from going out. The magic would burn it off faster than usual, but I'd have more time than I needed. The bigger problem was that I had to keep the mask out of the sun.

Yes, you heard that right. In the middle of a bright Miami day, the mask had to remain within shadow. Failing that, it would burn away in a flash of fire and my guise would strip away.

To most people that would be a problematic feat, but to a shadow charmer like myself, well, let's just say I could bend the rules a bit. I knew where the sun was. I knew to avoid looking in that direction. The brim of my cap provided minimal shade. My spellcraft could thicken and stretch the shadow to encompass my face.

Before you ask, yes: in direct sunlight, this is difficult. And I can't enlarge shadows and then draw from a greater well of power. It doesn't work like that. The strength of the shadow doesn't increase, and the overall net effect is wasted energy on my part. In other words, this isn't a magical loophole that ignores the laws of physics, and it's not worth doing in most situations. This just happens to be a perfect counterpoint.

I strolled to the street and circled the block. As I approached the gate, I realized this would be difficult as I'd be facing the sun on the way in. Nothing to do about it but keep my head down.

The gate opened before me. "*Sak pase*, little player?"

Crap. All the shadow in the world couldn't help me with Creole. I opted for the universal lubricant. The fist bump.

"Same old, *nèg*," I said in the kid's voice. The Saint nodded and I passed without another word.

With my head and brim lowered, I couldn't see more than a few steps ahead of me. I also realized that I hadn't bothered to pay attention to where the kid walked once he'd been inside. One wrong turn could betray my ruse. I trusted in the mask and pressed forward, hoping the other bangers would forget about me.

Between the hat and the shadow, nobody could see my face. I closed my eyes and guided myself from above like a video game avatar.

The human stumbles for a moment, unfamiliar with my perspective. He gets his bearings and moves blindly toward the sun. I show him the men in his path.

I rounded a building to avoid the wandering guard with the Rottweiler. A dog was the last thing I needed, as my shadow did nothing to mask my scent. I reached the area with the parked limo and approached the building Namadi had entered. Several armed men huddled at the base of the steps. The bokor, Jean-Louis Chevalier, stood outside the open front door at the top.

I'd already had two run-ins with the bokor. His caution made up for his lack of power, and he'd likely be ready for my tricks. It would be best to avoid him.

The other end of the structure is less occupied. The human goes in that direction and confronts another.

Now that I hugged the wall of the building, I could look up. The sun was blocked here in a small strip of shadow.

The new guard I approached wasn't a man at all. He was a zombie, and not a very good one. The half-rotted corpse stank of blood and sulfur. A thrall like this could only pass for alive from a distance.

I wasn't sure what it saw when it looked at me, to be honest, but I didn't give him a chance to react. I lightly blew my silver whistle and he froze in place.

Let's pause for a moment here and face facts. I know my limits. I was a damn good necromancer for twenty-four. Even at thirty-four I'm ahead of the curve. But this wasn't about my skill.

I work black magic in the voodoo capital of the United States. Other hot spots exist, of course. Pockets along the coast down to Key West. Hubs in Jacksonville and Savannah. Everyone knows New Orleans. It's a hotbed of hoodoo. And the *Santa Muerte* followers are gaining ground in the Southwest. But if you exclude the Caribbean and focus solely on the United States, no area manipulates the dead quite like the voodoo-centric Miami.

And here I was, not only in Little Haiti, but in the headquarters of the Bone Saints, whose officers all painted their faces like skulls.

So it should be apparent that I couldn't go around dispelling their dead without them taking notice. In a scrap, I'd do what needed to be done, but on the sly, I had to resort to other methods.

Standard zombies don't have brains like we do. Dogs have more intelligence. Probably squirrels too. We only begin to approach a match when we consider reptiles. Synapses, electrodes—circuits work to complete commands, but zombies function on muscle memory and instinct.

Balance. Walk. React. Anything higher level requires a suggestion. Guard this passage. Kill this man. Protect me.

Knowing that, it's surprising what a functional zombie can accomplish on its own with just a simple goal. They're dumb all right, but a lifetime of physical experience has honed them into machines with problem-solving capabilities surpassing the smartest AI, with dexterity that shames the most functional robots.

For anything very specific, necromancers use direct connections to their creations. Whether driving or not, this is the best way to handle delicate tasks. Without this oversight, zombies are left on cruise control. But even in this state, the link between living and dead is always present. If I severed that link, only the most inexperienced bokors wouldn't notice.

All this means, to retain my cover, killing and freeing this zombie was out of the question. In anticipation of this, I had another trick up my sleeve, compliments of Opiyel. Whereas voodoo is crude and mechanical, the Shadow Dog enlightens and obfuscates.

I pulled out a pair of knock-off sunglasses and placed them on the undead thrall.

The shades weren't enchanted themselves, but they served as more than just stylish flair. While not a fetish, they were an anchor for my magic, a physical item to enhance my spell and ground it in place. In this case, it gave me a link to the zombie after I moved away, and it gave me the darkness I needed to literally pull a shade over the dead man's eyes.

I might not have been able to quietly get inside the thrall's brain, but I could sure as hell control what images got fed to its eyes.

With that done, and the rest of the back stairway clear, I climbed up and opened the door of the apartment neighboring my objective.

The human climbs the steps. He moves inside and beyond my sight.

The interior of Saints headquarters wasn't exactly what I expected. Three teenagers, younger than any so far, huddled on a normal couch in a normal living room and played a normal video game. A first-person shooter in this case. Except maybe the game wasn't so normal. I realized I'd been gone for a while, but the graphical advancements in that time astounded me. The three boys turned to me and all I could do was gawk at the screen.

"Watch out for the grenade," I warned.

They faced the TV again. Here I was, prepared for a fight, and I was instead greeted with casual apathy. Score more points for the straw mask.

I moved to the screen door and happily confirmed that the balcony was entirely in shadow. The platform stretched across half the building, leaving a three foot gap between it and the next one. That next balcony was my objective.

"What you doing?" asked one of the kids as I opened the sliding glass door. He looked barely fifteen.

"Don't worry about it," I barked.

He stuck his lip out but didn't protest. I didn't know who he was, but it didn't matter. He was a scrub. It wasn't a stretch that I was legitimately securing the room adjoining an important meeting. And it was an easy guess that the kid with the gun that I'd knocked out had seniority over this punk.

I grunted and he turned away from me. Then I watched the screen again, amazed at the lifelike military simulation playing out. In what felt like a few days ago, I would've thought a game like that was the coolest thing ever. Now, I wouldn't even have a place to keep a flat screen and game system. It's funny how murderous plots can shift your priorities.

Before I could leave, the kid glanced my way again. This time his eyes widened. When the others turned to look, I felt it. The heat.

I jerked my head to the side. The cap and mask flung away from my face, the latter bursting into flame and dissolving in the span of seconds. Embers fluttered toward the kids on the breeze from the open door. Quiet time was over.

"Dead man!" they yelled.

"Shit," I said, pulling my gun. I rushed onto the balcony and slid the glass door closed to muffle their screams of warning. I hadn't exposed the straw to the sun. Something else was going on. I closed my eyes.

The boy runs from the shed, yelling. Causing a commotion. He presses himself against the gate and tries to climb. Others are taking notice. They approach him.

"Should've tied him up," I muttered. Whether intentional or accidental, the boy must've extinguished the candle. No flame, no shadow mask.

Around the corner, I heard the front door open. The three kids screamed for attention. I turned to the other balcony and saw a zombie guard standing there. This was getting claustrophobic real fast.

I took a few steps back and then ran at him, leaping over

the small gap between balconies. My alligator boots crashed into his chest and we toppled to the floor. The zombie brushed me away but I whistled him to stop. Again, I placed a pair of sunglasses on him. It might've been too late for stealth, but a hidden ace always came in handy.

A gunshot rang out. I ducked behind the thick, concrete balcony walls.

Below you. Two men.

They couldn't hit me for shit at this angle, but that wasn't the worst of it. Screaming people were one thing, but nothing gets everyone's attention quite like a gunshot. Everyone on the property was now aware of impending danger.

I dashed to the glass door. Another gunshot rang out. This time, the wall beside me chipped into dust. One of the next-door kids fired at me from his balcony. I opened the door and jumped inside.

Two topless women wearing G-strings cowered against the far wall. Beside them, a heavyset man slammed a metal door closed. It was the type of security door you see on front porches, but this was inside the apartment, leading somewhere deeper. It was a safe room. And one of the thugs had just locked it.

I caught a flash of movement behind the sofa. A guard peeked out with a gun. I jumped to the side as he fired, throwing up my shield. I aimed at his position, behind the couch, and he ducked away. I emptied half the magazine anyway—right through the fabric, and the wood, and the stuffing. He slumped out of cover with a broken curse.

The other guy didn't have a weapon, but he wasn't done. He went for another door, a second one that covered the metal gate. This one was just plain wood, but to me it looked like a bank vault. Runes had been carved along its length with bloody knives. Wards. This door took longer to close, but it was Baptiste's main defense. The thug chanted as fast as he could, unable to close the door until he activated the wards with the right chant.

"Stop," I ordered, pointing my gun at him. He ignored me. "Stop!" I warned, but the bastard was loyal if nothing else.

The front door, meanwhile, had been open the whole time. Reinforcements finally arrived. The yelling outside must have distracted them until they heard the gunfire.

I pulled the trigger at the first person who entered. Unfortunately, it was a zombie, and those things don't go down from isolated flesh lacerations. The undead don't need to worry about things like blood loss or failing internal organs. After one round penetrated its chest, I adjusted my aim to who followed. Chevalier. The bokor was quickly becoming a thorn in my side.

I fired a couple shots his way, but he predictably used his pet as a body shield. The damn thing didn't even notice. At the same time, the zombie on the balcony crashed through the glass (even though the door two feet to his left was wide open). What did I tell you? Lizard brains.

The fat man finished chanting and shoved the door. I didn't have a lot of bullets left, I was surrounded, and I needed to get inside.

I pointed the pistol at the ceiling fan above my head and fired, popping the single exposed bulb. The entire room darkened and I lunged for the door. The wards began to glow. I could feel the gap in the door filling with charged energy, the Intrinsics solidifying. But it hadn't fully shut yet. With a foot of space, I slid into the shadow and phased forward. Between the door. Between the bars of the gate. And inside the safe room.

A door slammed behind me and I materialized within the meeting room. A seal of red flashed around the seam of the door, then faded out. It was invisible, but we could all feel it. This room was locked down. No one else was getting inside.

I turned to the central table, taking in the stunned occupants, the leadership of Haitian voodoo in Miami. I smiled and tapped my gun on the door.

"Looks like we have a little time to talk."

Chapter 31

At first, nobody moved. That's how shocked everybody was. Two men, two bodyguards, and dead silence.

Max interrupted the lull, as I should've guessed. She had a temper and she hated me. After our last scuffle, I didn't blame her. She marched around the table until I pointed the gun at her. I didn't think it could kill her after last night, but she hesitated. Cotton stuffing or not, the bullets would hurt.

Still, she had something inside there, maybe even a heart, because she lifted her staff aggressively.

"Stand down!" snapped Laurent Baptiste, thrusting to his feet.

Max obeyed.

Laurent and Max appeared much as I'd last seen them, except the bodyguard looked as healthy as ever. I guess I couldn't cry foul considering I'd been shot too. A smirk played across her face. She'd been waiting for this reunion.

The other two in the room were new. Namadi Obazuaye had flinched when I first entered, but otherwise had remained calmly seated. He was slightly older and overweight, with the kind of stocky frame that held strength. He watched me carefully with striking eyes.

The single flinch at gunpoint was impressive. His

bodyguard hadn't even given me that much. Like the community leader himself, the bodyguard waited, supreme confidence on his face. I could see why. In fact, I now understood why Namadi didn't need a contingent of security today.

The bodyguard was an imposing man. The tallest in the room. The broadest. The most still. Besides a flash of recognition, his face was stone. His arms rested over his barrel chest, casually gripping large curved hooks, nearly full circles, in each hand. He wore a set of strange armor, metal plates on his shoulders and chest. His boots, even, were made of metal and extended into pointed tips over his knees.

His size and dress weren't the worst parts. Don't get me wrong. Those were scary. But the thing that stood out most about the bodyguard, to people like me who know these sorts of things, was that he wasn't human.

That's not to say I knew what he was. An ogre, maybe (although I'd never seen one before). The man didn't look especially dim-witted, but it was my best guess at the moment.

I turned to Namadi. A plain man with a curious smile. He didn't look like a mage but, if he had a bodyguard like that in his employ, he knew a trick or two. Walking around with skull paint was one thing, but I've learned that the ones who hide their skills the best, the ones who appear the most normal, are the most dangerous.

Periodic bouts of muffled shouting exploded outside the safe room. Guards banged against the door and argued with each other about how to get in. Most of it wasn't in English. The guard who had sealed the door wouldn't be able to open it, otherwise an intruder could force him to do so. I smiled at my fortune. Luck was better than cleverness, and using the Saints' defenses against them was a masterstroke.

"Bravo, *blanc*," announced Laurent coolly. It didn't surprise me to see him talking instead of fighting. I was, after all, the only one in the room with a gun. "You've succeeded in securing an audience with me."

I scoffed. "What's the matter? No snakes today?"

Laurent smiled. "She will need to be replaced, unfortunately. As will my security staff."

"Kids with guns, you mean."

Namadi showed Laurent his displeasure. The leader of the Bone Saints cleared his throat and attempted to curtail his anger, but it was seeping through like a leaking dam. To his credit, his voice remained even.

"You think you have accomplished the impossible," he chided. "But getting in this room is only the second most impossible obstacle."

"And the first?"

His smile vanished. "Getting out."

Yup, I'd walked right into that one. I sniggered and pointed the pistol at him.

"I could kill you," I told him. "Maybe I should. But believe it or not, I'm not here seeking your audience." The gun's aim slid to the Nigerian. "Namadi, I presume?"

Strong brows arched over his eyes, tightening the skin on his bald head. "It is Mr. Obazuaye to you."

"Let's keep things pronounceable. Maybe I should just call you Asan?"

The mask on his face fluttered. It was so fast I almost missed it. I knew then he was guilty, no question about it.

Namadi turned slightly in his seat to his bodyguard behind him. The large man only moved his eyes for a moment before returning them to me.

"What is this?" demanded Laurent.

The Nigerian put his palm out to silence him. For a businessman with no gang affiliation, Namadi was a confident man. "And what, pray tell, shall I call you?"

"It's Cisco Suarez," I answered. "But you already know that, Namadi."

"Why would I?" he grumbled. He turned to Laurent. "How do you know this man?"

Max took one step closer to me. I swung my aim to her, and she backed off with a sly smile. "He's been attacking us. A servant, but an adept one."

I spoke through clenched teeth. "That's over. You hear me? I'm nobody's fixer. If you weren't so bloodthirsty, you'd see I'm trying to help you."

Max's expression didn't soften, but I saw the gears turning in Laurent's head. I may have killed his older brother, but he knew he had other enemies.

Namadi's deep voice rumbled over my thoughts. "Mr. Suarez, what is your business with me?" The man pulled his chair closer to the table and leaned into crossed hands.

"Business?" I laughed. "This isn't business. This is payback. But first I want to know why."

Namadi's eyes narrowed. "Why what?"

"Why you killed me!" I screamed. "My family!" I stepped closer to the table and brought the pistol in line with his head. "Why you've kept me as a slave for ten fucking years."

His bodyguard edged closer, standing right behind

Namadi. That wouldn't be close enough to stop a bullet. The Nigerian and I threw hard stares at each other. The commotion outside increased again, but they weren't even close to breaching the wards. After a minute, they quieted.

Namadi took a breath. "I do not know of these things."

"Bullshit. I saw through Martine's eyes, Asan. You killed her and you tried to kill me."

Baptiste slammed his hand on the table in a show of force. "This is an outrage!" He eyed the Nigerian but didn't dare get close to the bodyguard. "You are this man's master? You, who do not serve the Barons of Death?"

"I am a businessman," insisted Namadi. "I take only a scholarly interest in the loa, but I am not capable of doing what this man says. I do not practice." He turned to me in earnest. "If I did this thing to you, why would I kill you?"

"Because you were losing control."

"I never *had* control. What benefit would I get from doing so? Do not listen to his nonsense, Laurent."

He was desperate. Shaking. It was a far cry from his earlier confidence, but facing death will do that to a man. As his armor cracked, I sensed something else about him. A darkness. Familiar maybe. If Namadi didn't know magic, I'd eat my boots.

"I was your hit man," I said. "Don't play dumb because you're surrounded by the people you ordered me to kill."

"Impossible!" he protested. "Peace! I want peace within our communities. The gang violence must be contained and kept out of sight. I run community centers. I sit on the Board of Latin American Leaders. I head two nonprofit organizations and work with the city to spearhead redevelopment of poor communities."

I remembered what Evan had said about working with Namadi and extrapolated. "You mean you have city commissioners in your pocket."

That gave him pause and I knew I was right. The city commissioners. Evan's bosses. They were all on Namadi's payroll.

His eyes flushed. "I am *not* interested in your perspective. My aspirations for the community are large. I have attained much, but even after it all, there can be no true progress without a marked reduction in crime. A united front. A gang war destroys everything I've worked for."

The man was passionate. Even worse, he was convincing. But I could feel the black magic clinging to him. The aura he fought to hide. And there was something else...

Max's staff crashed into the small of my back. I buckled, stumbling forward. Another swing came down to my head and I continued my fall, diving away and dodging the attack.

"Max!" warned Laurent, but the woman was bloodthirsty. She feinted and came at me on my weak side, knowing my right arm wasn't armored. I absorbed the blow with my shoulder and charged into her, shoving her into the wall with a painful crash.

The other three men were spectators, with Namadi and Laurent shouting to stop the violence.

Max brought her knee into my side. The pain was welcome compared to her weapon. I grabbed the staff and tried to wrest it free, but she held tight with both hands. In a second, the staff was hugging me into her instead of pushing away.

Damn. The bitch was stronger than me too.

Instead of fighting it, I spun out of the lock and tried to

drop underneath it. Max was quick and had expected that. She leaned down with me. My head, now facing her, pressed into her chest.

Max smiled gleefully.

I couldn't move at all, and she probably could've snapped my neck from that position. Fortunately, my right arm had shot up while I had attempted to drop to the floor. Her eyes widened when she realized my pistol was pressed against her throat, stabbing into the soft skin under her chin.

I pulled the trigger.

I didn't know if Max was alive or dead, or what magic protected her, but I did know one thing: her head wasn't stuffed with cotton. Regular old brains splattered from the exit wound on top of her head. A mist of blood sprayed the wall and rained down over me.

I sucked it in, feeling its strength. "And then there were three," I said.

Max's lifeless body crumpled next to me as I stood. Laurent Baptiste was shocked. Namadi backed into his bodyguard, who stood firm. Unimpressed.

"Please, Mr. Suarez," pleaded Namadi. "There is no call for violence."

I approached the table slowly. "But that's what this is all about, isn't it? Violence in the streets." His eyes flipped between the gun and my face. "I should've known you were involved with the city commissioners. It fits in with the redevelopment projects. This isn't about peace—it's about starting a gang war. About making a bunch of politicians rich after they buy out depressed properties that plummet in value due to violent crime."

Finally, Laurent was convinced. He hadn't believed

Namadi had the magic, but he believed in a force of nature even more corrupting: greed.

"You sold me out?" cried Laurent. "You ordered the death of my brother?" His eyes were bloodshot and he shook with anger, but there was a tinge of helplessness in his voice too. Of the hurt done to him. He was a cold-blooded gang leader, but I felt sorry for him.

"Why not profit together?" he continued, squaring off against Namadi. "Instead, you call out for peace while whispering for death."

"I do not know this man," swore Namadi, finally rising to his feet. "It is a trick. How does he know this, Tunji?"

The bodyguard placed his hands on Namadi's shoulders and glared at Baptiste, daring him to attack. Nobody moved. After a few tense moments, Tunji the bodyguard sighed. With a quick motion, he crossed his hands and pulled the curved blades apart, slicing Namadi's head clean off. The poor man's arms were still in the air in the middle of making a point.

Chapter 32

"*Bondye!*" exclaimed Laurent, moving away. I wasn't too proud to back off either.

The Nigerian bodyguard scraped his two blades together, more focused on them than us. When Tunji finally spoke for the first time, it was in an offhand fashion. "What happened to you, Francisco?"

I cocked my head. I'd heard that voice before. His tone wasn't just familiar, but familiar with me.

"I was told you were killed," he continued. "I had my doubts." Tunji turned to me and his teeth flashed in the light.

His teeth. His metal teeth. Tunji was the man under the cloak. The one who'd killed Martine.

In a sickening crunch, the beast sank his teeth into Namadi's open neck. He chewed and slurped. It was gross. (Trust me. I'm a necromancer and I almost puked.)

"I'll have your head!" cried Laurent, and he charged the bodyguard.

Just like in Martine's vision, Tunji was strong and fast. He chucked Namadi's corpse aside as if it were a child's toy and thrust his knee forward. The pointed spike pierced Laurent's stomach and protruded from his back. The houngan splayed forward and wrapped his arms around the larger man, leaning on him for support.

And then a curious thing happened.

The voodoo priest deflated. Shriveled until he was nothing more than a sack of dried skin. Laurent Baptiste, after casting off his snakeskin, appeared behind the bodyguard. He flung white powder across Tunji's unarmored back. Flesh melted as if exposed to acid.

Tunji roared and blurred away. It looked similar to my shadow trick, only he stayed completely solid. He did it with pure speed. In a blink, the bodyguard had created distance between him and his opponent.

"Do you not think I know what you are now, Tunji Malu?" mocked Baptiste, readying another fist of powder. "The dead man used the name Asan. He thought it was Namadi, but it is you, isn't it? Asanbosam, a demon of West Africa. Strong. Fast. Impervious to attacks." The houngan laughed now. "But not so immune to my poisons, yes?"

An asanbosam. That's what Martine had referred to. Not a who but a what. First a trickster spider and then this terrifying abomination. Asanbosam are African vampire nomads. I didn't know much about them, but I knew this was bad. I wasn't prepared for this. As Laurent attacked, I raised my gun and fired.

Tunji Malu's metal hook flashed and deflected the bullet. The pistol clicked empty on the second pull of the trigger.

He threw the second blade at the houngan. The arm holding the powder was sliced open. Laurent grunted as a cloud puffed to the floor.

Tunji lunged, again almost too fast to see. Laurent

whispered an incantation and thrust his other hand forward. A loud clang deafened me as the open palm halted the asan in his tracks, from blur to solid. The two men stood at arm's length, frozen in place. Baptiste's open hand rested on the bodyguard's breastplate.

When I'd woken up in the dumpster yesterday, my chest had ached dreadfully. "Stopped my heart" was how Baptiste put it. Now I saw the same death spell firsthand, perfectly executed against a physically superior opponent.

Tunji grunted, and both their heads lowered to the point of impact. "That hurt," he said.

Laurent's jaw dropped and he backed away. With unnerving speed, the bodyguard slashed his blade in a horizontal arc.

They were both so fast, I wasn't sure what had happened. Tunji and Laurent stood facing each other, two meters apart. They saw each other for enemies, each beaming with hatred and the promise of vengeance.

Tunji sneered at the other man.

Laurent merely snickered. "The High Baron refuses to dig my grave," he said with ease.

Then Laurent Baptiste gurgled and wavered.

The houngan had a faraway look, like he was in shock, and took a few off-balance steps before falling backward into a chair. His arms fell limply to his side, and his head yawned back. A clean slit opened in the man's neck. His head folded over the back of the chair, spine half severed, but still connected.

It wasn't a clean beheading, but it was a killing blow. The voodoo high priest slunk deeper into the chair, each breath ending with a heave, each beat of his heart spurting more blood from his neck.

"It was all you," I whispered, suddenly promoted to Captain Obvious.

The asanbosam recovered his second blade and scraped them together, wicking off the excess blood.

"You see what you've done with this crisis of conscience?" he asked. "Namadi was only a pawn, but quite useful nonetheless."

"You served him."

"I serve Nigeria. As did you."

"I was a thrall!"

"Were you?" he asked, licking his lips. "Black magic compelled you. Soiled your mind. Yet here you are..."

I swallowed. The asanbosam must have been able to exert some influence over his victims. Compulsion was common to many vampires. I understood the connection. "Namadi Obazuaye was just your thrall. Not a zombie, but not himself."

"A true countryman. He furthered our interests until you exposed him." He kept talking about "us" like I was with him.

"And Baptiste?" I asked.

Tunji shrugged. "The man was full of surprises, but in the end, he was only a pretender. A perversion. A Westerner who siphoned the soul of my culture."

The guards outside banged the door, but without their previous fervor, as if they knew it was too late to fulfill their duty.

"What now?" asked Tunji. "Shall I take your head as well? Or would you return to service?"

The word tasted like dirt. "Service?"

"You are no fool, Francisco. You are more powerful than ever with us."

"I still am."

Tunji grunted deeply, causing his chest and shoulders to shudder. "You realize you are not invincible, yes?" The beast made his way around the table to me. "You can die, shadow witch. I gutted you once before."

Flashes popped into my head. Of me dying. Once. Twice. Of my family. Star Island. My childhood home. Martine's cookhouse. I couldn't separate reality from my horrifying imagination. I'd never be the same.

"Just tell me one thing," I said.

Tunji Malu paused his approach and crossed his arms.

"Just one question," I pleaded. "Why me?"

He smiled. "The Horn, Francisco. I need the Horn of Subjugation."

Ten years ago, when I was just another hustler looking to make a buck, whipping up potions with Martine and thinking voodoo was just a game, I must have stumbled on the Horn of Subjugation. I was young. Dumb. Ambitious. Frankly, it sounded like something I'd do.

"The one you killed Martine for?" I spat. "I don't have it. I've never had it."

The large man nodded. "Considering your position, I'm inclined to believe you're being truthful. But consider mine: You don't remember anything from the last decade. Your word is useless."

Who knew the West African vampire could present such a succinct argument? I pressed my teeth together and snarled. He spoke of my death as a minor inconvenience.

Tunji Malu took a step closer to me. "The Horn is

linked to you, Francisco. It calls for you. You found it once.
You can find it again. If you bring it to me, I'll spare your
life."

And that confirmed what I already knew. He didn't have
it. He didn't know where it was. After ten years of looking,
working with Martine and the Bone Saints and likely every
other death animist he could, even after forcing me into
undead service, the asan had still come up empty.

Which presented quite the little mystery to me.
Granted, at the moment the concern was purely academic.
Tunji's curvy knives were half as interesting but
exponentially more urgent. I think that's a saying
somewhere: don't bring an inscrutable problem to a knife
fight.

I knew the vampire could move fast—I'd watched it kill
three people—but I had more defensive magic than Martine
and (hopefully) the others. I could cast plenty on the fly. I
just wasn't sure it would be enough.

"I wouldn't even know where to start looking," I told
him.

He nodded. "I thought you'd say that."

I recalled Martine's initial attack. Her undead had tried
to hold him to the ground. Smart move considering his
abilities. Tunji was too quick to be let loose. But the asan
had been too much for the dumb strength of the undead.
He'd ripped her servants from the ground and rent them
apart.

I'd like to see him try that with a shadow.

Tunji lunged at me, but before he could get going, a
shadow tendril from underneath the table locked around his
foot. He stretched for me like a bungee jumper and the

hook whizzed dangerously close.

I hopped back and flicked off the light switch. The results were unimpressive. It was dingy in here at best—not dark enough to blind anyone—but at least I had some pockets of darkness to work in.

Tunji ceased struggling with his binding and turned to me. I phased into the floor and launched toward him. Familiar with my powers, he guessed I would slip past him and attack from behind. Hey, it's my move. He spun around to face behind him. But he was too fast for his own good.

I skipped out of the shadow early, attacking him head on. Except Tunji's defensive maneuver had now exposed his back to me.

The tendril around his leg vanished as I summoned the force into both hands and rammed into the acid burns on his back.

The vampire rocketed into the far wall and roared. A hand of darkness emerged from the wall and latched onto his shoulder. I mustered as much force as I could but still failed to force Tunji to his knees. Immobilizing him would have to be enough.

Tunji swiped his hooks in wide arcs to keep me at bay, but I wasn't going for him. I grabbed the base of the drawn mini-blind from the window beside him and ripped it from the wall. Sunlight flooded over the corner of the room and bathed the vampire in warm light.

I didn't know what I expected. Besides weakening the shadow hand that held him, he kicked me in the gut for my trouble.

I crumpled to my knees and instinctively threw my arm over my head. His blade clanged against my newly fortified tattoo. Blue light blinded him and he hissed, but he spun his circle blade as he pulled away, slashing the inner, unprotected part of my forearm.

I recoiled and he broke free from the shadow magic. I rolled away, trying to get back to the shadow. Back to safety.

He was fast. I ducked under the table as his heavy blade punctured it. He swiped again but I kicked a chair into him. I scooted back on my ass, still in sunlight.

Before his next attack came, I scooped Baptiste's white powder from the floor and blew it in his face. It was a lucky shot and wholly unexpected—the vampire even breathed some of the deadly powder in through his mouth.

Tunji howled and spun away, slicing a piece of the table off. I made it out of the sun and slipped backward, resting against the far wall. No more windows.

The former bodyguard spit out bile and blood, but he came at me again. The type of guy who doesn't take no for an answer.

"What did you think?" I challenged. "You'd kill us all and walk away?"

He closed in and I saw one of his eyes had fused shut.

"I didn't kill them," he said, coughing, but calmly. "*You* did."

He brought both hooks above his head and forced them down. I easily sidestepped the attack, but it wasn't meant for me. He pulled his swing away and struck the warded door.

Both hooks buried into the cheap wood, one of them slicing through a metal bar of the security door. A blinding flash of red exploded into the asan, but he withstood the magic and heaved both doors off their hinges at the same time. The metal gate fell away, molten and bent from the destructive blast. The warded door remained undamaged from the directional magic, but Tunji's two blades were planted in it. He sliced and diced with his knives, splintering the wood to pieces and freeing his weapons, still glowing orange from the residual heat.

Neat trick.

But it had cost the vampire. He didn't look so hot anymore. His dark skin was coated with whitened ash. He breathed heavily. But I suddenly realized it wasn't him I needed to worry about anymore.

Jean-Louis Chevalier burst into the room with two zombies and a gunman.

"Assassin!" yelled Tunji, sinking to his knees and pointing a finger squarely at me. "He killed them all!"

Something told me the screaming mob crying for my head wouldn't listen to reason.

A shadow limb swiped at the gunman's hand. My magic doesn't have the manual dexterity to manipulate a weapon like that. I settled for knocking it to the floor. At the same time, the bokor spit green liquid from his mouth, a deluge of projectile vomit aimed right at me. I phased through it, but only a few feet till I hit sunlight. There, I made a break for the window. One of the zombies grabbed my ankle and tripped me.

The thrall held me down in sunlight. I reached for my whistle, but Jean-Louis Chevalier was wearing his silver gauntlets. Right here, in his proximity, I was unlikely to hijack his servants. The bokor smiled and took a swig from a glass vial, ready to regurgitate again.

That's when I noticed the zombie holding me down

sported cheap sunglasses.

Breaking Chevalier's connection with his pet wasn't happening. But tricking the undead lizard brain was an easy bet. The shadow flashed, and the zombie saw things in a new light. I was his bokor, on the ground, and Cisco was standing over me. The zombie released me and growled, then tackled the new Cisco Suarez.

Freed, I sprang to my feet. Over my shoulders I caught the hilarious image of Chevalier struggling against his own servant, a baffled expression on his face.

Before I went through the window, I locked eyes with Tunji Malu. I think he was impressed.

There's something about a twenty-foot drop that's educational. Namely, it displays how frail the human body is. I shook the haze away and rolled in the grass, bullets thudding next to me.

I fired up my shield and retreated, searching for the threat. My black cat peeked out of the open, back-door window of the white Hummer limo. Either he was trying to guide me or he was moving up in the world.

I made a break for the pretentious vehicle, skirting the building to keep it between me and the gunfire. Since my pursuers had to run through the structure's shadow, I waved a hand and the ground tugged at them, gumming up their movements. For a perfect moment, I became an Olympic high diver, careening through that open window in rare form.

I didn't stick the landing. Despite hitting a soft seat, I managed to flip around and kick bottles and glasses off a shelf. I came to rest upside down with my hand in a plate of oysters. The high life, all right.

I righted myself. No one else was back here, not even the cat anymore. Strange since I'd just seen it. I started to get the feeling it wasn't a normal zombie cat.

Bullets peppered the limo and I kissed the floor again. What sounded like hail hammered on the windows, but nothing got through. The freaking Hummer was bulletproof. I rose, raised the open window and checked the locks, and allowed a half smile.

Then the entire back windshield exploded.

Gunfire ripped through the cabin. Enchanted rounds again. Had to be. Or maybe your garden-variety, armor-piercing rounds. I didn't want to test them against my shield to find out.

I threw myself to the floor again. The oysters had the right idea. As I crawled toward the front cab, I noticed movement. There was a driver. "Get out of here!" I yelled.

Bullets swept over my head. Windows spiderwebbed. Expensive decanters of single-malt whiskey shattered. The interior of the limo became the Normandy invasion, but the freaking Hummer still didn't move.

"Namadi's dead!" I screamed. "Get us the hell out of here or we will be too!"

When the car didn't shift into gear, I shimmied to the front like I was navigating a trench. Between bursts of gunfire, I checked the driver.

The dude was wearing comically large headphones and jamming to music. I swear, ten years ago, cell phones were smaller, limos were smaller, headphones were smaller. So much for a future of miniaturization.

I ripped the bright red monstrosities from his ears and repeated myself. I don't think the startled driver understood a single word I said. The next argument he heard was more convincing: automatic fire ripping apart the newly-waxed chassis. He threw the Hummer into drive and floored it.

The driver weaved over the driveway to avoid the guards. I squeezed through the little window to the front with only one uncomfortable bump in the groin to show for it. It was better than a bullet, anyway.

The guards at the gate raised their weapons. I grabbed the wheel and forced a hard right onto the grass. The tires peeled through the lawn and sped across the property toward Second Avenue. The driver understood the plan and picked up speed before crunching the Hummer right into the green metal fence.

I tell you, the perimeter fence was firmly rooted to the ground. Impenetrable. But Hummer limos at speed don't mess around. The irresistible force met the immovable object. We won.

As we sped away from Little Haiti, both our heads ducked safely below the windshield, we traded glances.

"Not bad driving," I commended. "How do you feel about whiskey and oysters?"

Chapter 33

What did I think was gonna happen? It wasn't just a single person I'd gone after, it was an entire gang. No shame in retreat under those circumstances. Hell, it was outright cocky to think I could've handled everybody at once. I guess old habits die hard.

If I kept it up, I'd die hard too. Again.

My breach of the Bone Saints compound (besides the undignified end) actually accomplished a lot (besides pissing off a collective Little Haiti). I now knew who my real enemy was. Not the Saints. Not Baptiste or Max or Namadi. It was all Tunji Malu. Everything had been Tunji Malu. The asanbosam. The West African vampire. He was the one who had cursed me. Knowing that was some mark of progress.

The smug look on his face as he accused me of assassinating the gang leaders drove me to anger. I demanded the limo driver turn around and take me back. He refused and reminded me that I was the one who had convinced him to run in the first place. I knew he was right but I was too amped up to like it. I hated turning my tail between my legs once again.

We drove south and the shock wore off. I realized I was sitting on a gold mine. Here's a life pro tip: if you want to get at affluence's dirty laundry, ask the hired help. The limo driver was quite enlightening.

For one, he was totally creeped out by Tunji. The driver didn't know anything about magic, but he was superstitious enough to be scared. He didn't hesitate to believe my account of what had transpired in the meeting. Not only that, he was smart. He recognized that he was a liability now. The poor guy decided to head straight for the Port of Miami and flee the country.

On the way, he answered anything I asked. Namadi had arrived from West Africa, with Tunji Malu in tow, twelve years prior. It was a rags-to-riches story, but I only got the broad strokes because the driver had only been employed for a few years.

That had been plenty of time to confirm my suspicions.

Apparently, while Namadi had been "the boss," his bodyguard had free reign to make power plays throughout the city. Namadi hadn't been a voodoo priest. As for Tunji, his full skill set remained to be seen.

My West African mythology is rusty, but creatures like Tunji Malu come in several categories. He could be one of the cursed, once human but no longer. They're sometimes called subhumans (but as a general rule never to their faces). Zombies are an undead example.

Conversely, asanbosam might be fae, any of a number of underling races from the Nether. I'm not too keen on the Nether. It's a wild place of twisted life and blackened blood. Anansi trickster spiders fall into that category. With everything I'd seen, I bet Tunji did too. Except he was humanoid. More intelligent. I was guessing he was a silvan or a fiend of some sort.

It didn't really matter whether the vampire knew magic or *was* magic. One thing was certain: he was otherworldly. He didn't fit in the natural world. Several times the driver referred to Tunji as invincible, his words a reverent whisper, as if speaking of a legend. I've learned that legends are overrated but often have truth to them.

On the more practical side of things, I got the address of Namadi's mansion in Coconut Grove.

The driver offered me the Hummer. He didn't need it anymore, but I didn't want any part of it. A respected community leader was now sans a head. The police wouldn't look kindly on whoever possessed his stolen vehicle. I settled for a ride instead and offered the limo driver a word of luck when we parted.

It wasn't until he dropped me off that I thought of the cat again. I checked the back cabin but he wasn't in sight. I couldn't feel his connection either. My best guess was that he'd taken a bullet. The disappearance was a bit unsettling, but I had larger issues to worry about.

I knew better than to stay on the streets. Of all the places to lie low, I ended up at a strip club drinking a twelve-dollar beer, staring at my phone instead of the girls. (Okay, I peeked from time to time). These joints weren't known for their sincerity. Ironically, it might've been the only place in the city I still had a friend.

For about an hour, I tucked myself in the back corner with a shadow over my face. That was usually enough to be left alone, but here a new girl offered me a lap dance every five minutes.

It was dumb in hindsight but, in my early twenties, I used to have fun in strip clubs. I knew the silicone and smiles were illusions, but it was a game I enjoyed. The flirting, the invented stories, the arms around your shoulder. Now I looked around and all I saw was desperation and sweat.

Wow, listen to me. Most people live a lifetime before they start sounding like their parents. Me? A decade flashed by in the blink of an eye and I'd just quoted my father.

It's always hardest to hear when you need to listen most.

I accepted another beer and drank, thinking about friends and enemies. Neither were turning out quite how I'd imagined.

"Care for a dance?" asked a voluptuous bombshell wearing a bikini top three sizes too small.

I leaned forward and let the shadow fall from my face. "Howdy, Milena."

She started. Her reaction was to cover up, which I thought was strange considering the venue. She went from modest to indignant real quick.

"Cisco, you asshole!"

"What'd I do now?"

She smacked my arm. "I don't like my friends coming here."

I threw up my hands in surrender. "I'm not here to start trouble. Honest."

A meathead who put those old posters of Arnold to shame suddenly appeared. "Is there a problem here?"

Before I could renege on my previous promise, Milena jumped in. "Sorry, Mike. We're good. I was just convincing my lovely customer here to buy me a Sex on the Beach."

He nodded and waved the cocktail waitress over.

"You know that'll cost me fifteen bucks, right?"

"Twenty," she said, taking a seat. "And it's watered down to hell. But you gotta pay for my time when I'm working."

"As long as I'm paying—" I started.

Milena cut into me with her finger. "Don't you even make jokes about that."

I shrugged. It was a sensitive issue with her. I could respect that. The waitress returned with what amounted to a juice shot in a martini glass. I gave it a puzzled stare, trying to figure out why someone would drink something like that.

"What's up?" asked Milena. "I can give you five minutes. Then you're outta here."

I sucked my teeth, both impressed and disturbed at the same time. This wasn't the same Milena Fuentes I had known. It wasn't just the meaty hips and generous bust, either. She'd come a long way. Milena was a survivor. Turned a bad deal on its head and made it something—not good, maybe, but better.

"Hey," she commanded, snapping her fingers. "Eyes up."

I nodded. "I need to borrow your car."

She shrugged. "That it? You had me worried."

"That's not it, Milena. I need your help. I know it's a lot to ask, but you're the only one I can trust."

She sipped her "drink" and leaned back. "Now you're just being melodramatic. You have lots of friends, Cisco."

"You'd be surprised. What I did today..." I stared at the beer in my hand. Anything to avoid looking her in the eyes. "It may have hurt Evan. His career. His family. His nice little life."

"What'd you do?"

"Just put the truth out there. It's the fallout that might hurt."

Milena put her hand on mine, drawing my gaze. "Cisco. No one will blame you for wanting answers. Especially not Evan."

"He wanted me to stay away and I didn't."

"He'll forgive you."

"I'm not too sure about that," I said. "He wanted me to get out of town."

"If people are trying to kill you, it might not be a bad idea," she reasoned.

"It wasn't for my safety. It was for his."

She shook her head. "That's crazy." With a gulp, she killed the last of her cocktail.

"I can't trust him, Milena. Not anymore."

"Evan would never betray you. He's a true friend."

I snorted more aggressively than I intended. "He's mixed up in this, Milena. Maybe he was my friend at one point, but ten years is a long time. I can't blame him for having new priorities now."

"This is bullshit," she said, standing up. "Listen, Cisco. My shift ends in an hour. Come back to my place. Relax. You'll realize I'm right."

My burner phone rang. The number was blocked.

"Here it goes," I said, holding the phone up to her. "There's only one other person who knows this number."

"Then maybe you should answer it, douche nozzle. He's probably concerned for you. To be honest, I kinda am too. Let me get my car keys. I'll meet you outside."

She walked away, flashing a smile at the bar manager. I should've known better than to come here. The last thing I wanted was to mess up somebody else's life. I made my way outside, shielding my eyes from the blinding sun. The phone had stopped ringing but started up again. I leaned against the concrete wall and answered it.

"What the fuck did you do?" demanded Evan.

"Do you even wanna hear my side?"

He ignored my tired sarcasm. "They say it was a mess over there, Cisco. A real bloodbath."

"You know me. Go big or go home. By the way, thanks for your intel phone call."

He sighed loudly into the phone, making it clear his decision was arduous. "You're gonna need to come in," he finally said.

I laughed. "And what? Tell the detectives I was a zombie for ten years at the behest of a Nigerian voodoo outfit?"

"We'll tell them you were a prisoner for ten years. It's true enough."

"Then what, Evan? I get charged as a mob accessory? It's either hit man or vigilante. Both spell outlaw." I paced away from a man lighting a smoke and lowered my voice. "I'm not going to the cops."

He sighed again. I guess that's his phone equivalent of hands on hips. "You're not giving me much choice here."

"And what choice did you give me? You knew the Nigerians had the commissioners in their pocket. You knew Namadi was a pawn. And you tried to brush me aside. Your best friend."

Evan's tone changed, like maybe he was repositioning the phone. "What are you talking about?"

"The community redevelopment deal."

"What about it?" he asked. "Namadi contributed to a

number of land deals in the Biscayne area. There's a citywide revitalization project underway. How does that implicate Namadi Obazuaye?"

"It's Tunji Malu who's implicated. He was the real player on that end. He killed me, turned me into his thrall, and ordered me to attack the Bone Saints. He wanted the crime up and down Biscayne to be very public. To drive real estate values down."

"Where did you get this from?"

"Don't play stupid, Evan. Who do you think benefits from bargain-valued land? The ones snatching it up. Namadi and your bosses. That's what this is all about. I finally see it. It's not about Nigerian culture. It's gentrification. More money for the rich, in the name of revitalization and safety." I spit on the floor. "You sold me out for a political career."

Evan swallowed calmly on the other end of the line, thinking over his reply. Instead of an immediate denial, he surprised me.

"I can't talk over the phone, Cisco. We should meet in person."

"And how's that different from turning myself in?"

He hissed. "You need to trust me, man. That's how."

My jaw was sore. My fist was clenched. I was wound up. But I wasn't stupid.

"I'll think about it," I said, and hung up.

Chapter 34

I commandeered Milena's tiny Fiat and headed south before rush hour hit. I passed through the Grove to check out the address Namadi's driver had given me. The shaded, winding streets led me to an isolated mansion with an imposing fence. The overgrowth made the property difficult to see, but the red and blue lights were hard to miss. The police swarmed the place like worker bees.

That meant Namadi's body had made the official rounds outside the DROP team's jurisdiction. Namadi's house was now an area of interest. No way I'd be getting in anytime soon. I looped back around to Downtown Miami.

The heart of the city was beginning to clear. Traffic was tight, but everyone was leaving at the end of the workday. It made for convenient parking. I walked a block and slipped into the coffee shop across the street from Evan's office. I ordered something called a pumpkin spice latte from someone called a barista. I'm not sure when the future got so confusing, but I didn't complain. The future was delicious.

I watched the clock and badgered the barista about the medium being called a large in Spanish. After a while I saw what I was waiting for: police detectives poured out of the task force headquarters. That meant, exactly three minutes ago, Milena had made the call to Evan. She'd told him I was at her place in Midtown. Backing up the info, if the officers checked, they'd find my cell phone on her coffee table. I thought it a long shot they could track my burner with just the phone number, but Milena didn't think so. I figured, in matters of technology a zombie fossil like me needed to take outside advice.

My heart grew heavier as I watched the police load up into squad cars and take off. That meant Evan considered me a hostile player. On the plus side, my friend didn't ride with his unit. Just like he'd said, he was more politician than officer now, remaining behind to oversee matters. The DROP team would arrive in Midtown and Milena would give them a sob story about how I'd barged in and harassed her. She'd be fine. The downside was that I probably couldn't stay at her place anymore, just in case they were watching.

When the street cleared out and Evan returned indoors, I quietly crossed. The downtown shadows were lengthening now. The day was nearing completion. The timer I'd set the day before was nearing its limit as well, so I had to be quick.

I snuck in the task force building, abandoning the shadow when I found it unnecessary. The main room was empty. Once again, Lieutenant Evan Cross was in his personal office. This time, he was standing by his printer with his back to me.

My red boots scuffed the carpet as I entered. Evan grew tense, then sighed and dropped his head without turning to me.

"Hello, Cisco."

"Hi there, buddy. Sorry I missed the cavalry."

Evan faced me with his hands on his hips, looking me up and down and shaking his head like he knew something I didn't. "It was just a precaution," he said.

I scoffed. "Looked more like the actions of a corrupt cop to me. You didn't send the call to dispatch. You got your own guys to move on me, half a town away. You're trying to keep things quiet."

"You idiot. That part was for *your* protection." Evan came around his desk and put his hands on my shoulders. "I know the kinds of questions walking into the precinct will spur. I don't want that for you. This office? It's my private world. I can run things off the books. Maybe there's a way to keep your name out of everything."

"That the plan for Tunji Malu too?"

Evan's eyes narrowed and I brushed free of his grasp.

"I passed by Namadi's house," I told him. "Is Tunji there?"

"Homicide has it locked down. Tunji won't risk going there. Like you said, he doesn't want police visibility either."

"I get it. So the bodyguard doesn't even need to clear his name. Your guys will just sweep his association under the rug. Even though he's the one doing all the killing."

Evan returned his hands to his hips in his self-righteous manner. "Hey, you're doing a fair bit of that yourself. I got nine witnesses in Little Haiti who say that was all you."

"You know that's not true."

"Do I?"

I got right in Evan's face. "Yeah, asshole. I told you what I know. Everything. I was killed. Made into a mindless thrall for ten years. I hit the Haitians on Tunji's orders. I stirred up the pot. And if it wasn't for a lucky shot from Laurent Baptiste, I might still be on the wrong side of things." I turned away and leaned on the back of the chair. A third of my life, vocalized in a few short sentences. "He thinks I have something. He killed Martine for it."

"What is it?"

"It doesn't matter, Evan. I don't have it. I don't have anything. That's what I know." I spun around in frustration. "You believe every word of it, too. I can see it in your eyes. You know I'm right. It's just your heart that's hoping I'm wrong."

My friend frowned and took an unconscious step backward. Rethinking his stance. Alone, Evan had rationalized his actions. He probably thought he'd done what needed doing. But that logic wouldn't slide with me present. Right now, I was his doubt personified.

"I do want what's right, Cisco," he said softly. "For all of us. Living with this weight on my shoulders has been tough."

"Tough?" I cackled. "Try sleeping in a dumpster. You're living the high life compared to me. I saw that yellow Vette in your driveway."

His face soured quickly. "Fuck you, Cisco. Fuck you and your self-centered attitude. You've been back one day and I'm already sick of that sob story. You weren't the only one that suffered. You, at least, deserved part of what happened. Your family didn't. And those of us who lived, who had to live with the consequences of *your* actions, we've suffered just as much these last ten years."

My words froze in my throat. I wanted to curse, spit, jab,

bite. Nothing would come. I turned to the chair again. The bastard knew me just as well as I knew him. Pushing the right buttons, striking the right nerves—it was easy for him.

Again, his voice softened. "They said you were dabbling in black magic, man. They said you killed people."

I shook my head sadly. "And you believed them?"

"You were never exactly a normal guy, Cisco."

I was never a bad guy either. Not until Tunji had gotten his claws on me. I wasn't stupid. I knew I had dug this hole myself. But I wasn't fucking evil. I had a heart, damn it.

"You were supposed to be my friend," I said. "You were supposed to trust what I said. Ask me. Not take rumors at face value."

Evan sat against the windowsill and sighed. "It's been a long time."

"It's been more than that. You're in bed with a West African vampire."

My friend was speechless for a second. I knew that was the last thing he wanted to hear. I also knew that, like everything else, he believed me. The horror on his face spoke of more than guilt.

"The limo driver came clean, Evan. Tunji wasn't just Namadi's enforcer. He acted on his own discretion. You could say he was in charge all along."

My friend came to grips with the revelation and nodded. "He's approached me several times. I always got the same impression."

"And you went along to get along."

Evan met me with a wry smile. "Look. Just 'cause I'm the boss in this building doesn't make it my show. This is a political detail. The commissioners make the assignments.

Are certain laws enforced more heartily than others? Sure. Ultimately, it's their call."

"And they're gonna need a scapegoat when this gets out."

His hands returned to his hips. "You don't get it, Cisco. You and me don't have power over these guys. It's the other way around."

More rationalizing. More passing the buck. After years of service, it was ingrained into Evan's logic. I didn't belabor the point. This wasn't about a logical fallacy. This wasn't about good and evil. As much as I hated to admit it, this was about me feeling hurt.

"Christ, Evan. I have trust issues these days. This is what you do to me?"

He stood up straight again. "That's *why* I did it. You'll never admit it, man, but I was always a better friend to you than you were to me. I always looked out for you. Tried to steer you in the right direction. Give you a hand."

"That's not true!" I yelled, getting my buttons pushed again. "I would've died for you!"

Evan stepped forward. "You didn't die for me. You died for power. You died for yourself. And it got your family killed in the process." The scorn came through his eyes now. "You turned your back on them. On all your friends. On your parents and Seleste. On Emily."

I decked Evan so hard he sprawled against the office window. He was slow to get up. When he did I slammed him against the wall. But I didn't feel any resistance. The dude wore two holstered pistols and never even reached for them. I had tears in my eyes, and they kept coming when Evan wouldn't fight back.

I released him and spun away. My friend dropped to his knees, breathing heavily, staring at the carpet.

I couldn't look at him. I wanted to end it. Our friendship. His life. But I knew I couldn't do that. Not like this.

"I didn't know," rasped Evan. "I swear. You were dead and no one knew anything. I looked and looked but there was nothing to find. I knew what you were into. I knew it was out of my league. It sucked, Cisco, but one day life moved on." Evan bared it all now, just unloading his conscience without a care. He finally met my eyes again. "I heard about your family a couple years later. I was heartbroken, man. And it was the same brick wall. Except I eventually got this appointment. I was finally in a position to make some moves for you."

I crouched beside my friend, listening intently.

"I wasn't lying when I said I looked into your murder. Martine wouldn't talk to me. Nobody would. I dug up old graves, man. The commissioner had already been working with Namadi. Our team began joint security for him. Tunji Malu introduced himself to me. He told me he'd kill my family just like he killed yours if I pressed the matter." Evan turned away. Scared. Ashamed. "I couldn't fight anymore, man. I was all alone. I had no idea you were still alive. You have to believe that. Everything would've been different if I'd known. You would've been the first person I went to."

I stood up again. It disgusted me, to see my friend beaten like that. A part of me hated that, but another part hated myself for blaming him. To him, Tunji was a demon. An unstoppable force. Would I have been happier if Evan had been killed too?

And it wasn't just him anymore, I knew. It was Emily.

I kicked the chair and sent it flying into the far wall.

I couldn't hate him for protecting Emily. I would've done it differently, but that would've been my end goal as well. Lord knows how kids figured into the equation.

I rubbed my face. My tired eyes. The new, sun-lined wrinkles that traced my forehead. I was beginning to get a feeling, I thought. Beginning to see things from another point of view besides mine.

I steadied my breathing and spoke evenly, without sympathy or indignation. "Just tell me you're not on his side here, Evan. Just tell me I can kill Tunji Malu and end this."

Still on the floor, he shook his head. "It's not that simple, Cisco. He's been working this for ten years. The whole time you've been dead. It's not just about money to him. That's what drives people like the commissioner. But Tunji? He's playing the long game."

I snorted. "And you say I got mixed up in black magic."

"I thought you were dead, man. You would've done the same thing."

I grabbed a pen and placed it on the edge of the desk. Then I pulled out the tattered business card Evan had originally given me, the one with his address on the back, and snapped it on the glass surface.

"I want you to write down the address where I can find Tunji. I don't want any excuses or stories or reasons why I shouldn't go. I don't want to hear how noble your actions were, or that you did it for me. Just the address."

He chewed his lip and mulled it over. "You don't need an address. Tunji has a safe house off Eighth Street in the Everglades. A turnoff just past Gator Park. You can't miss it if you're looking for it."

Calle Ocho. I nodded and checked the window. It was almost twilight. Evan brushed himself off and straightened his clothes as he stood. I headed to the door but paused and turned to him.

"You no longer exist," I told him. "You're dead to me. And that means something coming from a necromancer."

That was it. The last word. I walked out and would've left it at that. But Evan Cross was too stupid to leave it alone.

"I did it for you!" he yelled back at me.

I halted in my tracks and growled. I stormed back in his office with unfinished business. "You know what gets me? That once you weren't alone anymore, once I came back from the dead and walked into your office yesterday, you didn't come clean. You kept balancing your house of cards, trying to keep it up, trying to keep me out." I sneered. "Trying to get rid of me."

"I was trying to keep you alive, man. Happy. You're gonna get yourself killed all over again. And for what?" Evan stared hard at me. "There's nothing left for you in Miami."

I lunged at him again, grabbing him by the shoulders. "I get to decide that!" I yelled. "Me! Not you! Not Tunji Malu!"

He threw me off him but I came back harder. Evan and I flailed against each other, emotions getting the better of us.

"You're wrong again, Cisco! It's not about you!"

He shoved me into the desk but I rolled out of the blow. I swung at him but he was ready this time. He ducked and came back at me, connecting with my cheek and making the world blurry.

"You can't always make decisions based on *you*!" he yelled.

I'd about had it with him. Old friend or not, Evan was seriously getting on my nerves. Before he could vent out any more frustration on an old buddy, a slither of shadow peeked up from behind him and enclosed around his neck. I yanked it backwards, hard, and Evan tumbled to his back.

I'd never used magic on my friend before. It had always been off limits. In principle, it isn't cool for animists to take advantage of the general public. It's cruel and unfair, especially with anger involved. Even now, after everything Evan had done to me, I shouldn't have done it.

But I couldn't stop myself.

Evan was supposed to have been my best friend. He was supposed to have looked after me. Avenged me. Instead, he was in league with my killer. He was sleeping with my girl. He was washing over my life like it had never happened.

He choked against the shadow tentacle. I snarled. I didn't snap his neck, but I didn't let go either. My friend's face flushed red and hot. I didn't know if I could stop the hate.

"She's your daughter!" he squeezed out.

I recoiled, suddenly seeing my actions with open eyes. I shook away the rage. I dispersed the shadow. My friend rolled over like a recovering drowning man.

"She's yours, man," he continued between coughs. "Emily was barely pregnant when you died. She didn't tell anyone. She was afraid, Cisco. She didn't even tell your family."

"What?" I asked dumbly.

"She was right to do it, too. They were killed, but she was left alone. I watched after her though. I figured it out." He sat up but stayed on the floor, not risking another skirmish. "Once we got together, I couldn't risk them, Cisco. You... Your family... This was your daughter, man. The only piece of you anyone had left. The only piece I could protect. What other choice did Emily or I have?"

I quietly backed away, not sure how I felt about what he said. About what had almost happened here. If Evan had been even a little bit right, then maybe I was a little bit wrong. Maybe I was a lot of bit wrong. Maybe some of the evil I had done was a part of me now.

I blinked, trying to focus. Trying to sort out my thoughts. But they were a helpless jumble. I was a dead man. A cursed man. A wronged man. And I was also a father.

Evan rubbed his throat. "I didn't know you were alive," he muttered again, more to himself than me.

I forced my feet to move, one by one. I had to get out of there.

"It would've changed everything..." he said.

I walked out, leaving his tattered business card behind. "Everything changed anyway."

Chapter 35

Bad decisions are usually made without conscious thought. That extra drink that puts us over the edge. A subtle difference in wording that transforms misunderstanding to hurt. It could even be, say... I dunno—stumbling upon a mystical artifact named the Horn of Subjugation and receiving a one-way ticket into indentured service for my trouble.

Maybe I should've known the discovery would blow up in my face. Hell, maybe I did. It's hard to speak to something I don't remember. But what I was doing tonight. Going after Tunji Malu? That was a bad decision I had every intention of making.

Slightly less stupid (but every bit as necessary) was revisiting Saint Martin's Cemetery. I had started a spell the night before, one looking for old answers to old questions. This late in the game, considering my date with destiny, I wasn't sure how many more chances I'd get at this. That meant it wasn't an option.

It was dangerous to return here. But it was nearly twilight. I was on the clock. I had to know.

The Fiat pulled into the empty parking lot. I surveyed the block behind me for anyone on my trail. I'd been ambushed here once already. I couldn't let that happen again.

The sun dipped below the horizon, rushing my precautions, but I was satisfied with the outskirts. I phased through the gate. My eyes traced over every headstone, every tree, every shape in the fading light.

I hurried to the graves and knelt down, scanning my surroundings one last time. Cemeteries weren't inherently creepy to me, but something prickled the hairs on my neck. Was I really that out of practice?

I used the ceremonial knife to prick the palm of my hand, careful to avoid marring my tattoo. Then I plunged the knife into the dirt and considered my options.

He walks alone but always has a home. This grave... Death was my home, whenever I was done walking.

My curiosity got the better of me.

"I'll take door number four, Alex."

I squeezed a drop of blood onto the small pile of dirt clumped over my grave. Moments later, the dirt crumbled away and an earthworm emerged. I plucked it from the ground and laid it on the blood spot on my palm. It squirmed in the fluid, grit and ooze almost forming a paste.

If I were at the crime scene moments after death, or even a morgue, maybe, I could've used the death sight as I had done with Martine. Fresh corpses are much more susceptible to spellcraft. Given the right circumstances, getting a corpse to speak isn't out of the question. What I was working with, however, was decay. Rot. The elements. There wasn't anything left to talk to. I had to hope there was enough for my little spies to detect.

The worm turned in my palm, fully bathed in blood. I've

seen this spell culminate with the worm being eaten, but I'm not much for French cuisine. It can be done other ways. My preference? A whisper and a waiting ear. I cupped my open palm to my ear, listening to the report. A smile played across my lips. As expected, my casket was empty. No trace of spirit or body.

I released the worm to go on its way and repeated the process for my sister. This information didn't bring a grin to my face.

Seleste's coffin was filled with pieces of her. An arm. A foot. There was so little of her remaining it made me wonder why they'd bothered with a burial at all. But Catholics don't cremate.

After ten years, my sister's spirit was long gone. These coffins contained biological remains, not people. I released an empty sigh. I hadn't expected closure to feel so hollow.

There was something else. The worm detected faint Intrinsics, magical energies from a left-behind spell. It was odd for trace workings to stick around so long, eight years in this case, but the hallowed and undisturbed grounds could account for it. There wasn't enough left to identify the magic, but it was dark.

Thinking about Seleste broke me up a little. Imagining her final moments. The horrifying barbarity of being torn apart, unable to fight off a magical foe. I needed time to process but twilight was running out.

I moved to the next grave. Lydia Suarez. I paused, unsure if I could handle the same image with of mother. I skipped her and went straight to Pops.

The worm took a little longer to surface. Either my magic was weakening with the sun's light or my little minion had better things to do. As I fetched him, a small clump of earth latched around my wrist.

I jerked back. The dirt fell away and revealed a bony hand gripping me. I pulled away but it didn't budge, and I couldn't slip into shadow during twilight.

Things went from bad to worse when something locked onto my ankle. Another hand, the right to the other's left, but twisted around in such a way that I knew it was from a different body. I was being attacked.

I searched for a link, a magical signature to whoever commanded these undead. It was absent. If true, that meant these corpses were acting alone. I'd never seen anything like that before. Then again, besides historical accounts, I'd never known of bodies this far decayed being animated either.

This couldn't be happening. What the hell had my little worm dug up?

I reached awkwardly across my body for the knife planted in the ground.

Another mound of dirt surfaced beside the first. It shook violently, and I did my best to recoil. They had me. I stretched and finally succeeded in grabbing the knife, then watched in horror as the dirt fell away to reveal a moldy skull with patches of flesh.

"Francisco," it uttered.

The voice was ragged. Ghostly and empty, but with a tinge of longing.

I ceased struggling. The knife went limp. "Dad?"

Impossible. This rotten skull, the voice—they were beyond the realm of the living, but they were unmistakable. I realized both hands were part of the same body—one skeleton, not two. My father's separate pieces, hacked apart.

"How is this possible?" I asked. This sorcery wasn't my doing. I hadn't called the spirit, and the worm sure as hell should've gone unnoticed.

"Possible?" he rasped.

"To come back. From the dead."

"Dead?" A few inquisitive humming noises resonated in the skull. "Oh, yes. I remember now. Waiting a long time."

I gazed into the dirt-filled eyes. This thing, the physical remnants before me, was unnatural. Putrid. But I needed to navigate past that. To lean on long experience. To lean on my heart.

"Put down the knife, son," said the skull, its voice practically shivering.

Hearing the fear in my father's voice, however supernatural, shook me. I threw the knife down. My body shuddered as the emotions came out. My family was supposed to be far beyond my reach.

My voice broke. "I'm back, Dad."

I wanted to reach in and hug him, but that was impossible. The unyielding hands still held me in place. Still squeezed.

"Yes," he said slowly, understanding. "Back. Back far too late."

"Where are Mom and Seleste?"

My father heaved wistfully as the earthworm crawled over his face. "Lydia is in a better place now."

"And Seleste?" I asked. The face grumbled and twitched in the dirt. "Dad, why are you still here?"

"Lost," he whispered. "Elsewhere."

"You're not lost. I'm with you now." My eyes watered

but I blinked away the tears. Twilight would be over soon. I needed to focus. "You can tell me, Dad. You've waited all this time for me. I'm here now. You can tell me."

The skull hacked out a bitter laugh, like my father had sometimes done after a bout of drinking. It was a grating sound that set me on edge.

"My son," said the spirit. "It is not you for whom I wait. It is for Seleste." The hand around my wrist tightened. "She will return to me."

I squirmed in the old man's grip. Elsewhere. "Return from where?" My father sounded mad, speaking in incoherent loops. I wondered if Seleste was like me, a zombie. But no. My sister was dead. Her body was proof of that.

I grunted and tried to pry his skeletal fingers loose. "What can I do?" I asked desperately.

My father nearly growled. "You have done enough, Francisco!"

He tugged my hand down to him. The soil was loose and gave way easily, swallowing my hand.

"No!" I screamed, struggling. "I'm sorry!"

"You should be the one in the dirt, my son. My blood." He dragged my foot under. "It is *you* who should be dead. And *us* who should live."

The feeble bones were strong. I recalled Tunji ripping Martine's servants from the ground. The vampire must have marvelous power. I didn't.

"You're right," I said. Tears leaked from my eyes like a dam threatening to collapse. I shoved them away and gritted my teeth, pulling hard against my father. "I never meant for this to happen, Dad. I never wanted any of it."

Although I couldn't escape the ground, the corpse ceased tugging me under. He took a long, wheezing breath that sounded like his soul escaping. I wanted it to be over, but he spoke some more.

"I do not care for myself, Francisco. You are my boy. My blood."

I nodded. "I love you."

"It has been a long time."

His grip loosened. I imagined him smiling. Maybe it was silly, but I needed the peace.

"I missed you," he said. "I miss Lydia. And Seleste. Where is everybody?"

I shook my head. "Dead and scattered because of my mistake..."

The skull rolled in the dirt. "Dead? I'm dead?" He squeezed my hand and began to shake again. "Drop the knife, son."

"Mmm?" My left hand was still bleeding. Still empty. The knife was in the grass beyond my reach. "I don't have the knife, Dad."

His empty eyes flashed. His broken jaw widened in horror. "I couldn't stop the knife, Francisco. Too strong." I pulled away again. "You were too strong."

"Dad, what are you—"

"You cut us up, son! Hacked us to pieces! You murdered your own blood."

"Dad!"

"You killed us, Francisco. You came into your home and slaughtered us in the name of your dark power. And now you come to me for forgiveness?"

"It's not possible!" I protested.

He yanked harder, and my arm sank to the elbow.

I panicked. At what was happening. At what he'd said. At the awful, horrible, unspeakable truth. I felt it in my heart now, on the verge of bursting. I felt the slick of the darkness on my soul.

I thrashed in the old man's grip. I brushed dirt into his face with my free hand and pressed down hard, doing whatever I could to bury him. To bury the memory. To stuff it all down in a quiet, dark place where it never needed to be seen again.

"Dad!" I screamed again, seeing flashes of the memory behind my eyelids. The blood. The shock on their faces. The images weren't hallucinations or my wild imagination. They were real. They were what had happened.

My father. Mom. Seleste. They never had a chance against my black magic.

They never had a chance against what I had become.

I couldn't hold them anymore. The floodgates. All semblance of discipline and control burst into flames and scattered like ashes. My tears came heavy and hard. I buckled over and ignored the outside world.

I stopped fighting. I stopped pulling away. My father, his ghost, his corpse, embraced me. Crushed me. Started to drag me under. And all I could do was sob.

I couldn't remember the last time I'd cried. *Really* cried. And not just because I'd been dead for ten years. My life had been full of so many expectations, so many disappointments, so many loves and losses and bitter defeats that I'd given crying up. I'd locked it away as something unnecessary. A mark of weakness.

I didn't care about that anymore. I screamed as my

mouth pressed into the dirt. All the breath escaped from me until I couldn't cry anymore. I rested on the grave, broken, deserving my fate.

And then the last of the sun's light faded with the spinning world, and suddenly my father was gone.

It was some time before I realized I was still breathing. The ground constricted my expanding chest as my lungs filled with air. The dirt was packed now. Impossibly hard, as if it had never moved. Even though I was only partially buried, it took all my strength to force myself up.

This magic—it was strong. It was unreal. Something powerful was at work within its engine. Something far beyond me.

But none of that made a blip on my radar.

My father. My hero. He had met a horrible end at my hands. Along with almost everyone else I loved.

I pounded the ground, demanding that he come back and take me. Demanding that he trade places with me.

I don't know what's in the Murk. The Shadow Dog has never shown me that, and likely never would. My mom may have been at peace, but my dad was a lonely sentinel, waiting in the shadow world for my sister, wherever she was. My family had been splintered in more than just this world.

The depths of my destruction continued to grow.

I collapsed to the ground and yelled some more, but it did no good. The dirt matted against me and scrubbed the blood and tears away. My breathing steadied until everything was quiet except for the footsteps in the grass.

"The sunglasses were a cool trick," announced Jean-Louis Chevalier.

I spun around on my hands and knees expecting another assault.

It was only the bokor. Alone. I laughed nervously.

"We didn't know who you were," he said, stepping slowly my way. "You had no name. No face. Just an expert assassin. But after following your scent here last night, seeing you by the graves, I wondered..."

I let my black pupils fill my irises, taking in the grounds in the fresh darkness. No one else was sneaking in my shadows.

"I see you again by these graves, white man. Are you not Suarez?"

My bloody palm closed around a clump of cemetery dirt. "I'm not in the mood for pleasantries, Chevalier, so you'd better get on with it."

"There was nothing pleasant about killing Baptiste."

"I didn't kill him," I said.

He frowned at my statement. "But why kill the African if you heeded his bidding?"

"Fuck you," I said, rising to my feet. A rush of blood left my head and I wavered a bit.

"You don't look so good, Suarez."

"Cut the threats. You can't take me all by yourself."

He chuckled. "This much is true."

I saw the ambush too late. Three blurs—no, birds—speared through the air toward me in a tight cluster. It wouldn't do much unless I got lucky, but I tossed the fistful of dirt their way. At the same time, a shadow javelin spiked up from the dirt, narrowly missing one.

I forced my mind into them. Felt their single-minded presence. They were closed off, somehow. Armored. With their master present and their current bearing, there was no time to break them. No time to reach for my whistle.

Another spear of shadow shot up. Another. I finally grazed one and sent it off course, barreling into the ground. The other two were almost upon me.

The bokor hadn't thought to bring a flashlight this time. I pulled my fist back and drew in the darkness. A heavy gauntlet gloved my hand, and I propelled it forward just in time to smash into the remaining birds just three feet away from me.

Just in case I missed, my left forearm swung in front of my head to protect my eyes from razor-sharp claws and beaks.

It wasn't necessary. The gauntlet shattered the hollow bones of the two birds. They exploded in a sickening crunch. But it was fulminant. More like a pop powered by escaping gas.

A green fluid—not blood—hurled from their destroyed carcasses, still carrying their momentum. My arm bar was useless. The rotten substance sprayed all over my hands and face.

It burned. I fell to the dirt immediately. I grasped for loose soil and rubbed it against my skin, hoping to neutralize whatever it was.

I tried to regain my feet, but my body reacted violently. I keeled over, coughing. Spitting up blood. My empty stomach vomited bile. My muscles grew lazy.

I heard the bokor laughing over my gasps and coughs. I tried to wipe my eyes, to focus on my assailant, but they seized closed.

My hand pawed the ground, struggling just to crawl.

Closer. Closer. As the footsteps neared, I wrapped my fingers around the bokor's knife. Chevalier pressed it to the dirt with his shoe.

"What did you do to me?" I asked weakly.

He kneeled down and recovered his knife. "I only needed the proper preparation, my friend."

Bad decisions, I thought.

I puked again and tried to shake the nausea away. If this was a magical poison, it could be done. But I couldn't wrap my tethers around it.

"What do you think I should do with this?" Chevalier placed his blade against my neck.

"Not like this," I pleaded.

Another amused chuckle. "Most do not choose how they leave this world, Suarez."

"Let me," I urged, my voice growing stronger with desperation. "Tunji Malu. He is my master." I forced my eyes open and saw the bokor considering my words. "Let me kill him."

Jean-Louis Chevalier cracked a sly smile and plunged the dagger into my neck.

Chapter 36

My eyes opened to a rush of breeze. A concrete overpass stretched above. The sound of vehicles speeding overhead drowned out the rest of the world.

I didn't bother crying out. It would be futile here, on the outskirts of the city. At least I was still alive.

I tugged at my limbs. They were chained, staked to the ground. I was sprawled out on my back in the shape of an X. Flashbacks to the house on Star Island rushed through my head. The time of my first death. Tunji had gutted me there. I could vaguely recollect it now.

But this was different. As I scanned my surroundings with blackened eyes, I didn't see the trappings of ritual. This wasn't magic, it was muscle.

Someone outside my vision approached.

"I don't feel sick," I said plainly.

Chevalier stepped around and looked down at me. His silver earrings hung over his cheeks. The painted white skull left hollow, black holes over his eyes, but the albino irises within were even more unnerving.

"I alleviated your pain," he explained, holding up the knife. "I cut it out of you. Sucked the infection from your arteries." He cocked his head. "Until I decide whether to give it back or not."

I nodded. When he'd stabbed me, it wasn't to take my life. He was casting a spell, undoing the disease.

"We're not in Little Haiti," I noted.

The white skull grinned. "If we were, you would be in pieces right now, being fed to the corpses, never to be seen again."

I shuddered. "Yeah. Thanks for that."

Chevalier kneeled over me. "Baptiste was a warmonger," he said with distaste. In a split second, his blade was again at my throat. "But Max was my friend." I believed it. The bokor seemed to be on a last name basis with everyone except her.

My body twisted against the bindings. I was locked down tight. Still, the Shadow Dog was legendary among the Taíno for escaping all ties. In the darkness of the night, I slipped down into the shadow.

A searing pain jolted my wrists and ankles. I screamed and jerked back to the physical world, taking heavy breaths and checking on my extremities.

The bokor chuckled. "Iron binds those of spirit."

I now noticed the four handcuffs that held me to the ground. Iron is the bane of creatures of spirit, of many things not of this world. Me? It didn't hurt me, but it sure as hell kept me down. I guess when the Taíno were creating their legends, they hadn't come across iron yet.

"Max tried to kill me," I said quickly. "I told her to stay and she didn't."

He flashed his teeth. "She was a stubborn woman, Suarez, but your accusation falls flat. Her charge as a bodyguard was to defend Baptiste."

"I never meant him harm. None of the Bone Saints. I was there for the Nigerians."

The bokor narrowed his eyes into slits.

"It was Tunji who sliced their heads off," I told him. "I only killed in self-defense. Think about the kid I left alive, the one who blew my cover. It would've been more convenient to kill him."

Chevalier pulled the knife away and leaned back. "And so you still live. What was your business with Obazuaye?"

"To get the truth. To expose it. What I knew, it should've helped Baptiste."

The bokor tapped the knife on my chest impatiently.

"They've been playing you for fools," I said.

He countered with a defiant glare. "Obazuaye was brokering peace. I have heard him speak on it myself."

"Maybe," I conceded. "He wasn't a bokor, he was a businessman. If you ask me, it was only about money to him, not unity. But Namadi doesn't matter. That was our mistake. Namadi *never* mattered. Tunji Malu was the architect of the betrayal. The assassinations to your leadership—"

"Carried out by you."

"*Ordered* by him. Tunji had me under some kind of vampiric compulsion, same as Namadi. Whatever Baptiste did to me in that dumpster must've shaken the black magic away. I figured he was using me to ignite a gang war."

"Impossible. The Nigerians are few. They would not be so bold."

"So I realized. They can't meet your numbers. They could never control the streets. So Tunji wielded me, a third party, someone without a link back to him. He acted to create instability during the pretense of peace."

"To what end?"

"Property values. Buyouts and redevelopment. I have a friend with the police who admitted as much."

"A friend." The bokor pondered my words closely.

My face darkened. "Not anymore."

Chevalier rustled silver-armored fingers, twiddling his knife. "Politics. Police. Property. These do not sound Haitian or Nigerian. They sound white, Suarez. Cuban."

I frowned and kept silent. The bokor was right. Tunji said he served Nigeria but how was he furthering their interests? I squirmed against the cuffs that bit into my wrists, hoping the bokor would spare me since he understood the true evil. Chevalier's expertise meant he knew just how mindless my actions had been. The conspiracy wasn't mine. Or his. We were just soldiers in different armies, fighting different wars.

A fleet of trucks passed overhead. The sky rumbled and relaxed. The bokor waited until it was quiet again to speak.

"Tell me about Tunji Malu."

I swallowed. My life depended on my ability to convince Chevalier about this next part. "He works a dark magic. Like ours, but different. West African. He came stateside with Namadi seeking power. At some point ten years ago, we crossed paths and he killed me."

The statement was true enough. I kept out the part about why we had crossed paths. I didn't need word of necromantic artifacts getting around.

"He killed my friend," I continued. "My family." More lies. More shadowing the truth. "Laurent called him an asanbosam."

Chevalier's eyes widened. "This is impossible. The asanbosam were exterminated from the continent a century ago."

"You can't exterminate what lives in the Nether. A hole can open up anywhere and anything can crawl out. I was attacked by a trickster spider too."

The bokor chewed his lip. The Nether is a strange place with lots of names. Its creatures have sometimes been a blessing to humankind but, more often than not, they've been a curse. Where Nether creatures walk, atrocities follow. From the troubled look on Chevalier's face, I could tell he felt the same.

"How were the asanbosam killed in Africa?" I asked.

He cocked his head. "Influenza. Disease. Their blood is volatile. Powerful, but hyperactive."

"It's unstable," I concluded. "Baptiste hit him with a poison that melted his skin. When I did the same, Tunji was weakened. That's when he opened the warded door. I hurt him."

The Bone Saint chortled. "He recovered quickly after your escape. He blamed the attack on you and never mentioned your association." Chevalier's face darkened. "We allowed him to leave safely. Now he is in hiding."

I smiled wickedly. That was my cue. "I know where he is, Chevalier. He's in the Everglades. A safe house. Unchain me and I'll kill him tonight."

The bokor leaned away from me, considering my offer. I had to give Jean-Louis Chevalier credit—he knew I was manipulating him. Unlike some of the Saints, the bokor was no stranger to guile. "Perhaps," he hedged. "But you are still a danger to me. Once you have surrendered free will, it is easily taken. I may find you siding with your master again."

"That's why Tunji needs to die."

The bokor stood. "You assume the vampire is your master."

"He's the one," I said. "There's no one else."

Chevalier shook his head. "No one else? You yourself spoke of the anansi. A connection with Namadi. With other bokors."

"All dead," I reminded him.

Chevalier flashed his teeth. "Let us not talk about death as the greater populace might. You, too, are a dead man." The bokor clasped his hands behind his back and paced around me. "Tunji Malu still has living ties. The police. Other animists."

"There's no evidence of that."

"Suarez, I have never heard of an asanbosam who could wield magic."

I gritted my teeth. The dark magic that draped over me could've been anything. Enchanted venom. A curse. It didn't need to be human spellcraft. "You've never seen an asanbosam before Tunji Malu. We don't know what they're capable of."

The soldier frowned. "If he is as capable as you say, chasing him alone is a death sentence."

"Win-win for you, isn't it?"

He considered. "And if I unbind you? You agree not to attack me?"

"A full truce," I promised.

He nodded. "Until the vampire is dead."

Of course. The bastard still wanted to kill me. Maybe it

was for Max. Or maybe just his dog. In any event, being chained to the floor was a weak bargaining position. I nodded silently.

Jean-Louis Chevalier withdrew a set of small keys and unlocked the handcuffs. I sat up and rubbed my wrists.

"The asanbosam are said to be swift," he warned. "Able to absorb physical attacks."

"I've seen him in action. Like you said before, we just need proper preparation."

The bokor laughed heartily. "We, Suarez?"

I regained my feet and nodded. "What you hit me with. Sickness, right? That's your magic. Pestilence. A special kind of death."

Chevalier clenched his jaw and looked me in the eyes. I told him my plan.

Chapter 37

The air in the Everglades was thick and humid. Plant life and swampland, mostly untamed, met with the sun-bleached asphalt road. The turnoff was right where Evan said it would be, past an aging alligator attraction, little more than rocky swale to cars speeding by. When I pulled off the road I noticed a dirt road heading into the brush.

The area was pitch black. Abandoned. Barren of the lights and sounds of the city, but alive with fluttering insects and animals scurrying in the brush.

This time was my time. The night. The blackness. This was when I was strongest and sneakiest, when my magic would garner its most potential.

As I studied the path cut through the grass, I knew this was where I had to go. I knew this was what I had to do. I also knew I might never come back.

Nobody would lose sleep over me.

For a lot of people, my disappearing would be the best thing that happened to them. Evan could go back to raising my daughter, Emily to moving on. Kasper and Milena and anyone else wouldn't need to suffer like my family had, like Martine had. Even the Bone Saints would be free of my menace.

In a world of saints and sinners, why is it only the sinners who get second chances?

All those close to me had paid for my sins. That wasn't fixable. What I did now was for vengeance, not salvation. My soul was already too black to wipe clean; staining it some more couldn't hurt.

I stood outside the Fiat and waited in the peaceful night, feeling the world for the first time. The breeze. The ticking of the car's engine. The insects buzzing and biting at me.

Any outcome tonight suited me just fine. Either I snuffed out a great evil, or the vampire snuffed me out, this time for good. Either way, the balance sheets of the world would tally a little brighter.

Headlights flashed over me as a vehicle bounced from the road to the grass. A work van with an empty cargo rack on the roof parked behind the Fiat. Chevalier exited the vehicle with his usual grim presence.

"It is ready," he said. "But I think it is not enough." The bokor was decked out in full gear, skulls and silver, yet he didn't move. He didn't share my death wish.

I kicked at a stumpy wooden post along the road and turned down the path without a word.

"Don't forget, Suarez," called the bokor, flipping the ceremonial knife in his hand. "After you finish him, if you live, we still have business to attend to."

I continued without acknowledging him. He would help me or he wouldn't. For now, I walked alone. It was better that way, unencumbered by others. I wasn't sure what to expect, and I needed to be free to use the shadow.

Cisco Suarez was nobody's thrall, man or fae. My mistakes were mine alone to make. As cheesy as it sounded,

I'd rather die free than live in servitude. Tunji Malu could pry my silver whistle from my cold, dead hands.

The path was well beaten. Twin tracks of dirt ran through the grass like scars, signaling regular (but light) vehicle passage. Foliage encroached on both sides, even as a swamp lined the southern portion. Eventually, I reached a patch where the trees cleared and a concrete embankment sloped into the water. A dock for lowering boats into the river. That's why the dirt road existed. I walked over it and stopped just short of getting my feet wet.

I scanned the swamp. None of the stars above were reflected in the murky water. The eyes of an alligator, barely peeping above the surface, watched me. I glanced at my red boots, rapped them on the concrete, and winked at the predator.

"Don't even think about it," I warned.

It didn't move at all. In fact, the water itself was completely still. Come out, come out, wherever you are.

The worn tire tracks gave way to thick vegetation. I continued along the grass. Wild, but still trodden upon. This began to look more promising as a hideout, and my patience was rewarded when I came upon a small metal utility box in disrepair.

Something, at least, was out here.

Further down was a large, concrete structure. Barely a building. The windows were boarded up with plywood. The roof was a single layer of corrugated metal. It was more like a permanent shed on a concrete platform, but it was two stories high.

Drat. I didn't have good luck with sheds.

A metal access door was barred shut with a heavy chain.

Opting for silence, I didn't touch it. Instead I made my way to the concrete platform to the side, which I realized was really the front of the building. Not only that but the structure was much longer than it looked from the side. Multiple large enclosures spanned the face, like a fifteen-car garage, except this was an old boathouse.

Tucked away and forgotten, this was Tunji Malu's hideaway.

Ever quiet, I crept across the cracked cement, peering into the shadows for any movement. I suppose it was too much to expect an army. Tunji Malu wasn't a king in a fortress, surrounded by animist allies like Chevalier had suggested. The vampire acted more like a frightened animal, cowering in the darkness with the rats.

Around the other side of the building were more boarded up windows and a metal door. This one was not chained closed.

It would be ideal to slip in silently, through the shadows, but there was no space for that. I tugged softly at the door. It scraped against the frame as it pulled away. The hinges creaked and set my teeth on edge. Even worse, the racket echoed throughout the inner chamber.

So much for stealth.

I stepped into the pitch blackness. Except, to me, it wasn't dark at all. I could easily see every detail of the open room.

As a West African vampire, I was betting Tunji could see just as clearly.

He stood at attention along the far wall, watching me.

Chapter 38

The vampire growled between taut lips. "Francisco."

I stepped inside, letting the door hang open. The building was essentially a large corridor with a high ceiling, the two of us squared off at opposite ends.

"You didn't think anyone *else* would come for you."

Tunji Malu licked his lips. "Perhaps not. You were resourceful to track me to Little Haiti through Namadi, but he was a public figure." The vampire's brow knotted. He cocked his head, flexing the muscles in his neck. "Finding me here is ever more curious."

He hadn't been prepared for my appearance. He didn't have his armor on. Just boots and pants. His bare chest was thick and ropey, his flesh a hide of dark leather. The metal in his teeth glinted, so I figured it for a permanent fixture. The knee spikes and curved hooks, not so much. The monster recovered his knives from the floor.

"The necromancer Martine knew of this place, but I dealt with her before she could've told you."

My face remained a passive mask.

"You still have friends in this city then," he guessed. "A secret ally? An old brother?"

I shook my head. "Thanks to you, I have no friends."

He laughed. "Ah, then a lost love, perhaps." His eye gleamed.

Whatever front I'd been holding up shuddered. The possibility that he knew about Em horrified me. My face flashed with anger. "There's no one!" I snapped, but the protest was too ardent.

The vampire smiled. "Perhaps Martine was not enough. I will need to flush out and destroy all other vestiges of your previous life. Or I will command you to do so."

I hissed. "Just like you did with my family?"

Tunji's confident smile vanished. "You remember this?" He stepped forward and studied me. "Your knowledge surprises me again. It was no accident we wanted you with us. Your potential is vast." He narrowed his eyes suspiciously. "What else do you remember, shadow witch?"

My stomach turned at the banalities. "Why'd you have my family killed?" I demanded. "Why'd you make *me* kill them?" My chest heaved as I waited. I flexed my arms, reminding him that I was strong too.

Tunji Malu arched an eyebrow and shrugged. "I will tell you if you explain how you broke my hold over you. How you come to me now, no longer a dead man?"

I ground my teeth. He was toying with me, having fun with it, but he wanted information too: Who sold him out. Who broke his control. The facts I wanted weren't so strategic: A rational explanation. Some meaning to the madness.

"Laurent Baptiste dispelled your aura with his palm of death," I explained.

The vampire smiled, then broke into a chuckle. "Impossible. You overestimate his power. Even if he had been capable of such a feat, it would have left you a corpse. No, Francisco. I wish to know how you still walk this earth."

I scowled. "I don't have that answer."

"And the Horn?"

"I don't have that either."

The vampire nodded and looked me up and down, measuring me. "Of course not. A blind man swinging at shadows. For all your cleverness, you remain a disappointment."

"Tell me why you had me cut down my family."

He sighed so emphatically it was almost a yawn. "Because I *could*, Francisco. Your family was irrelevant, ignorant of our dealings. They never *needed* to die, but I made it so. It was a test of your loyalty. My brother, dealing death from the shadows. I had to know if you could be a fully trusted member of the Covey."

"I'm not your brother," I spat. "And I'm not a part of your covey."

"But you were, Francisco. Once you slaughtered your family, we knew you were one of us. We gave you free reign of the city." The monster's eyes lit up. "And what a wonderful reign it was. For eight years, we held Miami in our clutches. This great city was at our mercy. We were an incredible team."

Tunji was trying to rile me up, but I was past that. I recovered my calm and spoke with measure. "Only my family calls me Francisco. I won't stand you doing it again."

He licked his lips in amusement. I paced closer to the vampire and glowered. "I was never one of you, asanbosam. If you think this meeting ends with me pledging service to you again, you're dead wrong. Look to your pet spider, the anansi, for a more likely outcome."

The vampire frowned and scraped his knives together. "We are all pets," he said. "He and I were equals. As were you. You just don't yet remember."

"I wasn't your equal. I was your thrall."

Tunji chuckled and shook his head. "We were brothers. And we shall be again."

With a flick of his wrist, the vamp hurled one of his hooks. I phased to the side and the metal whizzed past me.

Tunji charged in a blur. As I rematerialized, I waved my hand and muddied the floor. The blur slowed considerably.

Still, Tunji Malu was impossibly fast. Reduced to the speed of an Olympic sprinter, he quickly bore down on me. I gathered the shadow from the surroundings and solidified it into a wall between us. The vampire slammed headfirst into it and roared.

He'd be dashing around more carefully after that.

He swiped his blade at the wall of ether and I was surprised to feel resistance. Walls like this could take time to build properly. I gritted my teeth and refocused the darkness, pressing the surface into him.

Another flick of Tunji's empty hand, this time back. It took me too long to notice the magical tether.

The curved hook he had originally thrown reversed direction and thudded into my back. I grunted and attempted to phase away, but I was hooked. Trapped in this world as with the handcuffs. Tunji laughed and yanked me closer.

I couldn't believe I'd fallen for a Mortal Kombat move.

I fought against his pull, grimacing as the blade pierced

further into my hardened skin. An awkward twist allowed me to hook my arm in the middle of the circled edge. I braced my armored forearm against the metal and slid it from my body with a groan. Blood spilled from my back but I wasn't in dire trouble. With my arm against the hook, however, the vampire still had me tethered.

We struggled in a tug-of-war, using might against metal against magic. He pushed into my wall and pulled me closer with his blade. I leaned away and shoved my shadow against his mass. I was hoping the tether would snap, but its magic was strong. Absolute.

He did wield magic, then.

"How did you take me?" I asked, forcing the words through clenched teeth. "Ten years ago."

Tunji snarled, enraged at being unable to reach me. "Death took you," he answered.

I grunted against his power. I couldn't risk manifesting a shadow because that would dissipate my wall—the main thing keeping me alive.

"What magic?" I forced out.

He laughed, growing confident.

In that moment, I spun around and twisted my arm out of the blade's loop. It shot over my head directly at him. In the same instant, I dispersed the wall of shadow. Suddenly without resistance, Tunji stumbled forward. Off balance and surprised, he raised his hand to catch his blade.

He missed.

The rounded knife plunged into the vampire's chest and he tumbled to the floor.

I watched him on all fours a moment before continuing my interrogation. "I'm not only here to kill you. I want answers, Tunji."

"As do I," he breathed, yanking the knife from his chest. He let the bloody weapon clatter to the floor. "What did you do with the Horn before you came to us? How was it you broke free? There's no way that houngan could have done it. That fool was weak."

As Tunji climbed to his feet, the locked door on the wall behind him flew off its hinges and bounced past us. Impressive considering it was designed to open outward.

"Misconceptions," stated Laurent Baptiste harshly. The voodoo high priest casually strolled inside and smiled a set of double teeth.

Chapter 39

Tunji Malu shied away from the new threat to avoid being surrounded. His gaze shifted between me and the leader of the Bone Saints. "This cannot be!" he asserted.

The high priest grinned and the scar on his neck seemed to smile as well. He had no cigar now, no snake, but he wore his death outfit to full effect. Tuxedo. Top hat. Bony fingers. He stood with resolve now and his voice boomed.

"I have told you, demon. The Baron refuses to dig my grave!"

Tunji and I remained tense. It was only Baptiste who appeared calm.

"I have killed you once," said the vampire. "I can do so again. You are both dead men."

Laurent countered. "You think a master of death can be so easily killed?"

Tunji let out a blood-curdling cry and lunged at the houngan. A sliver of shadow grabbed his legs and tugged him back just short of his opponent. As he twisted in frustration, the voodoo priest emptied a bag of powder onto him.

This wasn't a simple handful. I held the vampire down and Laurent unloaded his entire stockpile. A cloud of dust mushroomed over Tunji Malu. It overtook the houngan as well, but he didn't react.

The vampire screeched and convulsed, pulling against my tether. I fought to hold him steady as his skin bubbled. Smoke and pieces of burnt flesh filled the air.

Hidden in dust and smoke, the tugging at my shadow stopped. Tunji's screams weakened to subdued growls. It took a moment for the air to clear. When it did, the vampire was on one knee. Laurent Baptiste stood beside him, with a hooked blade in his stomach and another embedded in his chest. The man stood motionless, without expression.

"You think," growled Tunji Malu, "that I will cower against pain?" He stood and snarled as bits of his skin curled away from his body. "You can flay me. You can impale me. You can burn me. But I will not succumb."

The vampire grabbed both blades and pulled the houngan close. He flexed massive triceps and tore his weapons free from the man, slicing him in half in the process.

I backed away as Tunji buried his face in Baptiste's open chest, slurping and gnawing at the red juices. The vampire watched me from the corner of his eye as he feasted. I didn't interfere.

With a triumphant smack of his lips, Tunji rose. Refreshed. Already his skin had stopped burning, his eyes shone brighter.

"You could have been one of us," he said, reaching for his blades. "We offered you glory. But I think I shall taste your blood instead." The vampire stretched his arms wide and then cracked his neck.

I readied myself for any quick movements. "Is it so

satisfying," I asked, "to kill a dead man?"

Tunji smiled, then quickly shook it away.

"You were right," I explained. "Baptiste really was dead." Tunji narrowed his eyes and turned to the body. "I know, he had a neat trick or two, but you killed him back in Little Haiti. For a man of his power to go down so easily, well, it's embarrassing really. The truth is, he couldn't pull off a resurrection like that. Nobody can return from the dead."

The vampire eyed me carefully. "Except for you, is that it?"

I shrugged. "In his case, anyway. It was me that brought him back. Not alive, but as a zombie."

He scoffed. "That was no dumb zombie."

"Sure he was," I said. "An automaton being driven."

"You did not control that man. I would've seen the tether."

"You're right on that count. Would've been too obvious. I had help from a bokor on the outside. He smuggled the body out of Bone Saints headquarters." I presented my whistle from my pouch. "I did the hard lifting, of course, but the bokor has other talents."

The vampire approached me slowly, grinning. "Tricks and shadows. But what have you accomplished? The houngan is still dead. And you are soon to follow."

He snatched at my neck with a clawed hand but I phased behind him. "It's not him that's important," I said as I backed away. The vampire sneered and turned to follow me. "It's what was done to his blood. Specifically, the blood you drank."

Tunji Malu froze in place and grunted. He shook his head and wiped his watery eyes. Black lines, like running eyeliner, streamed down his face. He stared at his hands and clenched them several times. When he looked up, black fluid was leaking from his nose.

Tunji spun and examined Laurent's corpse again. All the red blood painting the floor had now soured. It had darkened to black, like the blood of the fae.

"What did you do to me?" he demanded, then pitched to the floor.

I skirted his struggling form in a wide circle. "There are legends of asanbosam being obliterated in the motherland. Impervious to weapons, but devastated by blood-borne disease."

Tunji hacked up gelatinous gobs of blood.

"I can kill you quickly," I offered. "If you like. But first I want you to answer me. How did you enslave me? Why did you choose me?"

"You know this already," he spat, taking a feeble swipe at me with his hand. "It was for the Horn."

I hissed and a tentacle of shadow slowly unfurled. It leaned over his form and slowly undulated. "Why use me to get it? What does the Horn do? Why do you want it so bad?"

The vampire's body spasmed, but he remained on his elbows, refusing to back down to the last. "You ask the wrong questions. You ask the wrong person."

"Who then?"

He chuckled. "Pray you never know that answer."

The tentacle slowly wrapped around the asanbosam's neck.

Tunji broke into a fit of laughter. It abruptly cut off when he hacked out a piece of his lungs. The vampire smeared the blackness away from his mouth but it wouldn't wipe away. It tarnished everything except for his glistening metal teeth.

I tightened the darkness around his neck so he couldn't breathe. After a moment of struggle, I loosened it and the vampire gasped.

"No more abstractions, Tunji. I will have my answer or you will suffer. This covey of yours. If you're not its head, who is?"

"A being of primal power," he answered. "Magic personified."

My heart fluttered and I backed away. It was crazy to see the fear on Tunji Malu's face. Not of me. Not of death. But of the person he spoke of.

"Nothing you do to me can compare to his wrath," he continued.

"Don't bet on it."

He grunted. "Even now, he will save me."

I searched the darkness but no one was near. In a way, that unsettled me more.

"It doesn't look like it, Tunji."

He tried to laugh again, but groaned and twisted on the floor. "Then he will *avenge* me. And you will remain blind and swiping at shadows, Francisco."

His familiarity enraged me. Such confidence in the face of oblivion. With a wrenching crack, the shadow tentacle snapped the monster's neck. His body wriggled a little then ceased all movement.

"At least I'll remain," I whispered.

I stared at the crumpled form of Tunji Malu for some time. I wanted to feel something. Closure or satisfaction. All

I got was emptiness.

I dragged the vampire and splayed him across Laurent Baptiste's body. I snatched another sack from the zombie's waist and poured the powdered contents over them both. There was no sizzling this time. No smoke.

I studied the spoiled mess on the floor and frowned. This was supposed to have been a moment of victory. Now, I wasn't so sure.

I struck a match, adjusting my eyes to the small amount of light. Black tears ran down my face. I dropped the stick on the bodies and they erupted in flames. I added Tunji's armor to the fire. His blades and belongings too. It would all burn. Nothing would be left.

My walk along the abandoned Everglades path had less purpose on the return trip. The stars weren't as bright. As I trudged back to the road, I knew I had killed the man who had killed me. I knew I had avenged my family against the one who had ordered their deaths. But all I could think about were Tunji Malu's last words.

A primal being.

I didn't want to believe it.

Chapter 40

Chevalier sat on the roof of his van but hopped off when I returned. Between his stoic expression and the face paint, he was hard to read. I figured, by the slow way he approached, he was surprised I was still alive.

A lone car passed us on the road, bathing us in light for a brief moment. We stared at each other as the engine noise dissolved into the distance, leaving us abandoned once again.

"The vampire is dead?" he asked.

I clutched my wounded back and nodded.

"The bodies?"

"Burning," I said. The accelerant would make sure nothing but ashes remained of the vampire and the zombie. Our tracks were clear. With luck, or maybe with Evan Cross, the gang murders would be pinned on the bodyguard who disappeared.

"About the truce," I started to say.

The bokor smiled. With a quick snap, he produced the ceremonial knife in his hand.

I took a step back. "Actually, I was hoping we could extend our peace a little longer."

Jean-Louis Chevalier drew back his arm and flung the

knife. I rolled to the side and raised my shield.

A loud squawk was interrupted by a thud. The knife had missed me. It hadn't been intended to hit. I turned to see the blade embedded in a wooden street post, a beautiful crow impaled right through its mouth.

"You had a follower," explained the bokor.

In a matter of seconds, the beautiful sheen on the feathers faded and revealed a desiccated corpse. The bird hardened and dried, looking like it had died a long time ago.

Chevalier and I blinked dumbly.

"One of yours?" he asked.

"No."

He chuckled. "Perhaps you are mistaken, Suarez." He turned and headed back to his van. He pulled out onto the Everglades street and drove off without another word.

My gaze stayed fixed on the bird. I didn't know what was left of the bokor's debt to settle, but perhaps he thought I had a few of my own to settle first.

And he might've been right. This crow—I had seen it before. Back at Martine's house, it had watched me. Picking at her eyeballs. It turned out to be a zombie.

Expertly crafted, for me to miss it. But it was more than just voodoo.

Before being dispelled, the crow had appeared robust. Beautiful. Some sort of glamour had been worked on it to hide the decay.

I'd noticed other traces of glamour back at Martine's cookhouse. Her minions had been hidden in plain sight. The old gal had learned new tricks since back in the day.

I worked my jaw as I contemplated what the crow meant. Martine had been working with Tunji, but she was a liability in the end. I didn't know if she was a party to my death, but there was some evidence that she had remained my ally.

I closed my eyes and recalled her last moments of life once more. Her strange words. When it had become apparent that I was alive and Tunji would kill her, she chanted a spell. A riddle, maybe. The crow flies true, ever and only concerned with birdfeed.

Could she have known I would see through her eyes?

I supported the bird in one hand. Before I could pull the knife free, the dried carcass crumbled into dust and bones. Most of the remains slipped through my fingers, but I palmed some of the chunks. Of interest was a rusted metal chain wrapped around the knife blade. Attached to it, a sterling silver pendant lay in my palm. I blew away the debris and unveiled a relief of Saint Martin.

Sneaky bitch.

Martine had been helping me all along. Even in death, she'd left a cryptic clue in her final moment. Even in her absence, she'd left a servant behind to find me, follow me, and wait vigilantly until the time was right, with a prize in its belly.

Martine had gifted the pendant to me when we first started our voodoo partnership. She thought it was funny, the similarity of Martin to her name. Of course, the saint has much greater importance. Martin is syncretized with the High Baron, the patron from which we both drew our voodoo powers. This was my original voodoo fetish.

In this case, however, the sterling silver pendant had a different significance. I'm generally a patient person but, given the circumstances, I jumped in the Fiat and sped off.

After my last two visits to the cemetery, I couldn't deny dreading my return. The ambushes by Bone Saints shouldn't be a worry anymore (at least not for a while), but conversing with my father, learning the things I'd done—they'd shaken me much more than gunfire ever could.

I passed the statue of Saint Martin at the entrance. It held the same visage as the one on my pendant. Even though it had been used for spellcraft, it was a Catholic symbol. My mother had appreciated that I wore it. Even in the absence of my body, my mother, I was sure, would have had it buried in my casket.

Something was in this cemetery, and it was about damn time I found out what.

I went to my grave with a shovel this time. No more worms. No more magic. Sometimes you have to do things the old-fashioned way.

After digging for hours, the shovel rapped against my coffin. The worm could only have reported life or death within. I should've realized it couldn't have seen personal keepsakes. Symbols from the family. I admit, I was curious.

When I opened the lid, a bull horn rested on a single pillow. It was brown and white and capped with metal at both ends. It would've appeared entirely plain except for the gold plating running along its length. Ornate pictographs of objects and figures were etched in the precious metal. The symbols defied explanation.

I'd been expecting a musical horn or something. Curious indeed. And I think there's a saying about curiosity.

I swallowed nervously and picked up the Horn of Subjugation. I could've sworn it hummed.

I sighed and studied the large pile of dirt beside the hole

in the ground. I knew Tunji's death hadn't completed my business, no matter how much I wished it so. I'd at least figured I was in a place where I could slow down and breathe. Reflect. I thought I could take time to put the pieces back together.

Yeah, right. My life was a series of loose ends.

There was no telling what the Horn was capable of, but I knew it spelled danger. Just because I had finally recovered it didn't mean the trouble would stop coming my way. In fact, the Horn would probably attract it. The smart play was to rebury the artifact and forget all about it.

I grunted and tucked the Horn in my lap. In its place on the white pillow, I gently set down my Saint Martin pendant. It was meant to be buried with me. It probably had been until Martine dug it up and hid the artifact. I knew, since I was alive again, that my mother would have preferred I keep the pendant, but that wasn't me anymore. I had to bury the old Cisco Suarez.

I was a loner now. A black magic outlaw.

Yup, just a few seconds ago, I thought I was through the worst of it. Now, I knew it was just beginning. That was okay with me. Maybe it was time I finally did the world some good.

With a checkered past and a decade of bad deeds, I had a lot to atone for. *He walks alone but always has a home.* The streets of Miami were my new home, and I had plenty of walking left to do.

-Finn

Acknowledgments

Writing a book is a solitary venture most of the time, but I couldn't have done it without help. Special thanks to City of Miami Police Captain Dan Kerr, Deputy Commander, Criminal Investigations Section. I took liberties with some details but he kept me (mostly) honest. Thanks to my editor, Philip Newey, who saved me from featuring a "colander" of whiskey in one scene. (I swear, I usually know what words mean.) And, of course, I need to give props to James Egan. Judge my books by his covers. Please.

About the Author

I'm Domino Finn: hardened urban fantasy author, media rebel, and mozzarella sticks enthusiast. (Pro Tip: They should be scalding.)

Black Magic Outlaw will keep coming with the hits. Go to DominoFinn.com, join my reader group, and get the first word on sequels and cover reveals. I don't ramble, so no need to nod and pretend you're listening.

If you appreciated *Dead Man*, know that your kind words are vital to my success. Really. Please leave a review where you made your purchase, even if it's only a line or two. A few clicks from you go a long way.

Finally, don't forget to keep in touch. You can contact me, connect on social media, and see my complete book catalog at DominoFinn.com.

30746617R00174

Printed in Great Britain
by Amazon